Hope you enjoy reading this as much as I did writing it. Thanks for being an ear and a friend.

Brett Laurence

SHADOW GUARDIANS

Brett A. Lawrence

Martin Sisters Publishing

Published by

Martin Sisters Publishing, LLC

www. martinsisterspublishing. com

Copyright © 2013 Brett A. Lawrence

Martin Sisters Publishing, LLC, Kentucky.
ISBN: 978-1-62553-045-5
Editor: Kathleen Papajohn
Science Fiction
Printed in the United States of America
Martin Sisters Publishing, LLC

DEDICATION

To my wife, Sherry, who has been supportive in my ventures and is the other half of my wholeness, the wind in my sails. Then there are those, who over the years, have patiently listened to my storyline and other ideas that went onto paper. Finally, there are those at Martin Sisters who took an interest in this story and broke the years of sojourning in a desolate land.

EARTH

CHAPTER ONE

Abigail Webster listened to the voice that was almost drowned out by the static coming from the small plane's speakers.

"Piper alpha, tango, delta, 2-3-7 you are cleared for take-off. Wind is from the southwest at 15 mph. Visibility is ten miles. VFR apply."

Abby's husband, Dennis, turned to glance at her as the plane rolled forward.

"Hear that, Abby?" he said as their Piper climbed into the cold night air.

"Visual flying rules. Look outside. I scattered all these diamonds around just for you, my gift for our tenth anniversary."

Abby took in the city lights that stretched and faded into the chill, wet depths of the night. Here where it was warm they appeared an impossibly distant part of a secret universe. Tacoma, Washington was an enchanting city, once the magic of a winter night took hold. In the distance, she saw the dark swath of Commencement Bay and Puget Sound.

Abby laughed out loud and settled into her seat. Had she ever had a life before she met Dennis? She knew that her life had started when they met and it was comforting to know that the love she felt for her husband was returned in kind. No matter how frustrating a normal day could be, one of them always found a way to make the other laugh.

"I thought that delicious dinner was my present. Anyway, it looks like your throw missed its mark." She indicated what appeared to be a black hole in the middle of the points of light that filled Tacoma.

"That's Puget Sound, my dear. It must have swallowed a million dollars' worth of your diamonds. Now, just sit back and relax. We'll land in Everett in about thirty minutes."

To Abby, it felt that she and Dennis were tiny specks surrounded by bits of white in the middle of a snow globe.

She turned and looked at him again. "I love you, Denny."

"I love you too, Abby…madly! And you looked absolutely elegant tonight."

His smile broadened, and she noted the erotic quality to it. It was easy to guess what he was thinking. "I know that look in your eye," she coyly baited him.

"You do?" Dennis played along with a gesture to himself. It had that air of hand-in-the-cookie-jar innocence to it. He then dropped the facade in a dramatic *hummph*. "Then I guess you know me pretty good, don't you?"

"Hey, it's me, Denny. It happens to be my job."

Home for now was temporarily in Everett, north of Seattle. It was there that Dennis managed the initial phase of a bridge newly under construction. Abby sat back with a sigh and felt the day's tensions rolling off her.

Clearing the field, Dennis put them into a smooth climbing left turn. To the right and about two hundred meters below a hint of stygian ground and a few hazy lights dropped precipitously away to the black expanse of nothingness that was the abysmal, swirling void of Puget Sound at night. The tide-whipped body of water ended less than a couple kilometers to the east on the Tacoma side. There the city began at water's edge. Specks of urban illumination defined a vague boundary between liquid and solid ground.

"Isn't it absolutely a sight to behold?" Abby marveled loud enough to be heard over the straining engine. Raindrops splattered on the windshield, coalescing into rivulets that smeared up and past in the airplane's slipstream. Past uncertainties were for now forgotten, the magic of the moment a welcome distraction. "I like how the rain sort of smudges it like something from a dream."

They climbed over and past the twin Tacoma Narrows Bridges, a glittering binary necklace of slithering diamonds and rubies spanning the solid blackness.

"Uh huh," a busy Dennis absent-mindedly responded. Then abruptly trying to make up for his lack of attentiveness, "The sight below us may be beautiful, but your company beside me is better."

Abby hummphed but did not turn. "Nice try, Denny. You *are* always and forever the romantic." She reached sideways to stroke his arm then gave it an affectionate squeeze. What should have been a preoccupied hand found hers and returned the gesture with strong fingers.

She was tempted to suggest the idiotic idea of a nice, long circuit around Commencement Bay. She turned, caught him eyeing her. Even with the dim glow of the instrument's tepid illumination, she could easily see the tease in his expression and guess what he was thinking.

Once again, she sat back, basking in the warm glow of their mutual affection.

Suddenly, she felt an inexplicable twinge of anxiety. The hairs of the back of her neck stood up and she felt cold.

A raucous noise exploded without warning into the cockpit. It was the proximity advisory. Only a couple of moments had passed since Denny had last spoken to her, moments that now had him busy listening in on his radio headset.

"Has air control given you an explanation?" inquired Abby, raising her voice in order for Denny to hear her over the din. She peered uncertainly outside into the gloom.

For long tension-filled seconds, Denny continued to listen to the report coming through his earphones.

"The controller says that there's an unidentified about a kilometer off our five o'clock position, approximately one hundred seventy meters above us," he beat out.

Abby strained to look back and up, seeing only the vague outline of the wing stretching off into the darkness. It blotted out anything overhead and behind.

"They're still on the horn trying to raise the pilot of the unidentified craft," he said.

"Any indication what kind of problem?"

"Not a clue."

His terse comment gave her an icy chill. This was about the worst possible situation for any pilot to be in. At least Denny could hear the tower. They were flying deaf and just about blind. On a very slight positive note, it was still a big piece of sky, and the two craft more than likely would just simply pass each other, with nothing worse than some prop wash and a few jangled nerves.

"Which means they're blind to us, unless they have a proximity warning system too," she went on. "Wonderful!"

"That's the size of it," Dennis muttered. "Ground says that the problem's with the other pilot. They're keeping an eye on the situation and will advise on any change. For now, we just tiptoe our way around."

Abby trusted implicitly the unknown, faceless controller on the ground. They were a good lot, and she trusted them with her life. Such trust, however, did not extend to other pilots and their possible failures to maintain attentiveness or equipment.

Accordingly, uncertainty turned into worry, despite her attempt to hold it off. She nestled deeper into her seat. Maybe it would impart just a little more security against overwhelming forces that were drawing too close for comfort.

For a long, palpable minute, the plane's cabin was filled with the tension-amplified, penetrating drone of the engine. Abby squirmed in her seat and restraints for a better look

"I still can't see anything, Denny. Maybe the controller…wait a minute. I think…"

The burgeoning intensity of her voice was cut off by the urgent scream exploding in Dennis's headset that even she could hear.

"Abby…hold on! They've turned our…"

His explanation died in his throat.

Dennis hauled back on the control wheel. At the same time instinct took control, and he threw the plane into a gut-straining evasive left turn.

It was too late.

There was an explosion of sound and movement.

In that same instant the little plane shook violently, like a toy smacked on a floor by a rambunctious child.

Abby let out a shriek but it was lost in the violent screech of roaring engine, shredding metal, and disintegrating airframe.

Abby thrust her hand sideways, where it found Denny's arm. She could feel the iron-hard tension in it as Dennis fought a sudden life and death struggle with the wildly erratic control column.

By some miracle, the stricken aircraft managed to hold a tenuous straight course. Abby swept a glance past the altimeter…and realized their momentary respite was only an illusion: the instrument was shaving off altitude readings in a blur of motion. From what she could tell it was about ten meters every five seconds. They were level but headed down.

There was only one ultimate, grim conclusion with that kind of rate…unless Denny could pull something off. And why they were not in a wild, gyrating free-fall or disintegrating altogether she could only speculate.

Dennis hauled back on the wheel all the harder. The altitude readout slowed just a little.

Abby threw her own one hundred twenty seven pounds into the fray, for all it was worth.

"Abby…" Dennis forced out through clenched teeth, "get on the radio…tell 'em we're hit, going in!"

Denny yanked off his headset and flung it sideways to her.

Driven by her own adrenaline-fueled terror, Abby only clawed her slender fingers deeper into her own control wheel.

"ABBY!"

"Okay!" she blurted. Shaken free, she reluctantly let go.

"Good. Tell 'em I think the vertical stabilizer's sustained damage and the elevator's just about shot. I can only guess what else."

It took a long moment for her to wade through her own turmoil to concoct a mental report. It was a moment they did not have. Whatever she was going to say, she had to say it now, while their transient fragment of control remained. Unfortunate, and that was a big unfortunate, their descent angle was much too steep for ditching. Fixed landing gear did not help matters either. They would simply flip upon contact with the water, and that would be the end of that.

Terrific!

Again she checked the altimeter, groaned in dismay. One hundred twenty meters slipped past.

Abby shook her head in bewilderment. One minute they were just flying along, enjoying the sights and the next they were seconds from a grim, cold, ignoble demise at the bottom of a very big piece of water that rose toward them like a demon out of the night.

Abby managed to make the call then threw her strength back into the tandem control column. She dug her boot heels into the cabin's metal flooring for leverage. The results were not worth the effort.

Something snapped in the controls.

The plane lurched in a sickening motion, pitched over even steeper. Panic choked the breath from her throat.

In one semi-lucid thought, crammed amid the torrent of frantic ones, she had the fleeting impression of the plane simply giving up its struggle to stay airborne. It wanted to surrender to its fate and die. Their efforts felt so pathetic in contrast.

"Control's contacted Coast Guard, Port, and local authorities," she forced out on the tail end of a tight yelp.

"Wonderful! Somehow, I don't think it's gonna matter."

"Hey, I did what you wanted! At least they know!"

"Well, don't get your hopes up, love. If the crash doesn't kill us the cold will. It's winter, remember? We have only seconds left. Use them well…like for praying."

Abby began to weep, at first not realizing it.

If fate did not allow them to somehow survive what was to be a catastrophic impact, what did they have to look forward to? Would they be uninjured or even conscious? How long could they survive in forty-five degree water, at night, in the middle of winter, and with a running tide, no doubt? And those were just the known variables.

A lot of if's!

"Happy anniversary, Denny!"

"Yeah, same here."

Abby's gaze latched onto the altimeter with morbid fascination. From what she knew of Denny's flying, her best guess of their heading had them coming down just about smack dead center of Puget Sound, equidistant from any land.

"Noooo!" she mumbled under her breath. "Denny, what *is* that?" she stammered as a sudden, alien sensation washed over her.

"Abby, this *really* is not the time…"

"No, Denny, I mean it. I feel sort of…different. Something's wrong."

Thirty meters.

"Impending death…will definitely do strange things to you," he said through clenched teeth.

The cabin began to fill with a dim, thin, wavering mist of luminescence. It coalesced from the very air itself. In a second, it intensified to bright golden amber. The sound of droning bees, millions of them, overwhelmed the whining engine. Prickly static tickled and crawled along her skin.

All of it took only a second.

Abby screamed…or thought she did. There was vague awareness of a jolt. Unconsciousness took her.

But not completely. Not at first.

She sensed suspension, floating, though without a sense of warmth or cold. It was not quite flying, not quite swimming. There was no light, no dark, no pain, or sensation of physical touch or being. Time lost coherent meaning. She fought against the losing effort to focus, concentrate, to stay awake and aware.

Where was Denny?

Her mind refused to work; instead, it roiled in slow motion. She was adrift on a thick, formless, soupy sea. Then that left her. The universe about her folded in on itself and evaporated.

CHAPTER TWO

"This sure turned out to be a fine night to stay late," the young man grumbled under his breath. He made his way around the paper and file-cluttered table, collecting, sorting, and feeling the weariness of what had been a *very* long day.

Lindsey Maguire sensed his effort to keep his tone low and not sound too pessimistic and that he was losing the battle. She directed a stony, blue-eyed stare at him as he bit into his lip. The gesture barely kept his obvious frustration in check, from spouting something stupid. In the end it did not and she really did not care.

"It's necessary to get this done, David," was all she offered in explanation. And that was with an imperious air of finality.

"Yes, Miss Maguire," David Delosantos relented. His work took on a deeper, grudging, spiritless formality.

The two of them were the only ones in the executive office at this late hour. Lindsey had somewhere else she wanted to be, and the sooner she could break away the better. David could handle all of this, anyway. On his part it was his job as her administrative assistant. On her part it was executive privilege at his expense.

For a long moment, she contemplated her assistant as he carried on, unmindful of her scrutiny. Of a truth, David was a half-decent worker and as loyal as they came. But on the flip side, he was also a dreamer, a likable sort, but a definite pushover.

It was that last characteristic she saw as a definite flaw, little better than a festering poison. She had been so careful to remove from her own behavior any such liability as it related to her up-and-continuing career plans. In anyone else, though, it was an exploitable trait, a tool to be used to advantage. She had certainly gotten a lot of mileage out of it.

David will definitely go little farther than here, she mused. It was just as well. She had expended precious effort to train him to her standards.

Now executive vice president for international accounts at Premier One America Bank, she had come far since garnering a fledgling fiscal technician's position at another institution thirteen years before. It had been very far, indeed. Fortuitous timing, craftiness, and plain ol' good luck were her simple ingredients to success. The time invested had been carefully crafted into developing a respectable long list of lucrative accounts that translated into several promotions and transfers, not to mention a stint as a corporate lobbyist in the state capital. Still nudging ever higher up the career ladder, a presidency or a seat on the executive board was out of the realm of fantasy and within the grasp of reality in not too many years. Some pushing and shoving, a little elbowing, all wrapped up in the magic carpet of growing corporate profits, and anything was possible.

"Oh, by the way, David," Lindsey remembered. She nodded to a collection of folders, her tone set deceptively gentle. "After you finish what you're working on, I would like you to order these client account files based on each one's current asset status.

I want to look at them first thing in the morning for follow-up action."

David's countenance sank like a ship already going down and torpedoed again for good measure. A look of disdain took in the pile. He then graced her with a blank stare that threatened to collapse to hopelessness. She knew it was easily two hours' worth of work, to which she excised any hint of compassion.

"Yes ma'am," he gave in.

With that, she closed and latched her briefcase. She then reached behind her for her black woolen jacket draped over the back of her executive chair, placed there for just this moment.

"Would you like me to call security for you?" he offered, his tone flat.

She shook her head. She did not need to be patronized like a child under the doting care of a babysitter and seen to her car. She was a big girl. More important, she enjoyed the toady display, more as a reminder to him of his subordinate status.

"No, I don't think so. Eduard should be on duty in the garage. Thank you, anyway." She grabbed her briefcase.

David forced a grin, nodded slightly. "As you wish."

"See you in the morning," came her lackluster farewell.

*

David said nothing as upon watching her depart.

Even though about five years younger than Lindsey, he did find her outwardly attractive. It was enough so that it did, on occasion, stimulate something deep inside him. But it only went that far, and tonight was not one of those times. What a waste of humanity. With her, beauty was truly only skin deep.

On the inside it was an entirely different matter. She was a solid wall of ice when it served her, all coated in a shell of frosty, self-serving arrogance. Bright straw-blond hair, below the

17

shoulders in length and typically pulled back and neatly clipped rather than allowed to hang free, was her most standout feature. Piercing, intelligent, azure eyes and a small mouth gave her trim frame an attractiveness that he guessed would age well.

But it was a deception, an illusion. She was a siren...or a cobra, if stroked the wrong way. How she could come across so disarming, charming and, yet, at the same time be plotting her own self-serving career course at the expense of other... Well, that was beyond him. He had seen co-workers go by the wayside because of her, socially and professionally. All the while, she collected accolades from admiring superiors. That was one of the intangible fringe benefits of her position that she used to the max: the means of getting rid of any real or imagined competition on the way up.

David even came close once himself, a year ago.

In all fairness, she was a chameleon, on occasion loosening herself from her stony hardness to laugh and joke. She was even quite the comedienne when away from job and office. It just went to show that she could be counted among caring humans if it wasn't for the fact she was so...inhuman!

He continued to stare through a shuttered window, set partly open, as she strode across the outer office. Even her gait had a snobbish strut plastered all over it. He despised it.

A few more seconds passed and David put aside a sheaf of forms that he'd had all along. His eyes narrowed in a self-compliment of the wry smile creeping across his mouth, now that she was safely out of sight. Going the few steps to her large ornate desk, that was a not so subtle reflection of her personality, he sat and dialed her phone with one hand while the other hand tapped out a nervous beat on polished surface.

"*Yeah,*" a voice answered, almost a growl.

"She left about half a minute ago," David said.

"No problem. Everything's as planned. Sure you still want to continue with this job?"

"As planned," David nodded, satisfied at the report. Giddiness at the prospect of devious success began flooding his mind. He could be just as crafty and malicious as she was. She just did not make a secret of it.

"Unfortunately, she has me slaved here for at least another two hours, wouldn't you know?"

"Icing on the cake," the voice on the other end said in a confident chuckle.

It was too bad David's contact was in his hire: the contact and Lindsey were a swell match, each with personalities that had all the warmth of an Antarctic summer. They were definitely made for each other, and it was a shame circumstances were not different. Either way, she would soon see what a little sociopathic behavior from the other side looked like, up close and personal.

"Look at it as added insurance to keep things under wraps and you seemingly out of the loop. A fortunate inconvenience." The man went on.

David's countenance brightened. The drudgery that was there a minute before, now took on a new perspective he had never considered. "Right. I never thought of it that way."

"That's why I'm being paid to think."

David ignored the barb. With Lindsey about to get hers it was a small sacrifice to give up his own social plans.

A click from the other end signaled the end of the conversation, short and to the point with little fanfare.

Maneuvering about the solid oak desk, he seated himself in the high-backed executive chair like a petty subject trying on the throne of an absent ruler. Then lacing his fingers behind his head, he swiveled the chair to face the large panel window and the city of Seattle spread out below.

Reclining back and propping both legs on the desk corner in irreverent, secret contempt, "I do believe you will find the night interesting and very long, Lindsey Maguire. For you, it will be a very long one, indeed. Maybe I should cancel your engagements for you?"

*

The elevator opened into the cavernous subterranean parking garage.

Lindsey took in the cement slab chamber and noted it was nearly vacant. Perhaps two dozen vehicles were scattered about the expansive facility. Such was not an altogether unusual occurrence, considering another office tower shared the same business complex. From what she knew, a number of their employees worked well past even this late hour. Beyond that tidbit of information, she neither cared, nor really paid attention to who spooked around the lower levels of this echoing corporate tomb.

Directly across the aisle was the comforting presence of her glossy black Honda with tinted windows in its assigned stall. Two stalls to the left sat a windowless van, primer-splotched like somebody's perverted idea of makeshift camouflage. The original color was bleached out by the garish overhead sodium vapor lighting to the point that the exact tint was difficult to discern. She did not recognize it right off, and it should not have been there.

She shrugged off a twinge of concern. To the best of her recollection, the van had not been there when she went for lunch hours earlier.

Not to mind. Had she been its owner and working late, she, too, would have fudged and parked close to the elevator. Security, were it of a mind to do so, would merely search for the culprit, make mention of the infraction then give the requisite lecture about etiquette and consideration for others. A polite, "I'm sorry," in return would all but end the matter.

The solid footfall of her boots on the cement deck echoed off the garage walls in a rhythmic staccato. The building's security guard, Eduard, was down here somewhere, most likely in the security booth at the exit/entrance engrossed in a cheap novel. That did little, though, to keep from feeling a creeping uncertainty at being completely alone down here. Even one other soul, completely unmindful of her presence, would have been enough to dispel her situational insecurity.

Keys already in hand, Lindsey got the car door opened in quick order, threw her case in, and slid inside. She closed and locked the door, a little faster than normal. In an instant, her unease evaporated with the activation of locking mechanisms that securely cocooned her inside.

Inside and settled, she went to put her keys into the ignition. They instead fell out of her fingers and clattered to the floor.

"Oh, for the love of…" she muttered. She flashed through a few sample expletives in her mind for the one most appropriate for the occasion.

She leaned forward against the steering column and ground her cheek into the wheel. Her right hand groped about the floor.

The exercise would have been easier with better lighting or just plain getting out. She instead contorted closer to the floor…

The universe exploded.

Excruciating pain and a lightning flash of dazzling light engulfed her. At the same time, she felt herself irresistibly careen into a dizzying free-fall square into a pit of smothering blackness. Along with fragmented awareness, all other sensations winked out as unconsciousness overwhelmed her.

CHAPTER THREE

With grudging slowness did Lindsey become aware of a first sensation, if it could have been called that.

Actually, it amounted to a cloud of agitated fireflies of light skittering before her eyes. The only problem was, as best as she could figure, her eyes were closed.

There was no thought, no awareness of pain or self, only the feeling of treading water in a thick, opaque ocean of black unreality. A sharp hiss of radio-like static that came from the middle of her brain echoed off the inside of her skull and permeated the whole.

Then, from somewhere out on the periphery of the universe, she sensed movement. How or what she did not know, could not know. It was intangible, disjointed, undirected, a vague conglomeration of muffled sound and motion, present but unable to be interpreted.

The pervasive numbness short-circuiting her brain began to abate. New sensations, ominous ones, waded in like frigid water pouring into the darkened bowels of a sinking ship: burgeoning pain, tightness, persistent blackness, more pain...

She still had no idea what calamity had befallen her, but the next logical step was movement.

No use.

Next she tried to speak...

That, too, was useless. For all she could tell, her mouth was stuffed with mashed potatoes.

The mental fog lifted still more, a withdrawing window shade keeping out daytime. With its removal came an instantaneous, horrifying realization.

Then unadulterated panic!

"Might as well make yourself comfortable, sweetie," a gravelly voice sneered from close by. It was too close. "The two of us are going to sit tight here for a spell. Then, when it's time, we have places to go. As for you," and a sharp jab walloped her left hip, "you just stay nice and quiet and enjoy the rest. Any trouble and..."

Lindsey strained to raise her head.

Just as quick, her effort failed. It dropped back to the cold carpeted floor that reeked of grease, oils, and a nauseating miasma of other foul odors that were unidentifiable. The simple act of trying to lift her head was torture.

Slowly the sledgehammer pounding in her head subsided to a dull throb. So did her panic. Trussed up and hog-tied like an animal, blindfolded and gagged, it was quite obvious, after a little testing of her captor's thoroughness, that there was precious little she could do.

Except wait, wait on this maniac, whoever he was, and for the mental haze in her head to lift even more.

CHAPTER FOUR

"Miriam, did we reach them in time?" the man spoke toward the visual monitor and the waif-like human female face framed within.

His accent was articulate and understandable, despite a dialogue that sounded like a melding of Australian and Scandinavian. Yet its quality was gentle and patient, inclined to give conflicting impressions.

Filling the rest of the screen was a background of instrumentation that was not unlike the flight engineer station of an airliner flight deck cabin or a manned spacecraft. And that was reasonably close to the truth. At least it was from video monitoring he had undertaken in idle times. The man knew that she would be seated at the rear of the deck and to starboard at an L-shaped console that made up the sensor and computer suite.

Rather frail in appearance, she looked a tad pale and just a little malnourished. Her lively countenance and the apparent deftness of unseen hands on her instruments, however, told otherwise.

Intent blue eyes checked and rechecked readouts only she could see. Then she sat back in the bulky flight seat that was disproportionately large for her slight frame. A smile then graced her thin lips as her gaze met his. She nodded once.

"Good," the man said.

Acquisitions were usually and desirably cut close, and this one had been no exception. It involved an outright accident where even the last seconds held out hope that a tragic end could be averted by some miracle, making his and Miriam's intervention unnecessary. That was, then, the trick: interpreting the circumstances to decide whether to carry through and rescue or let it go.

This one proved easier than many, as there really had been no real hope for the male and female victims who were now his guests. The damage to their aircraft had been too extensive, too lethal. It was confirmed by the unwavering descent angle that had only one grim, final end.

"Are you sure about the next one?"

Miriam gave another nod this time. It was a cocky self-assured one, one in which her sense of the matter was as certain as any of the five common physical senses. Earthers referred to it as a 'sixth sense.'

"Then how about laying in the destination and your time estimate, before going back and getting our guests settled in prior to them waking up? This next one will be our last one. I am afraid we are pushing our good fortune the way it is."

Miriam mouthed only silent words.

The man watched intently, waiting until she finished.

"I know," he sighed. "This will be one of precise timing with more variables than I care to imagine. Crimes of violence typically are, from what I know of Earth culture. But I think we can pull it off without losing her or arousing the attention of that bhaktar who has her."

He turned a bit more upbeat. "And who knows? We may even be able to subtly force his hand...Yes, I am aware of the referendum protocols limiting our involvement in nonemergency surface affairs. They are clear enough...No, I think we can work around it, though...I am pretty sure...No, more subtle than that."

Miriam's expression conveyed only perplexity.

He knew that she was not completely convinced.

She started to mouth something but came up short. After a moment, she nodded acceptance anyway, and began working more controls. She was in this also. Then she pushed up with elegant ease and moved away from the field of vision.

The man poked at a button on his own instrument panel, shutting down the visual link.

*

Lindsey tried everything in her very limited ability to forestall the invasive loss of feeling in both arms and legs. Fortunately, if she could use that word, the throbbing in her head was something more tolerable. Instead of a body-wincing pounding it was just a dull throb.

She put an occasional, feeble effort into working at the cords that were cinched on her wrists and the one strung tight to her feet that were drawn up behind her.

Unfortunately, her efforts produced nothing more than frustration, more abrasions, and broken fingernails. And whatever was wedged behind the gag in her mouth proved just as intractable.

She groaned and gave up, resigned for now to being trussed up like a Christmas turkey.

The beast appeared to have drifted off to sleep. The rhythmic roll of heavy breathing, with an occasional loud snore thrown in, had relayed that much. Then all sound stopped.

Long silence…

Lindsey forced herself to guess the time, if for no other reason than to give her mind a frame of reference and a distraction from the torture. That, too, proved as futile as everything else she had tried.

Finally, and most acutely, she was cold, very cold.

It was a pervasive, penetrating chill to the bone, one that came from being inactive too long at a temperature where a sweater or light jacket would have provided sufficient comfort. Overall, she just knew the scant attention paid her bore no good for the near term.

There was a slight tremor around her.

"Okay, Miss Maguire," the voice came to life, like the foulest of odors among everything else. "I believe that is your name?" And, like a Washington winter, the voice was devoid of any warmth. "It's time for the two of us to get moving. First, let me enlighten you to a few things that might interest you."

Lindsey felt a blunt push against the side of her head. She winced as a wave of renewed discomfort pounded through it. She could only guess at the injury this pervert had inflicted upon her. The very thought that he had violently assaulted her in his efforts to subdue her lit off a flash of mindless rage.

"There, I thought you were awake. I hope you rested well?"

If only her mouth was free! Still, that did not stop Lindsey from attempting a stream of searing epithets.

Maybe the gag was a good thing. To have been able to cut loose would assuredly have brought on punishing retribution and that while unable to defend herself. She was being tempted to resign herself to going down with the ship without so much as a fight.

"To begin with, I'm sure that you're aware this happens to be an abduction," the man sneered.

How stupid of me!

"From what I've learned about you, this should be a fitting reward, considering your obvious pathologic tendencies." There followed an interlude of frosty chuckling that exuded unadulterated contempt. "My associate wants you unharmed and held safely until your family and/or employers are informed and come up with a modest, specific dollar amount. Then if things work out, you will be set free.

"On the other hand, I also have specific instructions to dump you if any complications arise. There are to be no 'tracks' that might lead the authorities to this little entrepreneurial venture." There was a slight pause, perhaps to let his explanation sink in. "Off the record, though, I would just as soon do the world a favor and be done with you. Nothing personal, mind you."

There was another laugh, one of malicious pleasure that could only be a natural inclination for this beast. At least the issue was settled, except for the reason why he had divulged as much information as he did.

In the back of her mind and pushing steadily to the forefront was the dread notion, unbelievable though it was, that she, Lindsey Maguire, was about to become another entry in the obituary column of the local newspaper.

That typically required a corpse, rather than a missing person report. But if it should come to the printed word, and if she was really fortunate, there just might be a few drippy, sweet words from some big-hearted soul about all her accomplishments.

She should be so lucky.

That thought evoked a rampage of naked panic through her brain. Just as quickly it exploded to white-hot rage. How dare he consider…murder!

Lindsey began thrashing about, squirming with the limited movement her bindings permitted. Screams and curses were little more than muffled whimpers, which only further fueled this brute's sadistic amusement.

Her tormentor threw something over her. She assumed it to be a blanket for concealment. It certainly was not for warmth or comfort, considering the travesty so far perpetrated upon her. For all intents and purposes, she was alone in the universe, a universe now much too big and impersonal, cut off from help, from hope.

The man maneuvered into the driver's seat and started the van. With all the nonchalance of someone who belonged, he pulled out and drove off. The security guard, more intent on his book, paid only scant attention to the van's exit, with a single nod and a limp wave through.

Lindsey's last hope of rescue evaporated in disinterest.

"All too easy," she overheard him sneer. Then, "Be polite and say good bye, *Mizz* Maguire."

This is a pathetic game to him! she fumed.

This thug was not going to have the final say in her fate, not if she had anything to do about it. It had never been in her repertoire to be pushed around and bullied by some two-bit outhouse slug.

Or murdered.

Not now! Not ever!

CHAPTER FIVE

For long metrines, the humanoid male perused the readout that scrolled across the monitor nestled among the other console instruments and gauges at the pilot's station. Reclined back and feet propped up on the corner of a small ledge he could have been reading the latest net news edition.

The data being gleaned from the myriad sensors sniffing every facet of Earth's immediate environment would be knit into the ship's computer memory banks with the information that had already been accrued. All would then eventually be dumped into his own civilization's vast reservoir of knowledge on galactic life.

For the time being, he knew that nothing was out of the ordinary for the unsuspecting populace on the surface below, at least from his long experience of covert monitoring. This was just another typical day for the locals with their crime, business, social activities, and weather forecasts, to name a few current events.

He yawned, he forgot how many times, and twisted in his seat through a skit of muscle-contorting stretches. Settling back again, he let his gaze drift up to the forward view port.

From his and Miriam's holding point at an altitude of fifteen thousand meters, they could have been lost in the vast reaches of space. The pure, black canvas of it was alive with an all-encompassing spray of iridescent diamond dust that was undiminished by most of Earth's atmosphere, its pollution, and the opaque swaths of clouds that stretched from horizon to horizon far below. The latter created a void of undulating velvety dimness that stretched off in every direction. They were drifting above a stygian sea on a sunless, distant world.

And like the yawns, he could not remember how many planets he had so far seen in his travels. A couple score? And that was just the ones that were populated.

Ah, the stars.

He let his eyes shift back to the monitor and was just in time to catch a message. Miriam's image followed it. Her expression searched for a response.

"Let them be. I will be back to awaken them," he mouthed in careful pronunciation for her understanding. "I think we got to them before they suffered any impact trauma. I am planning on heading back momentarily."

Mute since birth, she spoke in silent response as the man watched her lips move. It was a practice he had long since gotten used to, perfected.

"Do not worry. I will try to keep it short, no long-winded speeches. I promise."

More lip movement.

The pilot's face wrinkled slightly at the implied insinuation. In spite of her disabilities, Miriam had a penchant for quick, cutting wit. Flashing a teasing smile, "What is the matter, do you not trust me? Tell you what you can pilot us to the rendezvous."

The offer purchased an eager smile and a ready nod. Miriam had since become a competent pilot in her own right under his tutelage. Any chance she had to perform an extraction, with its inherent maneuverings, was always an opportunity to hone growing skills. Not that they weren't adequate already.

Her face moved out of the fixed field of view.

A pale, nondescript scene replaced her presence. It was a wall of metallic gray-green, starkly illuminated. With the limited view and a dearth of immediate detail, it could have been the inside of a grand chamber or a small closet. He sat back in his seat and stroked the several days' growth on his chin with thumb and forefinger.

Finally, he swung away and planted his feet, pushed up. He skirted around the half dozen unmanned stations crammed onto the flight deck and made his way to the back of the bridge.

When he approached a blank wall panel that looked as solid as any bulkhead or armor plating, an unseen sensor picked up the presence. In obedience to its program it scanned and correlated particular body features. It took an instant for the ship's security protocols to be satisfied, and it performed its sole function for those who were authorized passage. The panel went translucent, melted from sight.

Miriam arrived at the same time, bringing them both up short.

"She is all yours," he offered, stepping through. He ushered her past and onto the deck with a patronizing bow and sweep of his hand, but never letting his eyes leave hers as she took her place.

"Oh, by the way, please keep an eye on that number three repulsor, will you? It has been acting a little balky, and I want to make sure it stays in balance. No telling when we might have to depend on it, spur-of-the moment like."

Miriam nodded understanding, mouthed a sentence. It included a thank you.

He nodded too. "Yes, I know. There has been no sign of the others, in spite of reports. Despite the minimal risk, I will not rest easy, though, until we can safely set down and do a proper checkout powered down, not to mention some routine housekeeping chores."

Miriam nodded then moved forward.

Losing contact, the access promptly and soundlessly solidified into an impenetrable wall. For half a minute, he stood there, gazing at it in quiet contemplation, investing a passing thought at what lay before them.

At his feet, a fur-covered snake-like form began to undulate and crawl up his left leg. The creature coiled around and up until it reached his hip, where it then slithered with its three pairs of stubby paws and pulled itself up his back via his jumpsuit. It then draped itself about his shoulder and neck, slowly drumming its tapered tail end in a gentle rap against his chest.

He muttered something under his breath and began stroking the half-meter long creature.

It had no other discernible features, other than a complete covering of cream-colored fur that was banded by several darker, rust-tinted rings. It began to coo and purr in apparent contentment, making no further effort to move.

He nodded slowly, then turned and started off along the main corridor heading aft.

The passage was a utilitarian cluttering of access panels, ductwork, and equipment modules devoid of any thought for aesthetics. The tone and feel was obviously that of a working cargo or utility vessel, as opposed to the more comfortable amenities lavished upon the living, breathing manifest of a passenger ship.

Along it were five framed access portals with the same dissolving panels as those leading to the bridge. Two each were to the left and to the right. The last one formed the corridor's aft terminus. Each was replete with a small, square panel next to it that had a button and two lights. All but one of them had a single amber luminary that maintained a steady glow: the last one, on the left, was a bright green. That meant someone was present within.

The man walked up to that one. In the span of a breath, the hidden mechanisms of the door before him made disappear in an instant into thin air.

The chamber within was as unremarkable as the passageway, which was pretty much true for the rest of the ship. With his lifestyle the way it was, almost always on the road, as humans were fond of saying, there was no allowance for the extravagances of a settled-down existence.

The entrance was in one corner. Ten meters in the opposite one was a raised console. Between the two was the chamber's most prominent feature, a circular dais roughly three meters in diameter and rising a half meter off the deck. It pulsated in a gentle rhythm with an ethereal turquoise glow, accompanied by a faint hum that hinted at life, yet dormancy.

The half-lit chamber was rectangular in shape with all the joyous atmosphere of a tomb. Along two of four walls were tiers of stacked, closed, and darkened window panels that lent it its greatest mausoleum-like quality. Two stacks of three were on the short aft wall, while three tiers of three adorned the long starboard one. It was a quality he could abide, since many of his acquisitions had come to describe it as such. Was it any small wonder? Most had enjoyed only a heartbeat of time separating them from survival and eternity.

The man moved around the platform and approached the middle stack of sealed niches along the latter bulkhead. He stopped, bent slightly and stroked a button on a control pad beside the lowest one. He did the same for the next one above. Then he backed up and seated himself on the dais to await events that were about to unfold very soon.

In a moment, the enclosing panels dissolved. Inside each, a warm, diffuse, golden glow filled the space like sunshine, revealing their respective male and female occupants.

*

The tree trunk at Abby's back felt solid, secure, as she crouched low and tight against it. She only hoped it was broad enough to sufficiently conceal her form from her pursuer.

It was real against her back: she had seen it, touched it, marveled at the earthy redolence of its moist bark. Yet, some part of her brain could not be certain; she could not completely accept its reality, just as she could not accept the twilight darkness permeating everything.

The sun and a host of stars shone overhead. All were vague luminaries. The former was undeniable proof of full daytime, but its light was neutralized in some weird, incomprehensible way. One part of her brain could not agree with the other to make a final, definite determination about anything.

She looked up to where denuded, gnarled branches should be. Unfortunately, all she could see was a swath of drifting mist, and the anemic sun, an ominous presence she was unsure would provide her a friend or bedevil her as a foe. It descended in slow motion, with purpose, and had to have some meaning. Just what that meaning was, she could not imagine. As a matter of fact, an inordinate involuntary amount of effort went into solving the problem.

Her confusion only deepened. Any comprehension remained elusive like the mist.

Abby heard the plod of a footfall sounding from the other side of the stump. It was hard to gauge the distance, interfered as it was by the pounding of her heart in her chest and the gasping of the breath in her throat.

The presence had always been there, relentless in its stalking of her, like a predator on the blood trail of its prey. She could not escape it; worse, try as she might, she could not see it, identify it. All she knew was a deep abiding truth: it was malevolent, evil. Worse, it was faceless. That was the singular, terrifying aspect about it. Terror worked her lungs hard till they felt as though they would explode her chest.

The presence drew closer. The sound of its own heavy, throaty breathing and the plod of its steps belied its insane closeness. Despite the acute discomfort of her pulse hammering in her veins, she dared to creep around the edge of the hole.

Dread curiosity bid her to peer face to face at the unknown specter only a meter or two away.

She had to know, to seek the answer that beckoned as strong as the warnings that screamed in her head to cower deeper and deeper into the dead tree's presence. Each millimeter closer to the edge brought a corresponding intensity to each demand.

Finally, one millimeter remained. The chimera was all but on top her. From which side of her hiding place would it pounce, and for what purpose?

She committed, reluctantly, to erase the last miniscule bit of protective concealment. Her heart pounded one last, awful explosion in her ears...

*

The exhumation from smothering blackness, up through ever-brightening shades of gray, was beyond her control. Though it was the sweetest relief, the experience was disorienting and exquisitely so. She was being pulled from an alien abyss, from one reality to another.

Abby's eyelids popped open. Her first delirious impression was being on the far-flung beach of a warm ocean, bathed in glorious sunlight...

The hallucination promptly degenerated. In its place, a maelstrom of tangled mental images intruded upon her. Reality crashed in like a cannon round. Their lackluster anniversary date...light...collision...crash!

Movement proved chaotic like the deluge of those so recent memories.

She willed movement to hands, arms, and feet. Unfortunately, it felt as if a full dizzying second elapsed before her brain registered it. She had never been under the influence but guessed her current predicament was a pretty close approximation to what being inebriated was like.

In moments that melded into an agonizing span of time, brain and appendages managed to synchronize...in a fashion. She rolled in a clumsy motion onto her side and curled up...only to have a wave of nausea sweep over her. She closed her eyes hard against it, groaned.

This was no bad night's sleep she was coming out of. It was more like coming back from a dose of general anesthetic Maybe she was returning from the dead or near-dead. With grudging slowness, the insane affliction ebbed like the crawl of an outgoing tide.

She yearned to return to that beach.

A dull thud and an ensuing tight yelp from very nearby startled her to full consciousness. It could only be…

Denny!

She blinked to clear her sight. Her first image was the complete stranger seated only a couple of meters away. He was studying something below her. Even through the lingering mental fog, the last vestige of a grimace on his face was easy to interpret.

Abby pushed up on an elbow and steadied herself. For all she could tell she was on a ship. Not that she had ever been on all that many.

"Ouch!" Abby heard in exclamation from the unseen owner of a very familiar voice directly below. "Tell me I'm not dead!" he groaned.

Then on rising concern, almost to the point of panic, "Wait a minute! Where am I? Where is my wife?"

"Denny?" Abby's mouth was working, but no sound came forth.

She blinked at the flight suit-attired figure. He neither moved nor spoke. He only continued to exchange silent glances between her and the owner of the male voice, trying to decide who was the more interesting. The strange man's outfit was a dull green, giving the impression of military issue, though it was devoid of any visible insignia.

American, Canadian, some other nationality that just happened to be cruising by?

"Did you hear me?" Dennis now demanded, louder.

"Denny?" she managed to get out.

"Abby?"

Dennis shot up and spun around. Astonishment, relief, and confusion grappled for prominence on his face.

Abby slid out of the cushioned niche, found the floor. Her legs failed her, and she collapsed heavily into his arms. The all too fresh nightmare propelled the failure. Overwrought, she broke down and sobbed, clutching Denny by the shoulders. Words again were stillborn in her throat as the stranger got them both seated on the bottom niche and consoled her, as best he could.

Arching his left brow, "I believe the phrase is 'welcome aboard'." the stranger drew out.

Abby stole a peek with one wet eye away from her husband's embrace to take in their host. He wore a kindly enough smile, one devoid of either pretense or guardedness. This soul was friendly on the surface and definitely curious.

Together, she and Dennis could only return mutual confusion. It appeared the two of them belonged here or were, at the least, expected.

"My name is Milankaar," the stranger articulated without gesture. There was considerable accent, yet no hindrance to understand him. He was definitely foreign. "You can call me Mil." A clumsy pause followed, after which he offered a chuckle. "The last name, I am afraid, you would find hopelessly unpronounceable, in your language."

This Milankaar ventured into a moment's silence. He continued to smile, unmindful of the traumatic nature of what had only recently befallen her and Denny.

Now it was Dennis's turn to stare unresponsive into their apparent savior's face. Abby once more succumbed to the burden of their disaster and hunched over, despondent. They should have been dead, brutally dead and lost.

She wrapped her arms around her knees and buried her head in her lap.

Finally, she lifted it with weary effort as this Milankaar picked up anew. "I know you both have many, many questions," he said. "I will give you as concise an explanation as you are able to bear."

"I'll bet," Dennis sniped. "Just telling us *where* would be a good start."

Abby drifted her gaze sideways to Dennis, then back to this Mil. She blinked hard to focus eyes that were once again as out of kilter as her emotional state. There was no mistaking his straightforwardness that came through loud and clear.

"To put it bluntly," Mil began to explain, "both of you are on what your people would refer to as a spacecraft."

Dennis's response was immediate. He coughed, then shook off her hold like an unwanted encumbrance, rather than a feeble attempt at mutual assurance. He shot up to his full stature; Abby nearly fell off her seat but managed to arrest herself. Not so her mouth, which hung open, speechless. Obviously, her hearing was not yet up to snuff.

"You mean a UFO?" Dennis smirked.

Abby's gaze went from amused husband to the stoic Milankaar. Dennis would be gathering himself up for a tirade, but their host remained implacably patient. This, of all instances, was the wrong place or time for humor.

"If that is how you desire to look at it," Mil replied, his tone devoid of any defensiveness, "but I do find the comparison rather...inaccurate."

"Inaccurate?" Dennis flared. "Oh, excuse me. It isn't every day someone takes a spaceship ride, especially us. This looks like a ship all right, but a spaceship?" Then a little more menacing, "I think you need to start coming across clean with us right now. We were on an airplane and about to..." The rest of his assertion died on the air. He slammed his eyes closed and shook his head at the conundrum that confronted them. It didn't get much weirder than that, the boundary between life and death. And sometimes it blurred.

"This can't be happening! It can't be."

"The object you refer to," Mil continued to explain, ignoring for the moment, their consternation, "is something witnessed visually in flight, and though it is intangible, it has the appearance of reality. If memory serves me correct...it is a ghost, as it were. We, here," and he patted the solid presence of the dais next to him, "are not observable to prying eyes, physically or otherwise, but are as real as each of you is to each other."

"Invisible?" Dennis guffawed. The impact of the explanation was not lost on him. "Ridiculous!"

The irreconcilable difference of what should have been, and the here and now was, for the time being, forgotten. He ratcheted up his sarcasm by slapping his hands together, then folding his arms across his chest. Shooting a glare to Abby, "I don't think he gets it," he bit out. Then back to Mil, "You really don't expect us to believe that, do you?"

"I expect you to believe nothing. But in answer to your question: yes, at least as far as your people's current technological limitations permit."

"Oh, excuse me. I forgot about our primitive state of affairs."

"Quite all right. At least now you are recognizing a difference between your race and mine."

Abby felt her head spinning while Dennis was seething. Fortunately, he was doing nothing rash, being a lover rather than a fighter. Lucky for this Milankaar.

While she never cared for Denny's penchant for getting his feathers all ruffled, he was at least carrying the torch for both of them in this whole mess. In her current state of confusion it was a job she was unable to undertake at present.

"Then I take it this is some kind of…alien abduction?" she found herself asking. The query came forth more on autopilot than by conscious effort.

Dennis spun his head around to stare in surprise at her, mouth agape. The dialogue could have been just between Denny and Mil.

Mil also appeared to be caught off guard by the innocent question. He blinked once, twice, began stroking some kind of object draped around his shoulders. Abby could not be sure but it looked like it was moving.

Dennis turned to focus once more on Milankaar, awaiting a reply.

As Abby watched comprehension dawned on this Mil's expression. "Ah, now I see," their host smiled. He slapped both hands on his legs. "This is hardly an abduction! Hardly at all. Let us instead put it square in the category of a rescue." His expression turned a couple shades more sober. "And may I say a most timely one at that?"

Abby shifted an unsteady, perplexed look to her husband who, in turn, could only mirror it. This was going to be of no small interest, to say the least.

CHAPTER SIX

"Now let me see if I understand this," a still shaken Abby probed. Dennis, who looked completely skeptical, paced off tight circles before her, "You just happened to come along and snatched us from our plane at the point of impact?"

Dennis huffed, groaned. He threw his eyes up and shook his head in abject disbelief. Mil, on the other hand, pushed up and ambled over to the raised console in the corner to Abby's left.

"Actually, the timing was impeccable, Mrs. Webster," he clarified. "That is how it has to be. An instant more and you and Mr. Webster would have perished. Your craft flipped upon impact and promptly disintegrated."

Slipping behind the unit, Mil unwrapped the writhing creature and placed it out of sight on top of the panel. It stayed put. He looked up to face Abby.

"As a point of interest, the slower clearing of your confusion is lingering shock. It is due to the impact having occurred on your side first. Part of the violence transferred to you, but our capability allowed us to reach both of you at the same instant."

"Uh-huh," Dennis mouthed. He stopped at the point in his circuit where he faced Mil. Hope colored his expression. "In that case, it should be just a simple matter to put us back down. If it's anonymity you want…"

Abby turned an expectant look to Mil also, who appeared to ignore the query while playing with his pet. That alone spoke volumes, none of which hinted at any good. She climbed up, braced herself as best she could against the upper tier.

"Mil?" she pushed. Uncertainty shaded to worry.

The pause continued, long and heavy, until…

"I cannot return you," Mil drew out.

The terse, matter-of-fact statement had the impact of a bombshell. Abby staggered but otherwise managed to keep her reaction down to a couple hard blinks in exasperation.

"Come again?" Dennis snapped, irate.

Abby sidled closer to her husband, used his frame to hide behind. It was the next best thing to protection against unknown danger.

Mil flipped a final switch and looked up.

Staring was impolite, but Abby made no pretense of studying Mil for any shred of insincerity or contradiction that might otherwise betray him. Unless he was an adept actor or a practiced liar it would be difficult, if not impossible, to not let slip some hidden agenda onto his expression or mannerism. But try as she might, she could see nothing, no pretense, no nervousness. If anything, she saw regret, perhaps sympathy. She wondered if Denny also noticed, planted as he was in the midst of his tirade.

Probably not, given how worked up he is, Abby guessed.

"Let me correct myself," Mil amended. "It is not that I *cannot* return you. The fact is I can very easily. This unit," and he took in the console with an encompassing circle of his hand, "is what we call a matter pattern destabilizer. Put simply, it is a transporter. It is what was used to bring you aboard.

"Its purpose is to disassemble the molecular structure of a designated target object. It then transfers it as an energy stream, finally reconstructing it according to the pre-scanned pattern programmed into the unit's memory. Life forms are particularly complicated, though humans and humanoids are the easiest of the lot. That is due to certain universal, nearly identical characteristics. The whole process only takes a couple seconds."

"Nearly identical?" Dennis repeated, tone cool.

"You will find that I am basically human." Mil gestured to himself with an open left hand. "Except for a few anatomical variations, most of them at the cellular level, one of your physicians would be hard put to tell the difference between you and me at a casual glance."

"You mean…no!" Abby exclaimed. Her mind now grasped the enormity of what she'd just heard. Her hands came up to her mouth as she shook her head in disbelief, the absurd explanation bringing this whole mystery to a point. "I thought all this was some kind of top secret government project and you a military pilot, maybe a foreign operative, an alien national." Her mouth closed as she bit into her lower lip.

Mil shook his head, the quintessential picture of enduring patience. "Actually, alien is correct."

Dennis snorted.

"But yours is actually a common response, Mrs. Webster. I can assure you, however, that we have nothing to do with any of your world's various and sundry governments, factions, or groups."

"Ooookay," she drew out.

"You will come to find out shortly that human and humanoid groups are only a fraction of the sentient life populating the known portion of this galaxy. From our monitoring of your world's scientific endeavors, you all seem to have plenty of theories and concepts of parallel evolutionary development on extra-solar worlds."

"Yeah, right," Dennis brushed off. "That goes back years, decades."

Abby's knew her initial level of skepticism of this wild fantasy was "out there" akin where she knew Dennis's attitude to be. Her senses continued to firm, enough to begin to make self-inquiries. She had no experience in investigational techniques, but still…

There was something about Mil's candidness, his sincerity that started a creeping, nagging sensation.

"You mentioned cellular variations," Dennis brought back up, a degree calmer, for the moment.

Dennis continued to toy with Mil. It was a good bet her husband saw Abby and himself as little more than captives or hostages, in spite of a confusing lack of maltreatment associated with that stereotype. Dennis would be a tough sell, and this Mil, no doubt *very* intelligent, probably already had that figured out.

"That change involves your immune system, as it has evolved in time on Earth," Mil continued to explain. "Our race, consequently, has no protection from your indigenous microbiological elements, most of which your race have long since adapted to. Unless properly shielded, for me to leave the airtight confines of this ship to be exposed to your atmosphere or surface, even for the briefest stroll, would be a literal death sentence. I could expect to survive no more than…two days, three at the most. And my demise would be an excruciating, dreadful, drawn out affair.

"When we extracted you, the transporter adjusted your molecular structure to negate the lethality of your world to me, which is now the same for you, Mrs. Webster, and your husband. Designated microbes were filtered out and your immune systems biased to organisms my species is used to.

"Believe it or not, that to which you refer to as 'germs' are similar on both our worlds but with differences enough so as to be a problem. That means the transport design parameter has an unavoidable consequence that is beyond our current level of technology to ameliorate in your favor. What it further means is that, unfortunately, it is a one-way process meant to protect the both of us.

"After the transport, you were briefly anesthetized to counter the shock of your impending crash, any injuries sustained, and my abrupt appearance. It was at that time a decontamination procedure provided backup insurance, to keep this ship free of catalogued microbes dangerous to both of us."

"That would seem to be an easy enough problem to solve," Dennis countered. "I mean, how hard could it be to modify this transport process?"

Even as her thought processes continued to untangle other thoughts began to brush into her mind. Though Denny was the technical expert in the family, she felt herself the more pragmatic one, looking at any given situation in light of current facts. If the facts changed she modified her view as necessary.

Sad experience had long since taught her that this was the one great source of friction that arose on occasion between her and Denny, with him typically the unyielding one. She was afraid now was no different. But she was having to admit to herself Mil's candid explanation had started to sway her just a little, not to mention wanting to make her cower from what began to look more and more awesome with each passing second. Most important, there was no denying that they were here, now and alive.

"I could only wish," Mil sympathized. "As I explained, it is a purpose-built design feature meant to protect our respective species. Microbes familiar to us can be negated by the transport process, the adaptation cannot. You need only recall your planet's history of lethal pandemics."

"I see, Milankaar," a flustered Dennis drew out with frosty slowness.

Abby saw Dennis shift a sideways glance to the dais, then shuffle a half step away. What had been an innocuous presence now felt like an ominous one.

"Please, call me Mil," the more and more human pilot endeared himself. "Just a couple microbial strains that I am immune to could cause global plagues that would have no cure, at least not until many have perished before a cure was found and exploited."

"And if we do want to return?" Abby asked. "You did say you could return us."

*

Mil sighed.

This was getting to be a wearisome chore responding to the same litany of questions, especially an argumentative case wanting more than the usual proof. Sure most were intractable to a degree, but he sensed in the core of his being this one was going to excel at stubbornness. Never mind an advanced education.

A year ago he had relented, returning two extractions back to ground and what was certain doom. It was most difficult knowing souls he had saved from the very brink at great risk to everyone involved, and had gotten to know in a personal manner, were going to die. And it was all the more disturbing knowing their demise would be a painful one and without hope. Certainly Earth's medical technology was a full half-century behind that of Majora and all but useless.

But it had been their decision without duress. He could not and would not be blamed for a lack of strenuous suggestion on his part.

It did get just a little easier each time to deal with the remorse the event bequeathed upon him. But he knew it would always be a discomforting distraction, a bad taste in his mouth, till time formed a mental scab over the emotional wound. Be that as it may, he was going to have to see to some different terms when his contract came up for renewal, either that or else drop it altogether for something more conducive to a good night's sleep.

"Indeed, that is what I said. If you absolutely wanted to return, I would have no other choice. But you already know the consequences.

"You might also want to consider another quandary you will have to confront: you and your wife would have a very big mystery to explain to those you live among who know of your purported demise. Even now word is likely spreading of a small aircraft impact involving the two of you and an investigation in the process of commencing. The fallout and dry clothing would be difficult, at best, and most likely beyond your ability to deal with. Remember, the both of you *should* be dead, in the eyes of your world."

*

The sobering finality in his tone worked a cold chill that went to the very depths of Abby's soul. Images of the mortally wounded plane, the life-denying confrontation of impact, a watery grav….things that should have been, churned up in her mind all over again.

The shudder rebounded with a fury, making her shake like a leaf. Then there was that all too fresh memory of the smothering darkness and ensuing nightmare she had only of recent emerged from. It was an ominous dark, deeper than any she'd ever had the curse to experience.

If Mil and Dennis were conversing she did not hear it; indeed, the mind storm assault of their near demise left her numb with disbelief. The grave, one black, suffocating, cold, final, had been cheated, robbed. It had been so terribly close.

This time.

"…So far the others…"

"Others?" Abby snapped to. The word shot forth before she had even thought it. She blinked away the lingering distraction.

Abby stepped from behind the protection of Dennis's shoulder. A final spasmodic tremble had made the word waver a bit which, thankfully, neither of the men appeared to have noticed.

"All I ask is for you to have an open mind," Milankaar advised. There was a thread of pleading in his words, one borne of uncomfortable experience, if not just a little tired. "It will be plainly evident in short order. Neither I nor any of my associates intend any harm whatsoever to you."

"But why, Mil?" she wondered, herself now the one pleading. "What does this all mean? What kind of purpose does it all have?"

The query had just been voiced when an audible prompt blared forth from the console.

"Please excuse me for just a moment."

Mil's gaze dropped intent on only what he could see. In a moment, there came what sounded like well-scripted monologue. Abby traded confused glances between Dennis and Mil.

"Okay Miriam, go ahead and start us down. I am on my way forward." A pause ensued. Abby wondered whether he was reading script or another's lips. "No, I remember what you said...Of course, I intended on keeping it short. I promised, did I not? No, this time it just happened to be a little more difficult."

Abby saw mild surprise, then dawning annoyance, pass over her husband's face as it sunk in as to whom the subject of the conversation was.

"No, I am not worried about it, yet...Okay."

With that, Milankaar raised his head and sidled from behind the intervening console. "If you will excuse me once more, I have to leave. I would bid you to remain here while my companion and I tend to business. Should you desire to move about, however, access to and from the chamber is being programmed to permit you passage. I only ask that you refrain from touching anything until I have had a chance to explain our accommodations to you."

He smiled, picked up, and cradled the creature in both arms like an infant and paid a respectful bow to Abby. Then he was gone, heedless of protest.

*

When the access door closed behind him there was a slight shudder and a sensation of movement. It grew more pronounced. They were moving. Though surprisingly smooth, Abby and Dennis sat and huddled close together on the bottom niche.

Dennis breathed a long, despondent sigh. Shaking his head, "Of all the... Isn't this the biggest crock of slop you've ever heard of, Abby?"

Abby entertained other troubling thoughts. She did not know why, but something was…different.

"A spaceship, really! I don't pretend to know what's going on, but I, for one, am not going to stomach this fantasy of Milankaar's, or whatever it is he claims to be."

"Whomever," she corrected.

"Okay whomever."

Both spent a quiet minute staring at the deck, Abby forlorn, Dennis stewing. In absent-minded movements, Abby grated the toe of her boot against the dark purpose-etched metal decking. Any past quandary in her repertoire of life experiences was light-years distant from this, and that was putting it lightly.

She formed an opinion, both aware and wary of its consequences. It was the only logical one. She now raised her head and looked his way.

"Personally, Denny," she said, careful, quiet, earnest, "I think he's telling us the truth. I can't explain it, but I just don't sense any pretentiousness or hidden agenda from him."

Dennis was stunned.

"Abby!" he blurted. Both brows came together in cascading exasperation. Abby knew in an instant she had goofed. Denny shot her a hot glare that caused her to recoil. "Come on, don't tell me you've been taken in by this farce, not for one second! Besides, how long have you known him, ten minutes, and most of that muddle-headed?"

The expected verbal onslaught hit her like a slap. Stung by the scolding, her countenance sank back to the floor. She began rocking back and forth, despondent like a sensitive child scorned for no good reason.

"I guess…I guess I don't know what to believe," she collapsed. "I'm just trying to make sense of all of this. Maybe it's shock."

"And?" he wanted to know, faster than she was explaining.

"It was just an explanation, Denny. You're an engineer. You tell me. For whatever reason, good or bad, this is where we are, here and now. All I said was that I just don't feel any deceit or malice in him. He might be a sailor type, maybe. Who knows, he may even be our guardian angel."

"Now I've heard it all, Abby."

Abby cowered, further stricken.

"If you think for one minute that I'm going to submit to this…hoax, then you're just as…"

For just a second, there was a malignant pause that stifled the air as he teetered on the edge of his final phrase.

Then, "Just as what, Denny?" she demanded. She was wavering on the verge of losing it.

He came up short. It was like a seething volcano robbed of its explosive force. Mercifully, something had checked him before he'd uttered something stupid, some last shred of self-control. She closed her eyes tight, squeezed out hot tears, rocking all the more in an effort to stave off an expected continuation of the tirade.

Her world had all but caved in atop her, and it had to be Dennis, of all people, initiating and accelerating the process.

"Okay Abby," he surrendered in a sarcastic huff. He threw up his hands and dropped them, letting them slap against his legs, all dramatic. "I'm sorry. It's just that, well, look at what we're being told to give up, if all this does happen to be true." He shot an accusing finger at her like a spear. "Which it is not, despite of your beliefs. Understood?"

She nodded weakly. "As he said, no one's forcing us to remain here."

Dennis rolled his eyes, flustered, and shook his head. "Okay, okay. For all intents and purposes, though, we're as good as stranded up the proverbial creek without a paddle. Don't forget our whole life…everything…just happens to be down below, in case you haven't remembered. Sure he might be telling the truth, but how can we know for certain beyond your having a *feeling?* I mean, *really* for certain?"

"I…don't know," Abby replied. More tears streamed down, dripping off her chin and soaking the sleeve of her jacket. In desperation, she prayed for guidance into the pause between them.

"Well, he did say we could move about," Dennis said in a change of direction. It was a clumsy stab at trying to be more upbeat. He looked around and studied the surroundings as he slipped an arm around her shoulders. The casual gesture now stung on a par with his words a moment before. "Maybe this won't be so bad after all, for a while at least. Maybe. There must be *some* way to get off this so-called ship and back to where we belong."

He hadn't heard a word Mil had uttered. And Abby could not escape the growing conviction that home, their home, no longer had any meaning. Denny was right, in a way. Years of everyday reality, everything that had been familiar, all they had known and owned, was at the bottom of Puget Sound with the shattered wreckage of their plane.

The brutal truth of it left her mentally numb and physically exhausted.

For now just play along, she had to confide to herself. *We can do very little, anyway, at this point, except to sit back and see how things unfold.*

She squashed down a sniffle and just about choked on it. Even such a small bit of common sense was a good sign. Knowing that, she grasped onto it hard and drew strength.

CHAPTER SEVEN

Milankaar slid into the next seat opposite and a little forward where Miriam had been earlier. It was normally her place of residence when he was piloting.

He settled in, tapped a control on a switch and button crowded panel in front of him. Dormant displays, graphs, and gauges woke up as circuits engaged and drew power. They blinked, then held steady at the ready to do as commanded.

"Okay, Miriam, I am at engineering and monitoring ship's functions," he articulated toward the monitor and his mate's waiting expression. The familiar chorus of stresses, creaks, and groans born of atmospheric flight carried through the air. He flipped a series of switches and played with a dial, all the while studying a blue and gold bar graph display that fluctuated proportionately. "So far, number three looks good."

From forward, he could see Miriam raise her right hand above the seat and wave it once in affirmation.

To his left was a rectangular view port, a small creature comfort in an area that was all business. Outside they were already swallowed in a blanket of thick, wet clouds that were not quite black from the diffuse infiltration of lighting from the city hidden below. Occasional breaks made a procession of fleeting ghosts out of the fragments of tufted moisture that raced past.

Lower down the rain came, where splattered on the curved transparent pressure-therm panel that was the forward view port. He liked to watch it collect into small rivulets that smeared up and back. Affording himself a glance left, he looked out to see a silver-streaked granular mist that defied efforts to resolve it into what it really was.

Then they slid into clear air, save for scattered wisps of wet stratus that scuttled past. A scant few hundred meters below a broken tapestry of street and dwelling lights illuminated their immediate surroundings.

Mil became aware of movement behind. He twisted around. "Ah, Mrs. Webster! Good evening. Or should I say, good morning?"

*

"So, you were telling us the truth after all," Abby breathed in distracted wonder.

"Always my intent, Mrs. Webster. But at times, I find it is more prudent the truth be withheld rather than conveying an outright falsehood."

"You mean a lie," Abby clarified.

Mil arched an eyebrow. "I believe that is what I said."

She braced herself against the steadying bulk of his seat from behind and peered out the side port.

"Anyway, I took a chance and decided...decided it best to believe what you said back there." In spite of the lack of a detailed landscape, Abby was spellbound, letting her imagination do what her eyes could not. "But I never thought..."

"That there are little green men from Mars, as your culture is fond of saying?" Mil filled in.

Abby was caught off guard but managed to nod with a shy little smile. Really, the thought that little green Martians *existed*! She turned her head to give Mil a quirky look.

"Among our primary mission goals are the monitoring of your race's communications nets."

"You mean eavesdropping," Abby amended. She sent him a coy grin.

Mil returned the gesture. "Yes, very informative when there are few other means to learn, plus providing a certain amount of…um, amusement."

"I'm glad you find us so entertaining. I think it's absolutely distressing and depressing at times."

"Suffice it to say this is just such a point where most of the others I have had the privilege to rescue have come to a degree of comprehension. It is sometimes grudging but comprehension, nonetheless."

Abby's expression went to the curious. His familiarity with Earth was at the same time both comforting and enigmatic, not to mention a little unsettling. The thought of aliens spying on Earth and as close as a literal shout…

Things continued to clear up, especially since her marbles were almost back into a straight row. If it had not been for Dennis's assault…

She recoiled as sharp anguish lanced anew deep into her soul. For a moment, she closed her eyes hard against the too recent inflicted pain. She had to will strength to weakened knees. Mil gave no indication that he'd taken notice. If he did he was being polite about it.

"I guess I can understand that," she agreed. She swallowed the lingering discomfort. "I suppose that makes me normal and average."

"By all means and in a good way."

"Good. I prefer normal and average. It beats eccentric and just plain weird any day."

Mil chuckled as she craned her neck sideways in another attempt for a better view outside. The effort and the diversion of conversation was much needed balm on the open wounds that afflicted her psyche. More like an antibiotic.

"Obviously, you are not controlling this…uh, vehicle of yours, Mil." A memory swam back to mind. "You spoke of associates."

"Indeed, I did, Mrs. Webster." Milankaar gestured with his head to the forward most part of the flight deck. Abby followed the movement. "She is my closest associate, as well as my crew in its entirety. Her name is Miriam."

"Miriam?"

He gave her a confirmation in a nod. "In fact, she is human."

"No."

"Yes. She came into contact with our race under circumstances not dissimilar to that of you and your companion…I mean, husband."

Abby was mystified. It took a moment to form coherent words into coherent queries that did not sound too idiotic. Another human was here, now?

Maybe the simplest questions are the best questions.

"So, Mil, what is this all about, this rescue of ours?" she probed once more in gray-eyed earnestness. Her gaze was latched onto his. "If you have the time, that is."

"I am afraid the answer does require considerable more time than I currently have available, Mrs. Webster," he demurred. His voice also carried an undercurrent of hesitancy she caught hold of but decided was best to let go of for now. Somehow, it involved "others" he had earlier referred to, a reference that for some reason boded less than good. "I promise later that at a more opportune time I will answer any and all questions that you have to the fullness they deserve."

"I understand, and I will hold you to that."

"Fair enough."

His voice had changed in a subtle way, became more formal. It was not unfriendly or detached, just maybe…preoccupied. She decided not to meddle, instead contenting herself with watching and gleaning what answers would come by observation. And staying out of the way of whatever Mil and Miriam were up to was no doubt a pretty good idea, too.

Perhaps it was a good thing Denny elected to stay back and sulk in the chamber where he explored the environs therein. Now Abby could sift Mil's explanation for the truth without being fettered by his harping and griping.

Oh, how she wished to heavens he would be more understanding and talk without getting all worked up when confronted by hard questions that lacked ready answers! And him, an engineer even.

Speaking of her husband, "By the way, where is Mr. Webster?" Mil wanted to know.

Abby had discreetly, and with a good helping of timidity, tried to peer around the intervening dimensions of the forward seat and racks and consoles. So far, she had not been able to glimpse the mystery companion. Maybe if she stared hard enough, though, she could see right through the seat backrest. That meant she was no more than average in human size. Mil had used the term "human", but her imagination continued to conjure up pictures of ogres and bizarre aliens. This Miriam remained safely concealed from scrutiny.

"He said he might come up in a while," she replied, still staring. "He's getting a better look at that chamber."

Mil nodded. She watched him aim a finger at one of five identical buttons on the right side of his console. Pressing it and holding it down, "Mr. Webster, we shall shortly be doing some very tricky flying. I would suggest you move to the instrument suite in the corner. You will find a red-bordered switch by itself on the far right of the largest panel. Press that one and hold it."

Mil removed his finger and shifted a complimentary expression up to her, then over to the empty seat indicated on the starboard aft side. She had no problem understanding that gesture. She meandered over, sat, and began fiddling with putting the not unfamiliar seat restraints in place.

Abby leaned sideways and propped herself on her left elbow on some free space on the instrument panel. She took care not to touch anything that might cascade into further disasters. *Heaven forbid!* Another rectangular view port was to the side and a little above, providing a black hole of nothingness across which she glimpsed occasional flashes of small lights. She squirmed to peer out.

It felt more like being in an air shuttle coming in for a landing. When the craft banked every so often street and house lights shone in the distance like faraway beacons in the stygian gloom. A few sets of vehicle headlights and crimson taillights crept along and were swathed in vast patches of cold black that suggested a rural or semi-rural setting.

The ship lurched up, slid into a right turn, came gently back left. Then it leveled out. She had enough flight experience with

Denny to know they were following a water channel or a road course.

Unlike a more familiar aircraft, there was little corresponding rise or fall of engine noise that accompanied such maneuvering. To be exact, there was hardly any sound at all that might be construed as coming from whatever propulsion method drove the ship. A vague, distant drone summed it. It was entirely possible their passage went unnoticed by anyone on the ground.

Can anyone see us, she wondered.

It was just one more quandary in a litany of mind-dazing problems having assaulted her senses over the past few hours. And there was little to doubt that this was going to be the order of things for some time to come.

Continuing to peer below, a melancholic thought drifted like a dark cloud across her mind. Out on the very fringe of it a wave of panic hung ready to rush in. She and Denny were so close to home. So *very* close. In light of Milankaar's awesome revelation, though, the view was as good as an alien world. It was familiar and at the same time poisonous, close and yet intangible light-years distant.

Quite out of her control, her heart once more teetered on the brink of a meltdown by despair. Still fragile, her mended resolve began to soften once more like warm wax. Had it not been for the fact she was seated and restrained she might have collapsed into a pitiful heap.

She closed her eyes hard and strained to resist the emotional assault.

Maybe Denny was right, she confessed to herself. *Maybe I am too gullible. Maybe we should just ask to be let off here and let it go at that. Can it be so bad, since we are already supposed to be dead?*

She turned to Mil and was just about to make that request known.

"Do you have the vehicle on sensors?" she overheard him speak up, directing the query toward the console.

Once more, he was studying something not unlike a small television monitor. He was too busy to deal with her, anyway, and she too polite to interrupt.

"I know. I figured it out, too. I have no doubt that you know they will not release her alive. This crime is more than about financial gain. As a matter of fact, based on your insight, it has nothing to do with money. What was it you called it, revenge?"

Crime? Financial? Abby's mouth dropped. She gasped in realized astonishment, then slapped it shut.

"Maybe we can force the issue," Mil went on. "Give me a moment." He remained focused on the screen. At the same time, his hands worked in deft programmed movements, moving and manipulating a litany of controls.

"No, I am not talking about direct interference. There is nothing in the contract that I know of that precludes a little ingenuity, indirectly. I mean…Well, I am very much satisfied that you are my ever-present conscious…Okay, just keep them in sight until we have something figured out."

No more than a minute elapsed when a small blue light flashed for attention in front of Mil's face. It also caught Abby's attention. He began speaking again.

"Well, tell me what it is," he said.

There was a pause as his eyes scrutinized the screen. A nod signaled its end. Then his expression took on an air of expectancy in the ambient half-light. From what she could see, the item shared was conveyed on a positive note.

"You know, it just might work, Miriam. It could be real tricky, though. But it *just* might work. I will monitor the terrain ahead. When I find something appropriate we can get set."

Abby saw him glance her way. Giving her a coy smile and whispering as if Miriam could possibly overhear, "Confidentially, Mrs. Webster, I have to admit that sometimes I think Miriam is the smarter of the two of us," he confessed good-naturedly. "Her ability at foresight into certain human events does give her a distinct advantage over your normal Majoran, such as me. The truth is, none of this would be possible without her."

"Foresight ability?"

Mil nodded, turned back to his work. He left the cryptic statement unexplained and an abiding mystery. Maybe later he would be gracious enough to offer up an explanation. "We need to exchange seats so that I may monitor events that are unfolding even now, Mrs. Webster."

Abby readily played musical chairs in spite of burgeoning curiosity. Once more, she got herself secured. Mil had not shut down the station, and the plethora of graphs and readouts that entertained her were as alien as a calculus equation.

She gripped the seat's armrests as the deck underfoot rolled back and forth, steep and shallow, in an unpredictable pattern of banking maneuvers. They were still weaving around unseen landmarks and obstacles, any of which would swat them down before they knew what happened. Every so often, she thought she caught a glimpse of a dark apparition racing past the station's small window on the universe.

"Flat terrain coming up very soon," Mil announced. He looked away from a small auxiliary sensor panel. "There will in all likelihood be no more than several seconds to make this work within the window available to us. Give me a board flash when you are ready."

The banks and rolls continued...all done with an ease that surprised her. This had to be a ship of substantial dimensions and mass. Then they were flying level.

Abby stared at Mil's instruments from across the aisle, wondering what on Earth, a now slightly skewed term, was going to happen next. A thought went back to Dennis. He would be strapped into his seat and livid. He hated mysteries, and they were buried up to their collective necks in a grand one right now.

They did not get bigger than this. Not by a long shot.

Well, she sighed to herself, to understand just as often came by observing. If Mil wanted her to watch, then that was exactly what she would do. Watch and learn.

CHAPTER EIGHT

It was nearly impossible to hold together a lucid thought…almost but not quite.

Earlier uncontrollable sobbing had since expended itself, like a spent storm. It was just another proof of how every aspect of her being had so completely unraveled at the hands of a perverted criminal. And her mind, the last hold on reality with which she grasped hard onto, was slipping inexorably into an insane abyss of raw despair.

Lindsey figured her physical orientation was roughly in their direction of travel. Beyond that, time, day or night, morning or afternoon, was an imponderable concept without a reference point. How long had it been since all this insanity had begun? Two hours, ten, twenty?

And it was dark, incredibly dark, Maybe it was still night. Either that or else the beast had blindfolded her so effectively so as to render her completely blind. Either way, the result was the same.

A sharp yelp of surprise from close by split the monotony of the vehicle's droning engine, the road noise.

Much of her mind had been lulled to benumbed idleness, so much so that the commotion startled her with a reflexive spasm. The unyielding bindings gnawed wickedly into her wrists.

The vehicle jerked, producing a corresponding inertial, weighty pull back along the length of her inert form. They were accelerating…and none too gently. A string of half-muttered epithets let it be known that something had gone seriously wrong with this monster's macabre scheme.

It had to be the police!

A sharp jolt assaulted her.

Lacking restraints, she was tossed bodily a few centimeters up: just as violently she was slammed back down. Her head followed with an explosion of renewed pain.

She was not sure whether she screamed or not. Now she was on her side.

They were going to crash!

Visions of searing, grinding death crystallized in her brain. It pushed out every other consideration. Fire had to be the worst way to go.

Panic!

Then for some insane reason a wave of satisfying comfort in the prospect of such a horrific demise settled in. Maybe it was resignation to her fate, an acceptance that eased much of the terror. It was release. Death by collision was *infinitely* preferable compared to the drawn out horror her captor had in mind or any of the other means that crowded into her brain. It was oddly welcome, for that matter.

At the speed they had to be racing along at, coupled with hamstrung senses and mind, there would not be enough time to become aware of the object lurking somewhere ahead. That one would have her name written not just on it but plastered all over it. It would snuff out her pitiful existence in a blink.

Lindsey Maguire.

At least the nightmare would be over. And if there existed a thread of justice in this twisted universe, her tormentor would pay dearly for his crime too.

So much the better.

∗

"I'm afraid this is looking rather bad for you," she heard through her abiding torment. For the first time there was genuine uncertainty, rather than arrogance, underpinning his tone. "If they've found out who my associate is…"

The husky voice trailed off to another string of imaginative expletives. They were just about drowned out by the whining complaint of the vehicle and its tires.

The van's rearview mirrors blazed in a dazzling storm of cobalt blue and pure white. Instead of hounding him on his bumper, however, his pursuer was hanging back, pacing.

That was odd behavior for the police…and most confusing.

"Come on, fool, do something!" he snarled under his breath.

Still, the kaleidoscope of light stayed put.

"For your sake you had better hope he disappears," he snapped back to her.

So he was blaming her for this turn of events.

On her side, Lindsey strained to push the offending wad out of her mouth; instead, she almost choked on it. Maybe if she could rub her face against the foul-smelling, animated flooring…

The vehicle shifted hard to the left. Then it strained…lost momentum. Next came a vertigo-threatening roller coaster turn back to the right. It was less violent than the first one but enough to almost roll her bodily back onto her face. Several more turns followed in a mind-reeling convoluted series.

Outside, the flat mixed expanse of grazing land and woods had given way to winding foothill terrain. Part way into a particularly tight curve to the left, the van's right tires ran off the wet pavement onto the pothole-scarred shoulder.

Lindsey yelped at the shock of the corrugated surface rattling through her trussed up frame. More cursing, louder, filled the agitated air. The vehicle ground to a skidding halt.

As sudden as the intruding lights had appeared from behind they were gone. In actuality, they never followed from behind the last curve.

"Now what are you up to?" the man groused.

From the man's implied concern it was a ray of hope that the both of them were now of interest to at least one police jurisdiction. It faded back behind a cloud of gloom when he pulled back onto the road and brought the speed to a sensed slower rate. He was meticulous in keeping it there.

In what she guessed to be another five or ten minutes, she felt a sensation of braking; next followed the jostling of a rougher surface. Maybe it was a shoulder, pullout, or a gravel road, perhaps even a driveway.

There was no good to this as a knot of dread coiled in her stomach and slithered along every nerve. In spite of the excessive heat kicked out by the heater set too high an icy shiver worked its way through her body, tensing, pulling hands and feet against her restraints.

As long as they were traveling she was safe. Now that was no longer the case.

The engine idled for a moment, died. For too long, the only sensations to be felt were the heavy throbbing beats of her pulse in her ears and the dull drumming in her skull, interspersed by the irregular pitter-patter tapping on the vehicle's exterior. Not quite rain, maybe dripping water from a tree or a building eave. Otherwise, the silence was malignant, ominous.

Stirring and rustling sounded around her. There came a bump against the top of her head, followed by a whiff of something musty, dirty. She held her breath. She strained to raise her head a few centimeters.

"I think I have come to a decision, Lindsey Maguire," her abductor said. She did not like the air of evil finality attached to it. He was close now, too close. "As I mentioned earlier, if any problems came up I was to eliminate the cause of them."

Panic erupted all over again, carried on a wave of rising nausea. A few pitiful groans were her stifled efforts at protesting and pleading, begging for even a shred of mercy.

"So, I hope you will understand. It's really nothing against you, personally. Secrets have to be kept, you know."

What secrets, you swine!

His response was more indecipherable movement around her. Otherwise, there was only that maddening quiet. Tears began to stream forth once more.

It was not the fact of death that was so terrifying. It was also not the how of it. She had come to accept that dismal prospect. It was the abiding terror meted out in the meantime, the awful waiting.

Why…oh why…had they not just crashed and been done with it?

In a spasm of movement, Lindsey warred in vain again against the cords knotted as tight as ever hand and foot.

*

"Mrs. Webster, has there been any movement from the vehicle yet?" Mil inquired, preoccupied with his ship's balky drive unit.

Abby scrutinized the area of interest, having received a half-minute's crash course in sensor operation, after another round of musical chairs. It was good to have been on the periphery of Denny's instrument flight training. However limited it at least had lent her a mote of familiarity with the monitor and the array of controls before her. Unfortunately, the attendant script could have been in Chinese, for all the good it did.

"I don't think so," she said. She failed to keep uncertainty out of her tone.

"We have to be certain," Mil snapped back. "The nature of our extractions requires not only split second timing but constant vigilance leading up to and during the terminal phase."

She didn't need to hear that. Not during this most critical time. But it did remind her for a brief flash how very true it had been in her and Dennis's case.

The thought that perhaps one more half second aboard their doomed aircraft would have made all the difference between the here and now and the blessed ever after was enough to rattle her all over again. The memories were still too raw. It took considerable effort to focus on the critical task at hand.

"Speak to the monitor and command it to go to infrared," Mil added, a bit pointed.

Abby blinked, snapped to from her brief slide into inattention. Maybe later she could find ample time to give their untimely blessing all the contemplation it deserved. She hesitated at first, brushed away passing perplexity and complied, leaned closer.

Talk to a visual monitor?

She spoke to the dormant screen, tried not to look so obvious…or ridiculous.

It was like the device was waiting for the command. As the last word slipped out, the vocal override in an instant processed the request and in plain English. The solid, gray color painting it blinked, then transformed to a collage of vivid greens, blues, and darker violet.

She knew what infrared meant: heat emanation. Everything above absolute zero produced it, cold or wetness notwithstanding. That included mammalian life…and vehicle hoods.

The latter stood out in surprisingly sharp and familiar relief, like an artistic abstract and rendered in a bright peach hue. It was a coined-sized area that betrayed the still warm engine and the heat it radiated to the hood that concealed it. On the periphery of the monitor a few smaller spots of cooler scarlet were apparent. One moved with perceptible amoeba-like slowness.

Mesmerized by the display and its rainbow of colors, Abby only just sensed the presence behind her at the last instant.

"Welcome forward, Mr. Webster," greeted Mil. He glanced away from his own instruments just long enough to acknowledge the newcomer.

Dennis mumbled something akin to a reply. His gaze was busy meandering among the several workstations in passing interest.

"Mil, I still…"

"It can wait, Denny," Abby interrupted. The request was gentle enough but with a definite chill. She loved him dearly, but right now the wounds were still fresh. Besides, she and Mil had a most important matter to attend to.

Dennis drew a dumbfounded frown, his lips a tight line as he focused on her. Any protest was for the moment stifled.

Abby refused to break her hold on the monitor.

"I only wanted to say something else," he whispered to her with matching testiness.

"Fine. Right now our friends are in the middle of a delicate rescue. My job is to monitor."

"Sounds absolutely fascinating," he huffed.

Abby ignored it. "It seems the person Mil is interested in is a kidnap victim who is about to be brutally murdered."

Dennis's first response was immediate skepticism. "This can't be…"

He caught himself and straightened, perhaps to keep from looking any more idiotic than he already did.

Abby continued to ignore him.

But then, "You mean…murder?"

"Not yet, Mr. Webster," Mil overheard and corrected. "But your assistance would be much appreciated. It very well could make this intercept much more successful."

The wind snuffed from the sails of his ego all he could do was send a disgruntled look about the bridge and the Spartan crew manning it. "Of course…whatever you want."

"Excellent," Mil said. "Please return to the transport chamber. It can be operated from here; however, our current situation is requiring the full attention of three." Dennis's curiosity went to the forward seat and its unseen occupant. "The subject of our extraction will in all likelihood require assistance. You will find appropriate supplies stowed behind the transport console."

"I'll do whatever I can, Mil," Dennis reluctantly agreed. He stole a glance to Abby, but she returned a blank look. For a passing moment, his expression was unreadable.

His quandary and skepticism over all of this was still apparent. Abby then took the time to gesture with her head back to the exit. At least he was playing along, and that was good.

"Do as he says, Dennis, please. And hurry."

Dennis stiffened. She had no doubt it was her use of his proper name, rather than the endearing one she normally used, like with a child in trouble. If it made him feel guilt-ridden, even annoyed, then maybe that was fuel for a later discussion. That also went for her lingering hurt and indignation. He started off.

"Oh, by the way, Mr. Webster…"

Dennis stopped in the open portal, turned.

"Do not be in a hurry to climb onto the transport platform." Mil's expression was a study in experience. "Wait until the decontamination process has run its course. Since you will be there, I will delete the anesthetic phase."

"How will I know it's finished, Mil?"

"You will not see it."

"Right."

*

Free of the distraction, Mil turned his concern to the ship's finicky repulsor.

While it was not presently in the midst of a fit, the instrument readings were skewed just enough to shake his confidence in their ability to launch into space flight. Should the need arise. And should he have to take it off line, or, if it were to fail altogether, they would be limited to nothing more than terrestrial flight. That would make them little more than a high tech passenger hauler.

Of graver concern would be the severe handicap they would have to endure, should the others show up.

"Right Miriam," Mil acknowledged, "I am seeing it too. After we finish our task, one of us can go back to the drive section and do another manual adjustment."

He hoped that was all it required.

*

Lindsey was twisted and dragged across the carpet. One strong hand curled around her right upper arm like a steel clamp. Skin and fabric pinched painfully between his fingers.

The pulling stopped. Something cold and wet grazed past her cheek. In the next breath came a sharp splatter.

Rain.

There was a yank against her arms. A snap followed.

Thus freed, but with no sensation or control, her legs flopped heavily to the floor with a loud thud. In the same instant, she was hauled upright to sitting.

The abruptness of it spawned a tidal wave of vertigo that crashed over her. It was a condition that had lurked as a steadfast presence on the periphery of her brain. It ran the gamut from the mere dizzying on into the nauseating. He grabbed for her blouse and coat lapels and clenched onto them, keeping her from toppling over.

"Don't pass out on me now, cutie," the man sneered. "It'll be easier and faster with your help. As a little favor to you..." With a tug the blindfold came off, and with it not a few strands of entangled hair.

"Since this is the end of the ride for you, I guess it won't hurt for you to see your angel of death. A parting shot, you might say."

Lindsey grimaced. Whether from the terror of the revelation or from the eternity spent under the blindfold, she was unable to focus on this devil masquerading as a human. Again she screamed and struggled.

"That's very good, *Lindsey*. I like it." The man snickered. "You're actually quite attractive, did you know that? But you're also a snake, a deceptively pretty viper. And believe it or not, from what I've heard, that's not too far from the truth. You really should save the effort for when you need it."

An icy trickle slithered down her legs, nudging aside the numbness. With each passing second, they felt more and more like lead ingots. Then came the relentless onslaught of pins and needles tickling that intensified to being painfully unbearable.

Lindsey's vision cleared, firmed. She tried to focus on her tormentor but saw nothing other than hulking shadow with only a hint of discernible features, thanks to the darkness.

She hated not seeing her adversary, face to face. That went for anyone she could not face close up and overwhelm by the strength of her personality. This one was a coward, a demon that skulked about the night as a faceless, nameless specter hiding and doing his dirty work among the shadows and in the safety of anonymity.

Another hand laid hold of her and attempted to haul her up to standing. He relaxed to adjust his stance, letting her sag back down. She gathered what feeble strength she could, but it was in no way to help him with the evil plot he had in mind for her demise.

Lindsey did what she could in the brief respite available.

Despite bound feet and the continuing return of sensation, she bucked and kicked forward with her entire body, for all it was worth. Combined with the rest of her body mass, the shot went roughly in the direction of the apparition in one quick motion. With any luck, her aim would be good enough.

She connected.

Her desperate gesture, fueled by a blind instinct to survive this travesty, might have gained just a little more time. But to what end was more an exercise in instinct than the chance of any logical purchase, symbolic rather than practical. If anything, it would inflict a little retribution in payback for the abuses heaped, and to be heaped, upon her.

A small portion of her rage was satisfied, a grim satisfaction in the accomplishment of it. Wherever the blow had struck it had not been a glancing one but solid. The profusion of intermingled groans and profanity made that amply known.

Poetic justice, for whatever it's worth.

Retribution promised to be sure and punishing. She braced for it.

She went limp and fell backwards to the floor, used the momentum to roll onto her side. Head tucked in and knees drawn up into a tight fetal position she awaited the assault to come.

Instead, "Okay, sister, if that's the way you want to play it!" Anger quivered with discomfort. A sharp tug at her ankles felt like her legs were going to be pulled out of socket. "I'm more than willing to go along."

Vile hands grabbed her all over again. With irresistible force, she was hauled up to unsteady feet, now loosed. He shoved her into motion.

Actually, she was being dragged along, an unwilling, trussed up sacrifice being led to the altar, an altar of malevolent convenience for a twisted mind. Gravel ground and scuffed underfoot.

How she managed to keep her balance…

She tried to drop to the ground like so much dead weight. Through the tumult, she glimpsed some kind of structure…

Her mind exploded at the stark realization. Once more, her instinct for survival boiled to a feverish frenzy she had never before exercised.

Or would ever again.

CHAPTER NINE

"Kiss this life good bye, Maguire," the man spat, spinning her around. In the next instant, he shoved her viciously against the bridge railing.

Lindsey tried to plant unsteady feet on the wet, gravel-cluttered pavement. His strength and resolve was that of a Titan against her feeble resistance.

He forced her all the harder against the safety barrier, shoved once with irresistible effort…

Over she went!

"All too easy," the man chuckled, swiping his hands together. He could have been casting off a sack of garbage. Unconcerned with any telltale splash to indicate an end to his evening's work, he turned to leave.

"Hope you sleep tight tonight!"

*

Lindsey had no idea, nor cared, whether she screamed or not in her pell-mell tumble into oblivion. What came to mind was most odd, yet grim in its appropriateness.

In years past, during times of mental idleness, she had infrequently tried to finger her deepest, darkest fear. It was difficult, but one appropriate image now crashed back in exclusion of all else: being trapped in the bowels of a darkened, sinking ship with freezing, invisible water slopping at her feet. It would rise to her waist, chest, and last of all her mouth. Stifled, blind, and suffocating, she would struggle desperately and always in vain to find an exit to salvation.

That memory…the pitch-black blindness, the swirling water, the unseen deck canted at obscene angles…the utter aloneness…now flooded back in with exquisite vividness.

And what lay below stood ready to suck the very life from her lungs, her body.

She braced for what she knew must come.

Frigid water…blackness…helplessness…death.

*

"She's going over!" Abby screamed. Her eyes bulged aghast in horror realized, fixated centimeters from her monitor.

Mil's only physical response was a blur of movement over his instruments. He had said time was of paramount importance, and now what they had available could be measured in a few heartbeats.

A small tremor rumbled through the deck plating.

"Miriam, please keep it steady!" Mil exclaimed. "I am not locked on yet!"

Abby saw a drastic change in intensity in the infrared signature, a distressing change. It nearly disappeared.

"This is definitely not good!" she muttered into the energized air. "Mil, it's changed!"

"She is in the water. Almost…got her!"

The ambient illumination from the cabin and instruments faded just a degree as the transporter sucked the necessary power it needed to disassemble a human being. Abby noted but ignored it: her attention remained locked on the drama playing out before her very eyes on the monitor. Horror choked the breath from her throat.

This was cold-blooded murder, plain and simple.

A shiver coiled up her spine, one that wormed cold tendrils through every part of her being. To witness another living, breathing soul on the brink of eternity, at the hands of a twisted, perverted mind, whisked her mentally to the other's presence. Never mind this was an electronic rendition of a complete stranger.

The paralysis-induced shock of ice-cold water flooding throat and lungs, the naked panic of drowning, the relentless stampede of death…

Abby sucked in a breath in a loud gasp. She buried her face in her hands and pushed it out in an uncontrollable sob.

She had no idea how long she sat like that in a pitiful heap. So many emotions bombarded her that no single one was dominant. In their totality, they left her mind short-circuited and temporarily incapacitated. Then she levered her gaze up and dared squint through tear-blinded eyes to the sensor display. Certainly Mil had been too late. That could not, and was not, his fault.

Mil was up and shuffled toward her. "You can relax, Mrs. Webster," he soothed. She could only project bleary-eyed utter confusion. "She is aboard now. I will shortly be heading back to help your husband assist her. May I suggest that you accompany me?" Mil gestured with an arm to the exit. "There is little for you to do here."

Good news or not, the brief emotional storm, coupled with the swirling pursuit and rescue, left her drained. The effort it required to put animation to her feet, for the time being, failed her miserably.

*

Mil saw Mrs. Webster crying softly and paid her the deference of privacy with her private torment. It was uncomfortable and awkward to see this happen, but there was little he could do, no word he could really offer, except to comfort and counsel, should it be needed. Such assistance was not one of his contract requirements but an unwritten and no less necessary one.

Besides the rescues and extractions he was charged with, he was also responsible for observing his acquired charges and Earth with its plethora of cultures. He was the de facto rescuer and friendly soul. Mrs. Webster and the others and their responses to rescue were just one facet of what he was supposed to make note of. But it went without saying that Earthers, with their wide spectrum of emotional reactions, were not all that unique a lot.

Emotions were a universal truth among the many other sentient races scattered among the star systems populating this portion of the galaxy the locals were fond of referring to as the "Milky Way." Fortunately, Majorans were not too terribly far removed from the same range of emotions and behavioral peculiarities humans appeared to possess. That made for predictability.

Except for the presently insurmountable immunological barrier that separated the two worlds and their respective races, there was little reason they could not mingle and coexist. Yet there would of necessity be some inherent degree of awkwardness. Perhaps even comedy. That much was unavoidable. At least the similarities were greater than the differences.

Mil chuckled at the thought of such clumsiness. His time on Earth, such as it was, was extensive when he was not indulging in other business. His favorite snooping happened to be no more intrusive than monitoring local radio and visual broadcasting. From what he had seen, Earthers did enjoy comedy, and he could just imagine a shipload of Majorans trying to fit in. It was an easy temptation to think how many humans would suspect something odd, such as "extra-terrestrials", in such a hypothetical scenario.

All things considered, he felt himself a fairly adept interstellar anthropologist, of sorts. Maybe someday, Majoran scientists. more specifically those of his cultural persuasion, might come to terms with this microbiological barricade separating their respective races. Then he and others might not have to suffer with their quarantine entombment aboard a ship or any of a number of automated observation posts scattered about Earth's surface. They would then be able to intermingle freely among humans and *really* learn a lot, first hand.

And of the observation posts the closest happened to be not too terribly distant, in the central part of a territorial unit known as California.

He stole a glance to Mrs. Webster, who was still lost in the self-torment she had succumbed to. She came across as not much different than himself: soft-spoken and empathetic, a person of deep feeling who cared for those around her.

Unlike her, he could not allow himself to be embroiled in the emotional storms of others, though he had to confess at times it was difficult. He could not afford to and not be of any use to those he was charged with caring for. Still, he knew she would come around.

What was the term, resilience?

He would leave her alone for now. Maybe later they could get better acquainted, a behavior not particularly encouraged by his overseers. But she was also a lot like Miriam. Many of their hardier qualities lay subsurface under a quiet demeanor of reserve and elegance. They were gems beneath a pristine landscape, beauty atop beauty.

Mr. Webster should count himself most fortunate to have her as his mate.

Mil shifted attention and stroked a button that flashed a signal on Miriam's main panel. It brought her to face her visual monitor.

"Miriam, unless the repulsor starts acting obnoxious, I want to give this criminal an interesting time, a little something to remember this night by. For the moment, just tag along and keep shadowing him. I am going back to help out. I will signal when ready to proceed. Also lay in a course to get us back to the California station."

Miriam nodded ready compliance to his mouthful. He left the flight deck.

Over the years, he felt he had grown familiar with many of the global laws that were common among most of the local cultures. In spite of his own roguish beginnings, the years of contract work had instilled a settling of attitudes. While never a serious law-breaker, now he saw law and justice as the strong cord that bound societies together, kept them healthy and thriving. As far as he was concerned, part of his constitution was desperate to see justice done in this case. Unless he intervened this tail end of a slime yarkmah they were trailing stood an excellent chance of getting away free with his heinous act.

Vigilante? The local constabulary stood an equally good chance of missing this crime. Maybe his contract might not technically forbid interference, but it was the *right* thing to do. Just for this case.

Now if only his ship's ailing propulsion would cooperate.

*

The inert form lay twisted and deathly still on the dais, enclosed in a shimmering curtain of cyan energy. There was no sound, no crackling static that might normally be associated with an electric field. It certainly looked weird enough. In this case, Denny had no qualms about taking Mil's advice about not interfering.

Maybe he was right, at least until he found out more about this entire farce that was little more than a circus. Common sense *was* no doubt safer than innocent curiosity. Solving mysteries, much to his displeasure, would have to be put on the back burner, for the time being. At least until things settled down some.

Dennis beheld the phenomenon with growing wonderment. One thing was for certain: he had never seen anything like this, except in a movie. That went for most of the gadgets and knickknacks on board Mil's merry little space ship.

Just like Mil said, the field's intensity began to drain away. In a few seconds, it was little more than a few gnats of blue light swirling about, like skittering sparks caught on invisible currents of air. A couple moments more and even those evaporated.

In strode the big man, Mil.

Dennis saw the alien hesitate. By his body language and from the dip of his chin, he took it that Mil wanted him to move in. Dennis put himself into motion.

The person was obviously in need of help. At the very least, she was unconscious, all so very still.

An uncontrollable shudder shook him. There was every possibility this situation was worse, much worse.

She can't be dead! Denny felt the color drain from his face. *She just can't be. This is like something from a bad dream.*

He suffered through yet another sickening shudder. He had seen death before, his uncle and grandmother. Though it had been dressed and bundled up that alone had been tough enough. This, on the other hand, was not straightened, sanitized, tidy. No, this was about as messy as it got, up close and personal. This was the very front line of the eternal, vicious battle between life and death.

Death was never convenient, but at least with a funeral and a viewing the dearly departed was made to appear as if asleep. Finality was brought about. Fortunately, he had not been that close to either of them, making it easier to cope.

He fixed his gaze on where the chest would be. He hoped for Heaven's sake for some movement, any movement, that would dispel his dread.

"Come on, breathe blast it!" he muttered under his breath.

Then he thought he saw it.

He blinked hard.

He leaned closer, not daring to take a step.

Another breath came, nearly imperceptible, slow and halting.

Mil slipped up on the dais beside him. More respirations came, spasmodic and halting.

"Thank goodness," Dennis sighed in relief. It was bad enough being a virtual captive on an alien ship without having to deal with the formally living in same. He gulped hard, steeled his nerve to get ready to help. "Okay, Mil, you're supposed to be the big expert on this sort of thing."

Dennis saw that his comment was unnecessary. His host was already in motion and sinking down to his knees to attend to the limp form.

Now how long has it been since that first aid course, Dennis, ol' boy?

It was early on in college.

His mind raced, exhuming long-buried techniques that were never really driven home by any serious thought of usefulness in the future. The sole purpose for it was an easy two credit elective. Now he wished he had paid more attention, instead of daydreaming his way to a satisfactory grade.

In the modest illumination, it was obvious this person was soaking wet. That had to mean near drowning or something very close. A few dim fragments of long forgotten procedures began to coalesce in the back of his mind, like a jigsaw puzzle missing too many pieces. He gulped, drew closer, and noticed the bound hands.

Any previous hesitation went out the window as he dropped to his knees. By now, Mil had positioned the poor soul onto her side and started to work around the shoulders and head.

A gag! That explained the labored irregular breathing.

Dennis refocused on the task at hand: the knotted cord binding the wrists. The skin was pale, raw, wet, and ice cold. The arms were stiff in a pretty good approximation of rigor setting in and not waiting for the rest of the body to die off. In a pair of seconds, Mil had the gag off.

The female exploded into a body-contorting convulsion of coughing and sputtering. A wad wedged in her mouth shot across the chamber. The effort to free her wrists was another matter, hampered by her writhing so much. Somehow he managed to get the rope undone.

They eased her over onto her back. She continued to contort, hack, and sputter. Dennis leaned closer to her head and gently swiped sopping tangled locks of blonde hair from her face...

In a reflex, the female swung her right arm. It shot up and around to reward him with a belt to the head.

"Keep you filthy hands off me!" she snarled through another cough.

The force of the unexpected blow hurled him sideways with a yelp, more out of shock than any injury. He rolled backward off the platform and contacted the deck painfully on his right side.

"What'd you do that for!" he exclaimed when he righted himself, stunned.

Dennis found a sitting position and was already nursing what promised to be a sore jaw. In a moment, he regained his feet while the newcomer once more suffered through another spasm of coughing.

"So much for the good deed a day part," he griped into the air.

The Majoran scooted to the edge of the dais and eyed him for possible injury. "Do not be overly concerned about it, Mr. Webster," Mil consoled. To Dennis it sounded like the comment and event had only small significance.

Dennis felt a friendly pat on his left shoulder. Here he had just been walloped in the jaw with a smack that could have dislocated it, had it been a little lower, and his host was brushing it off like a minor disagreement. Even now heat began to rise in his cheek and effuse to the rest of his face. His ear was ringing away like an unanswered phone call. Following Mil's lead, though, he crawled back onto the dais and near the female on his knees but this time discreetly out of harm's way.

The sopping wet, disheveled female rolled over and in slow motion struggled up to hands and knees in an unsteady crouch. Her head hung low, the last part of her body to draw strength from a reserve just about depleted. She then rocked back and sat, crossed her legs and wrapped both arms around herself as reflexive shivering shook her body like a leaf in a strong breeze. She became more and more animated.

"This is a common response I have come to expect among your people," Mil enlightened. He could have been evaluating a specimen. "I would fully anticipate that for the time being, in her eyes, you and just about everyone else will pretty much be in the same league as the beast that attempted her murder. I would give her a little more time to adjust."

"And space. Thanks for the information. I'll believe that when I see it." Dennis grimaced, massaging his jaw. He now studied the female with the protection of Mil's shoulder, more than happy to let Mil be the Good Samaritan to his alien heart's content. "With my luck, she probably earned a black belt in karate."

Mil adjusted his posture with great conservation of movement, perused the new arrival for the most of a minute.

"You are…not him?" the female was able to ask. The last word barely stumbled past her lips.

Dennis was struck by how deathly pallid her complexion was, in spite of the lean illumination that did nothing to help. Maybe when she dried out she would look like something other than the next best choice to a graveyard candidate.

"Mr. Webster, if you will go to the supply compartment over there," and Mil pointed to a panel behind the control unit, "and open it. You will find some thermal wraps. Please bring one."

"Huh?"

"Blankets, Mr. Webster."

"Oh, yeah, blankets." Dennis complied.

The lady's eyes were now ablaze with fear. They darted about in anxious snatches but always keeping track of the two of them with ultra-heightened wariness. She was not affording an instant's inattention. He only hoped that, while a seething volcano of rampant paranoia, she did not go off in a dramatic way that required the full efforts of the both of them to contain. One definitely could not do it: two would have their hands full. Hopefully, Mil comprehended that little fact too.

In slow motion, the Majoran raised a finger to his right cheek. The female recoiled backwards a handful of centimeters. Dennis had the distinct impression this was a newly caged animal, one previously free and now surrounded on every side by perceived menace emanating from any and everything.

That sounded just a little familiar. Unfortunately, the comparison churned up a tenuous thread of calm he had managed to fashion, which made this whole charade all the harder to swallow.

*

In spite of Earth years of desensitization by personal experience, Mil had never completely come to grips with the remorse he suffered in the throes of such distress. Any creature of feeling would find it unavoidable. To not be so moved would be a tremendous moral injustice and trivialize his whole business. That included not just his business but life itself.

He hoped he never reached that point, to become as thoughtless and inconsiderate as a robot. It was a small token of identification with those he had to deal with, past, present, and future. Granted, those spells were becoming shorter, less intense. That he could deal with, especially since it meant a peaceful sleep period's rest.

What alternative was there? It was those tragic life-shattering events both humans and Majorans confronted that bred what he was now witness to. And he cursed it. It was all the more senseless when the circumstances were man-made. But the universe was full of tough careers and tough choices, and this was the one he had long ago opted for, in a more noble youth.

No regrets.

It was to make the universe a little better place, he had explained during the review of his application. Even now it was still true, but sometimes it sounded so...nobly neophyte. Experience had brought him far, taught him much, made him a seasoned veteran.

But unfortunate events *did* have fortunate outcomes. Miriam happened to be one of them. That alone helped make it all the more bearable, even worthwhile.

She had been one of his "extractions" during a catastrophic half-block tenement fire ten years earlier. Tenant records had proven less than accurate from the news broadcasts. In the weeks of follow-up investigation, he had discovered that she was never missed by those who kept track of such statistics. So much for covert snooping. Most fortunate.

A mutual fondness developed over time, and eventually he was able to wrangle a clause in his contract to include her in future work. In reality, getting her aboard was more like a well-placed threat to terminate the contract when his most benevolent overseers started to balk at the arrangement. It was a maneuver that had gotten him a lot of mileage in the past. Blackmail did have its uses, at times.

A pilot and consort were...well, frowned upon.

"My name is Milankaar," the Majoran offered in his best soothing tone.

"And I'm Dennis," Dennis added in from behind.

Mil tensed.

He had failed to tell Mr. Webster that he would handle this as a solo effort, at least during the initial interaction. Turning his head askance, "Mr. Webster, I would ask you to be quiet for the time being," he asked with a tactful, but firm, tone. "More than one voice is not normally a problem for someone under normal circumstances. With the chaotic state she is presently in, it takes only a small provocation to run the risk of forcing a mental overload. That goes even for an innocent unintentional one."

"Heavens, I would never want to do that," Dennis whispered, deadpan.

And he well knew the consequences could be predictably unpredictable. A potential Pandora's box, he had heard humans say on one or two occasions. She would need time and a lack of intrusiveness to settle down, to adjust and acclimate, assimilate. Some shelter of stability amid a storm of roiling emotions had to be gained.

Fortunately, she did not cower or jump to anything more drastic.

"Let us try again, Miss." In spite of the colorful brogue, he made sure his words were soft, slow, and articulate. He deleted any gestures. "My name is Milankaar."

The verbal medicine was now given in dose. Now they would see if a response was forthcoming.

Mil stretched an arm back, careful as much as possible to keep it out of view of their guest. A finger gesture bid Mr. Webster to hand him the packaged thermal wrap. He waited patiently until he felt the weight of it and brought it forward.

In innocent movements, he broke the seal on the tight book-sized package. Undoing a couple of the folds, he felt the gathering warmth as an unleashed chemical reaction began to infiltrate through the wrap. He then laid it on the dais, offering-like. One finger nudged it several centimeters closer to her.

"Here, you look like you could use this," he urged. "It will warm you up."

After a drawn out pause, the shivering female dared drop her gaze to the inanimate object. Then in a quick movement, she shot it back to Mil and locked stares. For the better, Mr. Webster was in full compliance with his request and stayed in the background while she kept full focus on him, one on one.

She remained mute, a coiled spring ready to let loose at the slightest provocation. And just as resolutely, he kept his patience.

"Just as soon as you are able, Miss, I would like you to take a seat over there." She followed the easy movements of his outstretched arm to the location indicated. "Then we can take care of that problem you had."

Mil glanced back to Dennis, whose mouth now hung open. Confusion hung like a heavy weight on his expression.

"Problem she had?" Dennis mouthed, sotto voce.

Right now, though, Mil would not explain. His guest would find out soon enough, with little explanation needed.

CHAPTER TEN

The van coursed its way along the darkened mountain highway. Its high beam headlights stabbed and scythed the wet darkness in an eerie sort of swordplay. At this late hour, there was almost no traffic, nothing or no one that had witnessed the deed only just concluded. Entering into a curve, the twin strobes highlighted for an instant the ghostly boles of ancient conifers and the knotted carpet of wet undergrowth that was the stygian forest's boundary beyond the road's shoulder.

His night's work complete, the man lit a cigarette and drew in a long breath. He held it briefly then pushed it out in a roiling cloud that hung in front of the windshield. Certain he had left no evidence beyond the unavoidable tire tracks on the road's shoulder he still kept the vehicle's speed casually within a few miles of the posted limit. No point in pushing a good thing.

Just to for insurance, he tried to remember if everything was in order: tail lights, headlights, turn signals… It would be his dumb luck if some bored deputy lurking on a side road up ahead had the slightest excuse to pull him over for something he had complete control over. Besides, coming to the attention of the authorities once already, with a sample of his handiwork in hand before his dump, was enough for one night.

The man drew on the cigarette again. The fiery tip flared hot orange, reflected off the windshield. He reached for the radio and turned it on. Scratchy static made him wince.

He groaned. *Blasted mountains!*

With the cigarette clenched between his lips and left hand on the steering wheel, his right hand fiddled with the tuning knob. A station, any station, would break the monotony.

Without warning, brilliant light exploded from close behind. He had not even seen a vehicle approach! How reckless!

"What the..." he swore under his breath. Panic was the order of the minute. "Not again!"

The harsh, pulsating blue and white glare besieged the van from the rear door window, side door, and rearview mirrors. He squinted harder at the blinding discomfort, using an arm in a vain attempt to brush it away.

Ticked off and unnerved, he swore again at this abrupt turn of events. For good measure, he threw in the *late* Lindsey Maguire and that sniveling loser David, his erstwhile co-conspirator, as he tossed caution to the wind and ground his foot into the accelerator.

How could he have been so inattentive!

He afforded a quick glance into the mirror in an effort to glimpse his pursuer. No use. They were practically on his bumper and blotted out by the brilliance. He turned back forward.

There was a sharp jolt...

No road!

The man had no time to hit the brake pedal before the van parted the guardrail and careened off into space. Even if he had it would have been a useless gesture. The headlights sought solid matter but instead found only misty night.

At first in slow motion, then with increasing animation, the beams gyrated as the vehicle lost forward momentum and began to tumble into an ever deepening arc. Only a muffled scream from within and the revving engine, whining in an effort by sheer force to keep the whole airborne, gave testimony to the plunge into oblivion.

So did the dazzling, oscillating lights.

They drew up to and hovered in silent witness over the mangled barrier. For a moment, they lingered while an unnatural, dull orange glow illuminated the black forest from below. Then the funeral pyre dimmed, a dying supernova settling down to something less dramatic. It was a pulsing epitaph of something once living and vibrant and now no longer.

The radiant luminaries vanished in an instant, leaving only the nocturnal sounds to fill the stygian forest.

*

With the pursuit ended, Abby made her way back to the transport chamber. Her entrance became the focus of attention, especially from that of the latest addition to the passenger manifest and their merry little family of refugees. The disheveled female remained cemented in her seat, preferring the security of the thermal wrap drawn tightly around her rather than the company of strangers. If a couple could be deemed company.

Mil and Dennis were out of their seats, the former acting the quintessential gentleman. Tentatively, "Mrs. Webster, may I introduce you to Miss…uh?" Mil tried to set up an exchange.

Abby drew up to but stopped a short distance from the still distraught female. She studied the new arrival with quiet expectancy. About thirty to thirty five years of age, she shot a look to Mil, then back to Abby. She blinked a couple times and shivered, then appeared to relax upon overcoming some kind of mental block.

Finally, belatedly, Abby heard a voice nearly cracking, "Lindsey...Lindsey Maguire."

That was that for the interaction.

This Lindsey's voice mirrored her expression, both clad in suspicion, all tight and guarded. Abby had no idea what had transpired back here between Lindsey's transport and her joining in on the group session. From the dialogue, it was easy to gather that conversation had not been a particularly significant or fruitful undertaking.

"Abigail Webster, Lindsey," Abby said in her best friendly, disarming voice. "You can call me Abby, if you want."

A collective relief deflated the tension-strangled chamber, like air from a punctured balloon. A flood was now pouring through the mental breech having opened up, and now the one called Lindsey crumpled forward and hunched over against the seat restraint. Hard, anguished sobs filled the air.

On an impulse, Dennis stepped forward to help, but an outthrust hand from Mil anchored him in place. At the same time, he motioned for Abby with his other hand to attend to the grief-stricken Lindsey.

Abby overheard Mil tell Dennis: "Mr. Webster, I think it would be prudent if we let your wife assist at this point. I would anticipate that for some time to come, she will harbor a particularly strong desire that all males of your race, and mine, no doubt, be damned to wherever it is such would be banished to."

"I think I see your point," Dennis conceded and just a little sarcastic. "I always did enjoy being the butt end of other people's problems."

Mil wrinkled his face in a frown. "I take this to be a…joke?" he tried to interpret.

"You catch on fast," Dennis smirked.

"Perhaps your wife's timely appearance, coupled with her being a female, broke the stalemate." There was a brief lull as Abby moved closer to Lindsey. "We should let them get acquainted, while the two of us tend to other business."

Abby nodded complete agreement.

Mil went over to the corner behind the transport instrument console and opened another square storage compartment. He rummaged around then withdrew an item from a drawer. Closing it, he shuffled back to Abby, who stood and moved back a little.

"Just a little something, should Miss Maguire wish to take interest." He leaned in closer to Abby's ear, his breath as warm and moist as any human's. Whispering sotto voce, "Over the last several hours, she has had very limited choices for her life, and the ones she did have were all bad and just as terrifying. It has been my understanding that even trivial everyday things, like hygiene items and other odds and ends, can go a long way in helping to stabilize one such as her. It has worked before. Humans, like Majorans, share many similarities and, consequently, happen to respond to many of the same stimuli."

Mil handed over a small flat box of black, reflective material, like hematite. A simple latch kept it closed.

She fingered and perused the object for a moment, then flashed understanding to Mil. "Understood. Hopefully this will get us some decent mileage."

Mil's brows came together, the metaphor apparently, like usual, eluding him. Then he nodded and smiled. He turned to Dennis.

"Come, Mr. Webster, let us go forward." Then he turned back to Abby when he remembered something. "Should you leave her company, Mrs. Webster, there is a yellow button on the right armrest of each seat. It will put you in contact with the flight deck. Please let me know."

Abby nodded silent acknowledgment. She went back to huddle next to Lindsey, like a doting mother or sister. Never mind she knew nothing of her beyond a name and a common predicament. She slipped a comforting arm around her still quivering shoulders.

In the same instant, she began to think the better of the gesture when a wee inner voice urged due discretion. She was not sure why, beyond an immediacy of feeling. And the fact Lindsey was pretty much ignoring her did not help explain it. The sobbing of moments before began to taper off.

Then, for better or worse, they were alone.

*

The flight deck entrance became transparent at their approach.

"I would like to know how that works," Dennis said, all mystified.

He felt he had settled down enough to let his professional curiosity, as an engineer, begin to answer many of the questions he had about this supposed alien ship. Most of what surrounded him had to be an elaborate hoax, of smoke and mirrors…gimmicks…to perpetuate all of this. Even so, some of the props were pretty good tricks and worthy of the mental effort to try to figure them out. Actually, they were pretty stupendous.

"It really is quite simple, Mr. Webster." Mil was first to step through and then paused to let Dennis pass. In his casualness, the Majoran could have been describing the workings of a toy. "Like many of the other devices you will come in contact with, it works on the same principle as the transporter's molecular disassembly capability, except on a selective basis. Security reasons."

"Hmm…anyway, as you were saying about this mission of yours. You also made reference to 'others'?"

Once on the flight deck and its detection field clear the access panel solidified back into place. Dennis considered it for a moment with lingering curiosity then accepted it for what it was. What he had so far seen and heard only started to alleviate his skepticism. Questions that led to what few answers there were only lead to a litany of new questions.

Well, no matter. Wasn't that his profession, to find answers to questions and solutions to problems? That went for technical ones, not personal ones.

Mil toyed with a couple switches on an overhead panel. In complimentary obedience colored luminaries flashed like holiday celebration lights, extinguished. This went on for several seconds, an amount that might have tried his patience, except he did have the big man's attention.

"The mission itself is easier to explain," Mil began to elaborate. "The reason behind it may be a little more difficult to comprehend. Perhaps by drawing off your own culture's history may be of benefit."

Dennis watched with passing interest his host's continued play with the instruments. That last comment came across as an indirect probe, or maybe even a challenge, rather than a teasing statement of historical fact. In spite of the Majoran's certain advanced education implied by the technology that surrounded him it struck Dennis that local history just might be a weakness for Mil. Perhaps on this subject they might even be more or less equal, the advanced alien and the village idiot. Either way, he felt a certain emboldening of attitude.

"That should make it easier," he said, trying to put a lid on his arrogance. "History used to be one of my favorite subjects in school. In fact, I did quite well in it."

"Good." Mil flashed a quick smile. "Then perhaps I stand to learn something? One can never get too much."

"I'm glad vanity isn't a hang-up with you."

Mil brought his brows together for a moment then brightened. "I will take that as a complement, Mr. Webster. Thank you."

Dennis's countenance diminished just a smidgen. He would have loved nothing better than to show Mil up. The latter's humble desire to gain knowledge, however, made that just a little awkward now. Well, there would be plenty of opportunity, to be sure.

"What it boils down to, in answer to your query, Mr. Webster, is the acquisition and trading of…"

Dennis sensed someone or something behind him, more than that fuzzy creature Mil had back in the other chamber. As he shifted his gaze, he noticed Mil did also, behind him. Dennis swiveled around.

A female.

"Let me introduce you to one of your own kind," Mil said. There was pride in his smile. "And someone who is also very special to me."

"By all means!" Dennis exclaimed. Casualness for the moment was forgotten. He straightened and adjusted his jacket. He almost stumbled over himself to be the consummate gentleman, as Mil had tried to be.

"This is Miriam," Mil introduced.

The newcomer slipped closer. A charming smile radiated from a tomboyish face. That one facet left Dennis first trying to guess her age. He wanted to figure not past twenty years, though he was probably off by several. *Forever a mystery*. It was a pleasant surprise, anyway.

With schoolboy clumsiness, Dennis extended his hand. The other obliged in apparent understanding.

She was string bean-thin, more than might be expected for someone her size. The flight suit, vest, and accoutrements she wore were as utilitarian as Mil's. They did little to enhance her appearance. Not that fashion happened to be the order of things around here. It hung loose on her, rather than being filled by a physique with more bulk. It was almost comical, looking like it could have been bought on the cheap out of a thrift store, with the hope it could be grown into later. On the other hand, there was an invigorating youthfulness to her countenance.

But was this an adult in permanent form facing him? Short, sandy brown hair, parted to one side, and just slightly scraggly, with her coy smile thrown in, only added to her teenage bearing. She did not attempt to speak; instead, she held him with eyes that were alive: intelligent, inquisitive, bright blue, like a pair of living, iridescent aquamarines.

It was Mil who broke the rapt spell of silence. "Miriam is in union with me, just as you and Mrs. Webster are to each other. We also share a joint contract, in particular because of her invaluable knowledge of Earth and the gift of foresight she possesses."

"Gift of foresight?" Dennis repeated, drawing a blank.

"I was getting to that, Mr. Webster."

"Then please excuse me."

"By all means."

"Well, I must say it is a pleasure to meet you," Dennis came back to her and greeted in his most amiable tone. For the moment, past skepticism was ignored. Now a tip of the head paid genteel respect. Miriam nodded in polite reply.

"You will have to excuse her," Mil spoke up. "Miriam is deaf and mute. She is, however, most efficient in being able to read your lips. She also has certain exceptional sensitivities that make up for any physical sensory deficit. One of those allows her to sense when individuals are about to be victims of violent acts."

"No kidding."

"No. Call it seeing into the future, if you prefer. If we are close enough to the event, she can feel it and, hopefully, some we can reach. As to how she can do this…"

He shrugged and shook his head. "Even I do not comprehend all of its facets," he chuckled on a thoughtful note. "The best theory is that it is an amino acid peculiar to our diet that only affects certain Majoran individuals. For those of Earth however, like Miriam, it could be a dormant genetic tendency the transport process manages to switch on. But for a certainty, the why and how of it remains anyone's guess. Even now, our scientists are still wrestling with it. One thing is for certain: it does appear to be completely random and a rare occurrence."

A brief shadow clouded Dennis's face at the pair of revelations afflicting Miriam. "I am sorry to hear about her disability," he apologized, a little awkward.

The young lady took note and nodded. It was a line she had no doubt interpreted more times than could be counted. That notwithstanding, her unabashed expression conveyed neither embarrassment, annoyance, nor any other emotion that might be exhibited when reminded on a regular basis of a handicap by an endless stream of well-meaning strangers.

In fact, her lack of any other emotion was just a little unsettling. Was she being genuine or just polite?

Something a little more in line with self-consciousness, even fleeting, would have helped him tailor any future interactions with her accordingly. Like Abby, and a brief flash of disappointment of her gullibility stung him once more, he liked to think himself as reasonably adept at sensing and interpreting the emotions of others. Tied in with that, he was pretty sure that he could see through even the best facades people sometimes erected to mask their true feelings.

Conversely, more than he cared to admit at the present time, Dennis knew Abby could see right through him, read his motives. Oft times it was outright galling not to be able to get away with the proverbial lie, or fudge his way out of a conflict. It was even hard to hide his true feelings when they bickered.

He loved her dearly, but to be honest, sometimes she could be so downright…well, right all the time! It was even eerie.

Then he remembered his goof. Actually, it was *her* goof.

He really did need to stand up to her misplaced gullibility. On the other hand, his delivery could have been a little more, well, fine-tuned. For longer than he could remember, he had been taught to stand up for himself when he knew he was right. But it was also to be tempered with diplomacy.

"Be right in your stance but keep the tone upbeat to keep the walls down," his dad had tried to instill in his young, tender psyche. Somehow being quick to cop an attitude and getting all defensive was an unfortunate character trait he had not yet quite gotten a grip on. It was one that had a tendency to poison any *discussion.*

Another lesson learned was just to shunt aside any unpleasant interactions and emotions and then move on. The sooner that was done the sooner he could get back to the business at hand. And that, too, did not always work out.

Dennis decided this human waif before him to be sincere. That only went so far with Mil. This Miriam's handicap had to be no more of an encumbrance than some innocuous scar, long since gotten used to.

"We can all get acquainted later," Mil said. He faced Miriam then spoke. "I will be back with that repulsor, just in case it decides to act up. Prompt me if you need anything."

Miriam nodded understanding, then flashed Dennis a final, friendly smile. She capped it with a tip of her head.

She and Mil went their respective ways. That left Dennis alone to take in the crowded assortment of lights and instrumentation. It was an engineer's delight. But in spite of how awe-inspiring all of this was, there had to be *some* way to alight to solid ground. Never mind what Abby took to be sincere truth.

One question bugged him, though: Mil and this Miriam trusted him to be on the bridge alone without escort. Such was the nerve center of any ship back home on Earth. He could do just about anything he wanted.

*

Abby explained the sum of what she knew of their predicament, once she sensed Lindsey Maguire could bear at least enough to understand. She had appeared little moved by it, including her personal testimony of her and Dennis almost being mangled and buried at sea.

The newcomer remained seated, restraints still securely in place. Both arms were wrapped tight against her abdomen, giving the impression she might fall out and plunge to oblivion. But Lindsey's bearing had mutated. Instead of terror and uncertainty her expression steeled more and more with each passing minute. If Abby was not mistaken, a hint of arrogance began to bubble through on her new acquaintance's expression. She had the weird sensation of being watched like a hawk.

Finally, "Even if what you say is anywhere near half the truth, there is absolutely no way that I can go through with this," Lindsey asserted. She shook her head in small, tight movements and shifted restlessly. She looked to be ready to put action to her words.

Abby kept her composure unruffled. "We happen to be newcomers too. As for myself, I don't profess to know all there is to know about our situation. Basically, what I do know happens to be very little. I also know *what* the alternative was…is."

Lindsey continued to eye her with an intensity that was oddly normal for her. This was a woman used to getting her way and no pushover at that. Her whole predicament had rattled her good, and she was no doubt settling back into her groove…and with a vengeance. It was just a first impression, and Abby hoped she was wrong. Perhaps just a little, she shrank back from this one who exuded such a dynamic will.

"That's your problem," Lindsey huffed, "and of no importance right now, as far as it concerns me. The fact is that I am alive, with a life and a career to get back to."

"So does my husband," Abby asserted.

"Good for him."

Abby blinked away the snide comment. "He said basically the same thing too. You also have to remember what I said would happen if you were to leave the confines of this ship without the proper precautions."

"Do you think I happen to be stupid enough to believe such a foolish delusion, *dear*?" Lindsey pounced.

Abby crossed her arms as she tried to hold her ground, unable to come to terms with this onslaught of vitriol. "But you have to admit everything you have seen here is way beyond anything either of us has ever experienced."

"I can't argue against that. But there could be any number of explanations for our being here. Lunacy just happens to be number one on the hit parade, in case you haven't noticed."

"I don't find any of this…"

"Which does not surprise me in the least!" Lindsey gave her a derisive snort. "Maybe they…or whomever it is running this vehicle…just fed you what you wanted to believe. You all have probably been abducted just like me, only these thugs are just a little less brutal about it, deceptive rather that outright homicidal."

Abby, just hang in there, she encouraged herself. *Consider the source, the situation. At some point, she is going to need someone to talk to.*

Impossible as it felt in her heart, Abby could feel nothing but compassion for the soul before her. Yet the callous disregard for her belief of their predicament stung, just as Dennis's chiding had. Maybe she was wrong not to join in on the mutual skepticism, but she just did not *feel* off base on this. It was an altogether settled matter.

Abby wished she could just reach out and embrace this fellow victim, but common sense popped off warning flares. Well, for the time they were stuck together on the same ship, she would do her level best to tolerate this tempestuous spirit. Lord knew she'd had to manage with Dennis, on occasion, when he was in a snit over a problem at work.

"Nobody fed me a thing," Abby denied. "I knew what we were up against, Mil explained our situation, and it jived with everything I had so far seen." She spread her arms in a slow, expansive gesture, to take in their surroundings and to let her conviction have whatever impact it was going to have. "I simply chose to believe this was the truth, our new reality."

"Then you simply chose to be deluded. You can stay here and play space ship with your alien friends if you want. Not me. This is *not* my life."

Abby determined to still believe Mil, in spite of the dizzying number of questions that even she had and this Lindsey was fueling. Hadn't somebody once said this was the realm of faith? To back down now would only make her look stupid at best and insane at worst.

Abby sounded a low groan. *As if there would be a whole lot of difference.*

Lindsey was being just plain ignorant, or contentious, and would probably never be convinced. Dennis fit that pattern too. Heaven help her if the two of them ever joined forces to become a united front of skepticism. They would bury her.

A thought drifted into her mind.

"If you think that I'm crazy, Lindsey, then why are you still buckled into your seat?" Abby asked.

Lindsey's expression flared....just as a bolt of guilt slammed into Abby. How could she have stooped so low as to trade barbs, insults, and innuendoes, like two boxers going at it?

Abby shook off the feeling, having a more immediate problem to deal with. Unfortunately, it was like a clearly posted quicksand pit and she had just jumped in...head first.

Had her counterpart's glare been a solid fist it would have knocked her over like a lightning jab. Yet Lindsey made no effort to free herself. If anything, she sank further down, fuming, arms folded all the tighter against her chest. This looked to be a healthy spell of sulking.

Abby stared past her for most of half a minute. Nothing particular came to mind, except the desire to do or say something that would help to convince this disheveled, miserable person before her of the truth of their situation, lousy as it might be. And like Dennis, it was, if possible, going to take time and self-realization. All she could do was to be there when the questions were asked. Better yet, she just wanted to be a friend to this one who had stood right at the brink of eternity and fallen in.

She hazarded a glance to Lindsey. The other's eyes were now closed, and Abby could only speculate what was running through her mind. The brittle cast to her expression gave a pretty good indication.

"You do not have to believe what I say, and you don't even have to like me," Abby ventured uncertain, soft.

"I don't think you will have to worry about that," Lindsey bit out, eyes still closed.

Abby blinked again, for a moment caught off guard. Then, "All I ask is that you try to be patient and open-minded about everything you see and hear. That's all any reasonable person should do. And you do strike me as being reasonable, Lindsey."

"Uh-huh."

Abby raised a hand in a slow, careful movement, the one closest to Lindsey. She slipped closer and reached over to lay long, delicate fingers on the other's shoulders. It was a small hope of encouragement. Instead, through them, Abby felt the blonde's muscles go taut. This friendly gesture was being regarded as an unwanted intrusion.

Lindsey's expression grew still harder, her lips tight. Her respirations were measured and forced. Whoever or whatever this wretch had been up until a few short hours ago, her present circumstance was a personal disaster at least on a par with that of her and Dennis. Maybe in some ways it was more so. Perhaps she wished she had just perished, instead of finding rescue.

Intuition suggested she back off. Abby withdrew her hand.

Just be patient, Abby, she encouraged herself. *It isn't your fault. Maybe you do happen to be the oddball around here. After all, you are the one who believes all of this so easily.*

*

Milankaar worked at the instrument console that ran the circumference of the alcove workstation in the propulsion bay. Concerning the ship's design, it had the appearance of an afterthought, situated in a nook between two tank-like neutral gravity fuel mixers. Compared to the other bays and compartments this one was cramped with the intricate workings of the four repulsors and all that was necessary to drive the ship and all its systems. This was a typical engine room, pure and simple.

He toggled a few switches then studied a bank of monitors above for any indication of a malfunction in the innards of the number three unit. The corner of his mouth wrinkled in growing frustration. Any problem should have been readily apparent. With circumstances calm at present *now* was the time he could dispense with the normal and deal with the abnormal. Later, he might be up to his elbows in flying and too busy to handle a glitch.

All the readouts were close to perfect. How galling when trying to discover a problem! The fuel flow and primary energy converter gauges were a little out of kilter but still well within limits. Old star-cruising buckets like this did have their quirks. So did aging Majorans. Well, he would have to keep an eye focused there. It was possible a fuel imbalance caused by the miscuing of a signal in a microprocessor might be the cause of the fault.

He manipulated a series of buttons and switches. In complimentary fashion, the smooth green wave on the graphic monitor readout bulged up then mutated yellow in caution. He tripped a final switch. The wave settled back down to its cooler green tint.

Mil frowned. He had tried everything in his acquired experience, and then some, to coax to the surface their mutual problem. He knew a real problem existed, in spite of being long on theories and short on answers.

The ship had been a former transport and slave runner in an earlier incarnation, confiscated by his home world's abolitionist government and auctioned off at an impossible to pass up bargain. There was one stipulation: he was required to engage in a year's contract, doing what he was doing now.

At first an entrepreneur and then an adventurer, depending on the size of his credit account, Mil had found such a lifestyle grueling yet liberating. In short, it was appealing…and he kept renewing his contract. *Unfortunately*, his ship, the *Starlight Mistress*, was more of a jury-rigged affair now, modified and customized at the whim of its previous owner and continued on by him. Despite his own thorough inspections, he knew there existed oddities and tidbits he was yet to become aware of.

For the length of a passing memory, Mil thought on the current situation between him and his people on their home world of Majora and that of their slave-dealing kin on the next planet in, Majora Prime. To make matters even more convoluted, the present diplomatic thin ice between the two made any discussion on the matter tricky, at best. There could presently be no accusations of endorsement or collusion in the off-world affairs of the other, even including ships and parts. So Mil and the others were unofficially official in their mission.

That left Mil and Miriam to develop their skills in resourcefulness and all its facets to scrounge for spares, parts, and equipment. Unfortunately, such were typically in short supply at best or, at worst, not available at all. To make matters worse, his contract remuneration did not allow for the kind of top-notch replacement parts and upgrades that were really needed.

Mil focused back onto the task at hand. In spite of a thread of uncertainty that continued to niggle away in his mind, he accepted the fact the diagnostics and instrumentation were in proper working order. As a last resort, he cocked an ear sideways, just on the hunch the faintest tone variation, click, or rattle over the peaceful droning pervading the bay might hint at the aggravating anomaly.

A passing thought came to mind. It was a comparison, really. There were the occasional stories garnered from his eavesdropping on Earth's telecomm systems, a few of which referred anecdotally to so-called transient glitches...*gremlins, that's what they called the*...that periodically plagued anything mechanical or electrical. Some individuals swore that they were living, breathing entities, as real as any person but yet curiously absent when it came to being dealt with. The concept was ridiculous, almost to the point of laughter, but he could see the sense behind it.

Well, I suppose it is not a phenomenon unique to Earth, he mused, giving in to a smile.

An audio prompt broke the narcotic hold of the chamber's throbbing song. That would be Miriam.

"And what can I do for you?" he spoke to the monitor, playful in feigning a patronizing expression. He studied her lips with the intensity of reading a good techno novel. "Fifteen minutes to the automated outpost, huh? I must have lost track of time."

She gave him a curious look, as though his last statement was an unheard of aberration.

"There was a communiqué? How long ago did it arrive?" Miriam mouthed her response. "It was not important enough to interrupt me, huh?...I see. Understood. Rendezvousing with them at the outpost will be fine."

So they were being requested to meet with the only other contractor in this hemisphere for now: the one and only Thalmond Garr.

Theirs was a cordial relationship. Insofar as contract work was concerned, Mil could generally trust Thalmond. As a friend that was a different matter.

Thalmond, or Tal, competent businessman that he might be, was too much into himself, for Mil's liking. Social occasions, thankfully far and few between, were typical times for the recitation of long since memorized deeds and glamorized exploits from a lifetime spent kicking around the galaxy. Mil had long since determined that Tal was not the kind of individual he would hang out with in a skyside café, killing time, or take home to meet the family.

"I imagine he wants us to handle a transfer for him?" Mil guessed. He made no effort to keep from sounding put upon. He noted the silent reply, sighed. "Okay, I guess a couple more will not hurt. This will cost him, though. I only hope he remembers his debt to me for the last run."

Miriam took on a noticeable sober look as she spoke.

"You say you reminded him of that already?" Mil wrinkled his mouth in a frown. If it was one thing Slick Tal could be counted on it was selective memory brought on by some vague head injury years ago. Or so Tal claimed.

She nodded, mouthed a silent couple words.

"That is what I thought you said...He does too. No, do not open the transmission link for a social chat. He knows better than

118

that. A stray signal could lead them right to the outpost. Just as a precaution, kill all the sensors, except surface navigation and short-range. I will be up shortly. There is nothing wrong back here."

Miriam nodded and the monitor blinked, went blank.

Mil groaned. That was all they needed. Despite his commitment to Majora's humanitarian efforts to rescue humans from slavers, extra passengers were an additional complication in any situation, especially on a ship handicapped with a temperamental repulsor. Though a run in with a slaver was a very rare occurrence, Mil worried that they could be spooking around too close for his comfort.

Keeping the ship concealed was not the problem. Still the chance of he and Miriam being discovered by slavers would make the two of them interlopers, infringing on what Majora Prime viewed as a legitimate business venture. They and their ilk, bounty hunters, were not the sort to take lightly business competition. It was like cattle rustling and vigilantes, to apply an old Western American Earth analogy.

Mil ran through a last diagnostic routine. He created and keyed in a repulsor system tag that he hoped would fish for, snag, and identify any future transient imbalances. That way, he would have a prompt for immediate attention.

And that was a big hope. He left for the flight deck and headed forward.

As he exited out onto the main corridor it was a sudden cloud of foreboding that settled into his mind. Slavers were bad news in *any* social encounter, and his line of work guaranteed it. Personally, he had yet to run into any in his many varied and sundry runs. Maybe it was predestination or perhaps just plain dumb luck. Either way, in spite of his abrupt trepidation, he hoped to stay covert and invisible.

CHAPTER ELEVEN

Lindsey was up and moving, stalking in slow circles about the now dormant ship's transport chamber. The solid, methodic drum of her boot heels echoed off the deck. Though still brooding, she was at least animated.

Abby watched in wary silence when Lindsey stopped every so often to absent-mindedly toy with a switch here or a fitting there. Abby had no idea what purpose the activity served, but were it a distraction it had to be a turn for the better…at least for now.

Abby stood to the left of the control console, right arm resting on the edge of the angled surface and trying to be as small as possible.

Lindsey just ignored her.

Abby managed to maintain a casual demeanor; however, each of the several times Lindsey passed centimeters behind her, and continued to do so in subtle intimidation, frosty hackles burst out on the nape of her neck. Maybe it wasn't overt in intention but the effect was just the same.

Did Lindsey exude such an aura of malicious arrogance and contention that she affected others this way, or was it just her? A front of self-control, hard as it was, had to be the best way to counter Lindsey's toxic vibes.

"At some point, you just might want to go down to the station, Lindsey," Abby encouraged. "You haven't been out of this chamber since you came on board."

"I'm glad you take such an interest in my welfare," Lindsey smirked. "But the only leaving I want to do is to get off this cobbled-together derelict somebody decided to call a ship. I want to get back to where I belong and the sooner the better."

Abby drew in a breath and steeled her resolve a few degrees more. She had not known Lindsey long, but she knew where this was going. Equally troubling, Abby knew this newcomer could easily, by force of will, run roughshod over her in any debate or test of wills. That was an event Abby had absolutely no stomach for.

"But that's not really possible," Abby replied. "Mil explained it very clearly: their transport process renders us helpless to the very germs we grew up with and became immune to. It's part…"

From across the chamber, Lindsey spun on her heels, nostrils flaring. It was so fast that despite the distance between them, Abby winced in surprise.

"Yeah, yeah, I know. So you think I should just remain a prisoner here?" Lindsey spat.

Abby shook her head in guilt-ridden denial. "Lindsey, please don't misunderstand. I just used the wrong choice of words. It's your choice whether you stay or go."

"But you think I should stay?" Lindsey asked. It was more a statement than a question.

Abby was speechless. She just shrugged.

"Look, I was just the victim of one abduction, and now it's happening all over again."

"Lindsey, if you would please just let me finish."

"Okay, so go ahead and finish your sad tale. Enlighten me."

"What I would hope of you..." Abby swallowed thinking about Dennis's simmering disapproval of her easy acceptance of their mutual situation, "is what I had hoped of my husband."

"He didn't buy into any of this either, I take it?"

Abby shook her head.

"That's good. That means one less sucker I have to deal with. But go ahead. Tell me anyway."

Abby's embarrassment grew more acute and uncomfortable. To add to that, Lindsey's attitude only helped make her feel lonelier than ever.

Abby was beginning to think that it might be entirely possible, that among the three of them and any others that might be rescued, she was the oddball, the gullible misfit.

"Could you at least have an open mind about anything you actually see and hear? Will you please think things through carefully before you make any final decisions?"

"I'm game. Shoot."

Abby launched into a brief overview of what Mil had explained to both her and Dennis. Mil could have the privilege of explaining all the technical stuff to his heart's desire. She would just divulge how she understood things, layperson-like.

Even after she let Abby finish, Lindsey made her feelings clear. "I find it plain ludicrous. It's just a story concocted to keep idiots pacified like dumb sheep. I have every intention of being returned, despite whatever you say. And if I'm not released, I can guarantee there will be a lot of trouble...big trouble!"

Abby was speechless before the tirade. It was obvious Lindsey hadn't considered a word she'd said. "No problem," Abby answered. "One of their requirements for doing this work is that whoever is extracted, like us," and Abby gestured to herself, "is to be returned voluntarily. If they do return, that is their choice, free and clear, consequences notwithstanding."

"Well now, that's exactly what I wanted to hear," Lindsey exulted.

The tension eased off just a little, but Abby knew what was just behind the happy facade her companion put up. Lindsey walked slowly back to her seat and lowered herself down into it.

Now it was Abby's turn. She spread both arms to rest her hands on either side of the console. Looking to Lindsey, *She runs on pure ego*.

Abby managed to have the last word. "Just remember one thing, Lindsey. The three of us are *supposed* to be dead. *Dead*."

*

If Mil's ship was less than a spacious affair, then the remote monitoring station was cramped by comparison. Dennis guessed it had about a third the space. A day's confinement here would be a definite test of one's sanity.

Their accommodations could only be described as intimate. Abby would say that. With the several of them aboard the ship, well, it was good to be by himself for a short while.

Mil had earlier been down below in the station but had returned to the ship to retrieve a memory module. Now he clambered back down the access ladder. Overhead, the dormant vehicle sat like a giant unseen bird of prey perched atop a massive boulder that was, itself, part of an avalanche field below a steep mountain face. In actuality, the slide was purpose-made during the station's construction for a ready and natural camouflage shield.

Dennis took in the surroundings that were not a whole lot different than the ship.

Mil stepped down onto the metal decking.

The odd creature that Dennis had seen him with earlier was wrapped loosely around his neck.

"I saw that interesting little monster earlier in your company," Denis struck up.

"Oh her?" Mil replied. His expression was one of an instant's mild surprise at what he no doubt deemed as a common fixture now having drawn attention to itself. He began to stroke it with all the casual care of a pet. The result was an audible cat-like purr.

"Her name is Kikki, a Lumeran Forest cat. I have had her about five of your standard years. Would you like to hold her?"

"Thanks Mil. Maybe later."

"So what was this you were telling me about Majoran slave trading?" Dennis asked.

"Not all Majorans, Mr. Webster," Mil clarified.

Dennis watched as Mil's attention left the animal, or whatever it was, and went to calling up some kind of a schematic on a visual display.

"Our race actually inhabits two worlds in our home star system, a star you know as Rana, or Delta Eridani."

"You still expect me to believe you come from another planet?" Dennis chuckled.

Mil came around. There was a frank earnestness to his expression that dampened Dennis's skepticism. Dennis's grin faded. "I would have expected by now that you, of all people, Mr. Webster, would have believed what you have both seen and been told."

"I *do*, Mil…to an extent. It's just that I still find all of this a mite too far-fetched to believe, practical man that I am."

"Your wife believes."

Dennis humphed. "That's Abby. You know, she's always been like that, easily duped. She should have…"

Movement out of the corner of his eye brought Dennis up short.

Mil looked askance also.

Abby had managed to slip down the ladder, any sound masked by conversation and the soft murmur of the surrounding machinery.

"Should have what?" Abby requested, touching down and suspicious. Mil's attention went conveniently someplace else.

*

All the hurt, disappointment, and humiliation came crashing back in, like water into a sinking ship. She did not have to hear much to know Dennis was talking about her in less than complimentary tones.

She closed her eyes and tried to swallow it, but it would not go away. It was a lump that stuck in her throat. She loved Dennis dearly, wanted him to care and at least acknowledge her own view, no matter how absurd it might be. Instead, she had never felt so alone, so abandoned. He was supposed to be the one person in the entire universe she could place her complete trust in. Disillusionment was getting pretty close to the quagmire she felt herself sinking into, especially with no end in sight.

"Nothing, Abby," he fibbed in a gulp. "Nothing at all."

"Your husband seems to think…"

"Mil, please!"

Abby darted glances of disbelief between the two conspirators. That was not quite correct: in Mil she found nothing but innocent, if not naïve, candidness. Folding her arms, she turned and retreated to a small nook beyond the two men, which was about the best escape that could be had without returning to the ship.

Abby pretended to explore. It was, instead, camouflage to allow her to sulk and expend the effort to nurse her injuries.

Unseen by either of them, she cradled herself in secret, rocking back and forth while hot tears burned down her cheeks. For once, she wondered if surviving their crash had been such a good stroke of fortune.

*

"Maybe you should not have…" Mil began to correct in a hushed tone.

"Oh, she'll be okay," Dennis minimized. Any concern for his wife's embarrassment was fleeting. "She just happens to be very sensitive to criticism. A little too much, if you ask me."

"Not necessarily a negative quality, Mr. Webster," countered Mil.

"Please, Mil, don't start going all psychological on me. I'm not in the market for some alien group therapy session."

Mil slipped a glance to Abby then came back around, a knowing half grin on his face. His course appeared unchanged. Ignoring the sarcasm, "It is a characteristic both your people and mine could use in greater abundance, if I may offer."

Dennis said nothing, letting a thoughtful pause ensue. Maybe, just maybe, he was being a *little* idiotic about all of this.

*

She had never felt so miserable, so staggered.

The anguish hung like a boulder around her neck, and it took effort to move closer to Mil. It took even more to face him. Careful to avoid Dennis's gaze, she could only imagine what kind of gossip he had foisted upon their mutual host, at her expense.

She was tempted to ask for an itemized list but decided her current pain did not need any reinforcement.

"I only came to let you know Lindsey's still refusing to come below," she relayed. "She's insisting on being taken back to the pickup point and returned."

Mil wilted just a little but recovered himself. He let slip a quiet, drawn out sigh.

"Must be pretty tough, huh?" Abby remarked. The conversation in the company of another troubled soul, however brief, would help.

"A situation I dislike intensely," he replied.

"There must be some way to convince her, to make her come around. I mean, considering what you said about the microbes outside now, she's as good as dead once she leaves the ship. Can she just do that?"

"Unfortunately…" Mil paused to straighten, the effort to force back some feelings on the matter obvious on his expression. "The freedoms that we enjoy, much as your own nation does, can often carry a heavy price. One is the right to make choices that are not always in the best interest of the one making them.

"And it is for the best. It is also a paramount contract stipulation, regardless of my feelings on the matter. While I might typically have to cajole or even plead, to do otherwise would make us little better than the slavers we are in competition with."

Abby paused to stare at nothing in particular, forming her response. "I guess I may not like it, but I think I understand. I might even have gotten to like her in spite of her obvious and many quirks."

"An interesting description, Mrs. Webster. But as always it is a shame. I believe she could have been a most productive individual on Majora. Thank you for your report."

"Please, Mil. It's Abby, just plain Abby."

She saw Dennis frown but pretended to ignore it. Her easy familiarity with their host was rankling him. If it helped him come to grips with his attitude then so much the better.

"Fine," Mil agreed, uncertainty threading his tone. "Please relay to our guest that we will grant her wish but only after we have concluded our business here. That includes provisioning ourselves for the flight out. In the meantime, I will shortly have something for everyone to eat. I believe you refer to it as breakfast?"

Abby arched a brow. The mere mention of food set off a rolling hunger pang that gathered momentum like an avalanche. With the stress of their continuing drama, nourishment had been the farthest thing from her mind. Just maybe a modest repast would help put things in a different perspective. Heaven knew Lindsey and Dennis could use a little new perspective. Then after a little stomach filling some decent rest might be in order.

"Most of our provisions are Majoran," he explained. "However, I have taken the liberty of programming the food synthesizers to suit your cultural tastes, as much as I am able to simulate them. I will prepare either, as you desire, but I think you will find the cuisine of both similar in some respects. I would assume color and texture would be the qualities most important to you."

"Sounds great, Mil. Thanks."

The distraction of the interaction lowered her guard, and she swept her gaze past Dennis. For a moment, their eyes caught hold. In that short span of time all the bound up hurt of the past night burst back to the forefront, of his unexpected verbal assault, of the criticism and curtness that tied in with the gossip she knew him to have relayed a few minutes ago.

In a way, it was more than that, now that she thought about it. The whole past year had somehow been different, ever since he had taken over as overall site manager for the firm. Sure she was acutely aware of not being attuned to all the nuances of being the consort of an up-and-coming business executive and all that such entailed.

In subtle ways, at times not so subtle, Dennis had reminded her of that, even to the point of chagrin on his part, embarrassment on hers. Yet, as the good-natured wife, she shrugged it off as occupational pressure or just her own ignorance. Always the next time she, Abigail Webster, would do better with her social and personal clumsiness, she promised herself.

Then again, he always managed to find something else.

The lid came off. Now unrepressed by the irreversible destruction of all that was familiar, it all boiled to the surface in an instant. Only the presence of Mil kept her from doing something way out of character. Her mind was another matter: the temptation by thought to do to Dennis what he had heaped on her was enticingly sweet...for brief moment.

It was called vengeance.

She turned away, closed her eyes in anguish realized. A wave of shame slammed into her. How could she have stooped to such an odious level in wishing to hurt Dennis in some way, the one person she had chosen to love and cherish? If there was any comfort it was that all of them, no matter their attributes or liabilities, were equals in a mess that had at least the singular quality of being a level playing field. They all had nothing, nothing except the clothing on their backs, their intellects, their health. Most important, they had each other and each had life.

Abby decided to retreat to the ship, at least for a respite, until the storm blew out and she could sort through the debris of emotions. Oh, how very exhausted she now felt. She sagged accordingly.

She now craved that rest. Perhaps just a portion of an hour, if it was not too elusive, might help her better deal with this mess.

*

Mil watched in quiet sympathy, lower lip curled inward, as Mrs. Webster disappeared above back into the *Mistress*. Once safely out of sight, he began anew to scrub the misgiving he had from his tone. Later, he might broach the subject of her discord with Mr. Webster. Were the two of them to stand even a remote chance of thriving through all that had befallen them, and what was yet to be, they would need each other. They would need to be on respectful terms, and that would be their only advantage.

"Our race inhabits two planets, Mr. Webster. Here, let me show you."

Under Dennis's watchful gaze, Mil worked about an island console that was the hub of the station's reason for existence. Round about the roughly rectangular space what equipment and machinery was not dedicated to cloaking, power, and life support went to local and planetary monitoring. The realms of weather and atmosphere to telecommunications and resources were fair game.

Next to the island, suspended at chest level, was a plain, gunmetal-gray metallic object not unlike a round, empty window frame. It hovered in perfect, vertical alignment between two small horizontal plates, one above and one below. These were, in turn, attached to finger-diameter tubing, one going up to the ceiling and the other down to the metal decking underfoot. The most remarkable thing was the lack of physical contact between the two plates and the ring.

Mil's fingers played around a central keyboard. In a few seconds, he had a three dimensional holographic rendition materialized ghost-like out of thin air within the ring. It was a golden amber marble of luminescence that even in its artificial brilliance cast spikes and rays just like a real star glimpsed through a telescope. Seven points of much less significant illumination attended it at various position angles and distances.

These were planets, and just as obvious this was not an extra-solar view of Earth's home system.

"This is a navigational plotter, or nav-plot for short," Mil explained. "There is a similar one on the bridge above. This one's primary purpose is to program the ship for surface navigation here on your planet. But it can also be used for many planetary systems located in this segment of this galaxy that both you and I are familiar with."

He paused to shove his hands into the pockets of his flight suit as they both studied the created scene before them. "This is the star your people know as Delta Eridani. The second and third planets are the Majoran home worlds. The inner is Majora Prime. The outer one, mine, is Leptis Magna, named for an ancient Roman colony city on the continent you call Africa, though the term Majora is interchangeable. We tend to take place names from other worlds for our own, especially when they are appropriate. Leptis was a colony of Prime long ago."

"Like you would know that much about Roman history."

"We know, or knew, of it."

"Don't tell me, your race visited there?"

"Of course."

"No."

"Yes."

"You're serious, aren't you?"

"Space flight has been a mode of travel for us for a few millennia. I do not recall for exactly how long but longer than Leptis' colonization."

Dennis shook his head. Mil could not tell whether it was from disbelief or from astonishment. Knowing Mr. Webster it was probably the former.

After a pair of thoughtful moments, "You mean to say this *thing* contains information on not just Earth but other systems, like an encyclopedia?" Dennis gawked.

"I suppose you could think of it as such." Mil had never thought of the nav-plot in that way, but it was a close enough approximation. "Actually, it would be closer to an atlas."

"If what you say is true, do you have any idea how much this would be worth?" Dennis's wonderment appeared to grow. Still, there was a coloring of skepticism on his words.

"Priceless would be pretty close," Mil deadpanned. "But please understand one thing, Mr. Webster. This is not a complete library of planetary information, interstellar exobiology, or any other 'space' science. It is merely a catalog of known stars, planets, and other phenomenon, their types, outstanding characteristics, and coordinates. All the data contained within the memory core is necessary for terrestrial and interstellar navigation for I and my associates."

Dennis moved closer to the visual display. Mil noted his mien was one of reverence, for however long, like he was standing in the presence of something omniscient.

Dennis maintained rapt attention on the device. "By the way, exactly how far is Majora supposed to be?"

Mil continued to fiddle with instruments on the console. He let a reply linger for a couple moments for his guest's benefit. Mr. Webster was an intelligent human, but he did nudge toward the boundary of self-righteousness, maybe even arrogance. Of course, the regal crown belonged to the one and only Miss Maguire.

He settled into a little thought-provoking interlude to elevate the suspense a bit. An air of casualness would also, he hoped, instill a little humility. Such was a quality that never hurt anyone, human or Majoran.

"Not all that far, Mr. Webster. In a straight line, that is. But straight lines are not necessarily expedient or safe. Objects like stars, to name one threat, clutter our course."

"I could picture that. So how far?"

Mil kept to his course. "Our journey outbound will require a rather circuitous route. It will include stops along the way at a few interplanetary way stations that have been set up to accommodate and cover us. The first will require only a couple days' flight."

"How far, Mil?"

"In answer to your query...twenty-nine light-years."

Dennis's mouth dropped open then slapped shut. "Twenty-nine...light-years?" he gulped.

"Remember, Mr. Webster, I said in straight-line flight."

"A flight like that would take tens of thousands...*hundreds* of thousands of years...with our current technology," Dennis stammered. "Surely it must be much, much less than that." Disbelief rolled off of him in waves. "No...that's preposterous." His head worked through a round of vigorous shaking.

Mil killed the display. Dennis's skepticism went to disappointment.

"Obviously," Mil said. He sent him a sober look that tried to convey no small experience in the matter, and the more the better. "Normally, we would require about a week and a half of travel time. But that is predicated on all going according to plan, as you and your kind reckon time."

"A week and a half?" Dennis echoed. He wobbled a bit.

"About that." Mil kept his tone light and casual. He could have been engaged in a conversation with a friend, rather than educating an outclassed neophyte. "That most direct route I mentioned would require a few days less. Among the other dangers are slavers and too many prying eyes, not to mention innumerable unsavory elements that have a profit motivation as their top priority. Some are not above selling out information at a fair price."

"Sounds like a bloody space-borne underground railroad," Dennis muttered.

Mil drew a complete blank on that one. He thought he was becoming pretty familiar with the more common local metaphoric expressions…and the not so common ones, too. That was one of the intangible benefits of his duties and a favorite pastime. Chalk up another entry into the data banks.

What was *plainly* evident was that every new contact produced new witty clichés and colorful metaphors that left him and the ship/outpost library wanting. Worst of all, it produced a social clumsiness that not a few humans found humorous, once they settled into their new lives. If he was good for a joke, well, that was an occupational hazard.

"Underground railroad?" Mil finally had to ask to sate his curiosity. Mr. Webster did appear to be the type to play it for all it was worth. He was game, though. Scratching his chin, "I am afraid I do not understand, Mr. Webster."

*

Dennis drew in a breath. This was going to be fun. It wasn't every day he had the privilege of imparting a language and history lesson upon an alien from an advanced extra-terrestrial race.

And like a scraggly student, Mil settled in to listen.

*

"I can bring down more trouble than you will know how to deal with if you people don't do as I say…now!"

Abby cringed. It was more from the screech of Lindsey's hollering than the threat. She had the acute impression of not just being caged up with a wild animal but of confronting one that was cornered and both threatened and threatening. A rabid one came pretty close to an accurate comparison. She realized her stomach now ached from the tension Lindsey exuded in all parts of the spectrum.

"And you will," Abby tried to assure her.

Lindsey Maguire was skating on the very last millimeter of self-control, and Abby hoped the tempest confronting her did not interpret her gentleness as a weakness and decide to pounce. This was a swell position to be in and she with no backup.

"Mil said it was an utmost priority for those who want to return. Once he…"

"Oh quit sounding like a sniveling puppet! Do you know how much I hate that?"

"Lindsey, please."

Lindsey sprang up from her seat in a bound, boiled to her full height. Her rage made her the quintessential picture of overwhelming intimidation. In two rapid-motion steps she was face to face with Abby. The cork was off.

"I thought I made myself quite clear, Ms. Scatterbrain. Either I go back immediately or else…"

136

"There's no need to resort to insults," Abby countered. She was wilting fast.

"Only where it's deserved." Planting both hands on her hips, Lindsey inched a nerve-frosting centimeter closer. The breath from flaring nostrils brushed her chin.

Abby retreated an equal distance but managed, barely, to keep her composure. That did not go for the cold sweat breaking out in the small of her back. Such a maneuver was not going to go on forever, and with no cover, she felt acutely naked. Their gazes remained in a mutual death-grip on the other. Then an odd memory wiggled up from some long forgotten bit of wisdom. It had to do with the eyes…

Yes, that's it. Eye contact!

They were the gateway to the soul. Every other body part or gesture might put on a convincing fraud, but it was the eyes that translated true intent. If only she could hold on until the storm abated or else help arrived…

Abby held out about as much hope for the former and peaceful seas as for a warm, sunny day in the Antarctic. The latter could be at any time, a few seconds or a few minutes. Unfortunately, even a minute was an eternity cooped up with a hurricane. Whatever it was Mil or Miriam saw in this one…

"Uh, Lindsey, perhaps you should really rethink…"

Lindsey cut her off. "Don't pretend to tell *me* what I *need* to be thinking!"

"I only meant…"

Lindsey struck out.

In a flash of incomprehensible movement, her right arm cocked back and rocketed up and toward Abby's face.

In the half second Abby saw it coming time slowed to an incredible crawl. Her reflexes off just a beat her body was about one step behind her brain. The recoil had just started when the blow crashed home.

The open-handed slap struck in a blinding flash on chin and cheek. Movement and force collaborated to send her sprawling disjointed in an oblique tumble onto the transporter platform.

Through scrambled senses, shock, and pain, Abby caught sight of another flash and an attendant blue haze. There was a crackle not unlike a static discharge: a tingling sensation that crawled over exposed skin before dissipating with the ethereal glow. It had to be shock from the assault.

Abby managed to find a sitting position on the edge of the dais. There was every expectation of a continuation of the onslaught with all its unabated fury. She tried to cower into the unyielding metallic surface.

The attack never came.

With ample wariness, Abby peered through stinging tears and shielding fingers toward her assailant. Confusion set in. Lindsey was not in a menacing stance over her, ready to deliver the coup de grace. Within arm's reach lay an unmoving heap that had not been there a few seconds before. It took almost that long to realize...

"What did you do to her?" Abby blurted upon seeing Miriam. She failed to realize she was yelling.

Then Miriam glided with effortless, fluid grace toward the inert form. She gave Abby a sideways knowing glance, appearing to use the gesture to instill a plausible explanation for the drastic turn of events. An object in her hand went to her belt. Miriam maneuvered down to kneel and straighten Lindsey out to help her.

"Oh, I get it," Abby said in a flash of comprehension. Miriam signaled with a hand that meant for her to assist. "You just sort of stunned her to protect me, something like a tranquilizer."

Miriam studied her face, in particular her mouth. Then her lips formed a silent word. Yes. The friendly smile that followed conveyed no pretense, just as with Mil.

Together they lifted the limp Lindsey to one of the niches. "Maybe she will wake up in a better frame of mind," Abby said hopefully. She contorted half inside the space's confines to put the unconscious form into a semblance of a comfortable position. A hand went to brush tousled hair from Lindsey's forehead. "How long will she be like this?"

Miriam tinkered for a dozen seconds with a monitoring switch next to the niche. She straightened and turned to look into Abby's inquiring expression. She had failed to hear the query.

"Oh, I'm sorry," Abby apologized in a little blush. "How long do you think she will sleep?"

Miriam's mouth moved, slow and deliberate but without any hint of self-consciousness.

"About half an hour, huh?" Abby repeated to be sure.

Miriam nodded once.

Their task finished, Abby began to massage the lingering numbness and heat permeating the side of her face. The other reached up with her right hand to replace Abby's and stroked and probed in a search for possible injuries. Then Miriam gave her an assuring headshake. At least they would not have to be searching out a doctor for a house call.

Abby made sure Miriam now saw her mouth, "Let's get down to the station. Mil said he was going to prepare us something to eat."

Miriam smiled, nodded agreement then moved sideways in the same easy movement to lead the way out. Abby lingered for just a moment, letting her gaze return to Lindsey.

For this one Abby felt true regret, in spite of the latent animosity Lindsey bore toward her. Yet it was tempered by the innocence of Miriam's amiability. And for that she was most grateful.

Miriam was a wonderful and mysterious soul she would like to get to know better. At some point perhaps she would, given time and the unknown that of a certainty lay ahead.

Unknown?

Abby trembled at the thought. It spawned a dark cloud that made the uncertainty of even the near future that more ominous. Maybe that was the reason for the warmth she felt toward Miriam…and Lindsey, to a degree. Danger shared in the company of others helped put things into a more comforting perspective. They would all need each other. That included Lindsey, whether she was capable of getting off her high horse and stooping low enough to admit it.

She followed Miriam out.

CHAPTER TWELVE

Abby finished eating the facsimile of scrambled eggs. She had tasted better…then again, there had also been worse. But Mil, bless his Majoran intentions, had done all right.

"So, Mil, tell me how you concoct your cuisine without fresh foodstuffs and supplies," she said after swallowing. "I have seen nothing in the way of bulk supplies stored here."

From across the rectangular stand up table they were gathered around Mil munched on a material she could not identify. With a near rhythmic tempo that was more casual than deliberate, he would pinch a small amount between thumb and the first two fingers and replace the previous mouthful. The pile on his bright tinware plate looked like gray granola. Color did not appear to be a significant consideration for Majoran culinary tastes. She hoped *that* was not a universal constant.

"You are right, Mrs. Webster." Mil licked his right forefinger. "Storage space on the automated outposts is at a minimum. Most of what there is goes to ship replenishment."

"Understood."

"This facility, nor any of the others, was intended for long-term habitation. But in reply to your original query, perhaps showing you would help."

Mil turned and led the way a few steps back to a stack of equipment modules that looked little different from everything else. Dennis and Miriam continued their own meals, though Dennis shared attention between the demonstration about to take place and his food.

The most significant feature of the unit was a square, dark, glass-enclosed opening. Various controls and instruments adorned it both above and below.

"Almost all the available food starts out as organic blanks," he began to explain.

He manipulated a couple controls, which caused a light in the recess came on. In a moment, a small beige block materialized within. It quivered slightly. Abby thought it looked more like tofu than anything else she was familiar with. His hand gestured to the item.

"It is then modified and processed by this nutriment synthesizer, which is basically a highly modified, programmable version of the transporter. Unfortunately, most of the examples we have of Earth nutrition come from trial and error, for better or for worse, and advice from previous contacts, such as yourself."

"Which means it evolves and improves with time," Abby deduced.

"Very astute, Mrs. Webster." He gave her a grin that conveyed an appreciation for her understanding. "It is an evolving necessity that, I would hope, will ease your transition. At some point, I will be inquiring of you for your input."

"Well, it really isn't too bad, Mil, but you will come to find out my tastes are pretty easy going. Others are more demanding. My food would have to be practically inedible before you would get a complaint from me."

"I dunno," Dennis chimed in.

Abby stiffened. She was not sure if this was going to be his attempt at some humor or something a little more sarcastic.

"You complain when I grill dinner and your meat's not well done enough," Dennis went on.

"Well, yours tends to be so rare, or raw, that it's swimming in its own juices...mooo."

"Ouch!" Dennis contorted his face through a mock grimace. "Yeah, I know, "give the steak a transfusion and it might survive"."

This was sinking into the miry depths of sarcasm, a place she had no intention of going to. Abby closed her eyes for a couple moments and shook her head, figuring now it the better part of wisdom to ignore anything else pitched her way.

"You are most generous, Mrs. Webster," Mil got back on course.

"Thanks. But since we are on the subject, to be honest, the coffee does taste a little odd, and there's a green tinge to the toast."

Mil wrinkled his mouth in a brief frown. The truth could be so brutal. "I can assure you that I do try my best, though my chef skills lag far behind my other strengths."

"Your secret's safe with me, Mil. A few spices and herbs and it will be just fine. I've been known to ruin a boiling pan of water or two in my time."

"Don't I know," Dennis quipped.

"Dennis, *puleeze*! Just..."

Mil's confusion deepened into the hanging pause. "How does one ruin a pan of boiling water, Mrs. Webster?"

Dennis rolled his eyes as Abby covered her mouth in an abrupt grin. "It means to mess something up that is basically unable to be messed up."

"Ahh, now I understand. As you can see, there is little opportunity to boil water here. The nutriment synthesizer does all the work."

"I think I like that, Mil," teased Abby. "No responsibility for culinary disasters. Just blame it on the machinery."

"So noted, Mrs. Webster."

Of greater significance, Abby knew that Mil knew a full tummy and the presence of familiarity, local food, in particular, went a long way in providing psychological stability in a universe turned upside down. He had said that. It was a tenuous link between a past existence now lost forever and one yet to be.

Speaking of stability, Lindsey and Dennis were both in definite need of stability. *Maybe the more food the better.*

Miriam, with her available knowledge, brought more to light about Majoran interests in Earth. From what Abby gathered on the positive side, plus that already deduced, active Majoran covert work centered on the acquisition of human "guests," all the while just wanting information. Mil's employment, if it could be termed that, was more in the line of a rescue effort. The "others" he mentioned on occasion were involved in what was tantamount to outright abduction and slave trading.

Back at the table, Abby listened with passive interest as Mil, Dennis, and Miriam carried on a discussion about Majoran work on Earth. In addition, secrecy was of prime importance to both factions. What could be less intrusive or suspicious than the covert garnering of humans on the verge of a violent demise, especially where the lack of a corpse was tragic but no big problem?

And for a moment, the awful truth of the revelation set off a frigid shudder that crawled up and then back down her spine. No wonder Earth was teeming with unsuspecting souls who just knew "extra-terrestrials" spooked about the galaxy in general and on Earth in particular. In a sense, tales of alien abduction had a ring of truth to it.

They were among us all the time. Wow! Abby realized.

For herself, Abby had always thought she was a little too sophisticated for that. They had been stories and delusions all along. But there were always the occasions where a co-worker or acquaintance would query her for her opinion during some pointless, idle conversation over lunch. Just as frequently, she would cover herself with the convenient deception of having an open mind about such things. Nice, easy, and tangle free.

Now on the face of it, those who professed outright were no more ridiculous than saying one thing and believing something different. All that had now changed. Those faceless, nameless individuals who had professed belief in extra-terrestrials and who had brushed shoulder with her had been right all along.

And here she stood, eating, drinking, and chatting with them in the flesh and blood!

But it was the secrecy of the operations of both the good and the nefarious elements that was hard to come to grips with. How long had it gone on, both sides extracting hapless people from the jaws of death? How long would it continue without detection, while the pros and cons of each side of the alien issue endlessly hashed and rehashed their differences?

Abby was half tempted to put forth to Mil a crazy thought, if colonies of rescued humans had been established around this part of the galaxy. If so they would be the seeds of humanity spread on the interstellar winds in a way no visionary could have ever conceived, unbeknownst to her brethren back home. She did not even want to think about those that were enslaved. With what had to be no hope of escape, no home, no family ties, and a meaningless identity, the hellish concept could only be worse than death. All the rotten details would come out in the open soon enough, she supposed.

"So how does Miriam fit into all of this?" she overheard Dennis inquire. "Despite the very brief time I have known her I find her the most intriguing part of this ship."

"For what we do here, Mr. Webster, Miriam is the key to this whole operation. She and those like her have gifted insights that seem prophetic in nature. They are able to focus in on the very short-term futures of those about to go through drastic alterations in their lives. Some can 'see' happier events. But it is Miriam and others who are privy to the tragic ones that, unfortunately, bring death and destruction."

Gifted? Abby wondered.

It was a grim thought how anyone could cope with what was sounding more and more like a curse rather than a gift. Had she been the one in possession of such an awesome power she was sure she would have long since gone insane, knowing how and when flesh-and-blood humans were going to perish. Miriam either had to have an extra special constitution or else she was so numb to the plight of those whose fate she brushed up against that it no longer caused her more than passing discomfort.

It was the former that she opted to believe, and for that she held a deep respect.

Abby heard little more after that. The whole concept was more than just a little eerie. And then there was that little snit fit with Lindsey on top Dennis's festering attitude.

"Hey, Abby, you okay?" Dennis spoke her way from across the usually stowed table/workbench.

Abby did not realize she had slipped off on a daydream tour. Her eyes met his and she blinked. Mild concern drifted across his expression.

"Oh, just thinking, that's all," she explained. "Actually, I'm mostly listening to you all. Please don't mind me."

He flashed a half grin. Then mild perplexity replaced concern, as if he suspected she was covering up something much deeper. Go figure. He didn't push the matter, though, which suited her just fine, for the time being. He gave her another smile, more forced for politeness' sake, and went back to his conversation.

It had not gone on for more than a few words when a device above them affixed to the ceiling, along with numerous others, came to life with a chorus of beeps, chirps, and warbles.

With no apparent urgency, Mil reached up and touched a button. There was a brief spate of hissing of transmission static. It stopped. An expectant pause ensued, giving time for the collective attention of all to focus on what was to about come.

A new string of sounds began to hustle in on the faintly musty air. It wasn't much different than the original hail, though more prolonged and strung together, like electronic notes on a poorly arranged musical composition. Whatever it was, Mil listened with heightened intensity to what amounted to a one-sided monologue. Then it ceased with a final, abrupt tweet.

"Thalmond Garr," was all Mil said with a combination humph and a slight smile.

Miriam mouthed a complimentary statement. Abby turned a questioning look to Dennis, though she knew he was hamstrung with equal ignorance like her.

"He says his ETA is ten minutes," he next added in Miriam's direction.

"Who is Thalmond Garr?" Abby asked.

"And the rest of the message?" Dennis added. "Even I know that was more than just a greeting."

Mil took a sip from his beverage. Setting the container down, he looked to Abby first.

"Thalmond is another contractor working the same general area as I am." Then to Dennis, "The rest of the transmission is ship and personal data, especially on the new arrivals."

Dennis was in mid-bite of one of those colored wedges of toast when the announcement stopped him. "Huh?"

Mil began to police the makeshift dining table. "All the acquired data in his computer to date is being dumped into this station's core." His expression evolved a little more sober. "More important, I should also mention he is transferring two of his extractions to us for our voyage out."

Dennis went wide-eyed. "You mean more people? And speaking of that, do you have to make 'extraction' sound so blasted impersonal?"

Abby cringed as Mil arched a brow. Dennis's rebuke had caught him off guard. The term had not particularly struck her that way, but in her estimation, Dennis was just spouting off. If Mil meant it even as a means to guard against the emotional baggage such work dropped on him, then that was fine by her.

"Then please accept my apologies if I have offended you, Mr. Webster. But, yes, we are taking on two more people. Thalmond and I take turns ferrying off-world. It happens to be my turn at the present time." He shifted attention to Abby. "He will not be docking with the station proper, since we occupy the only access port. He will instead transport one at a time. Once the new passengers are settled, we can depart."

Dennis said nothing, instead contented himself with rolling his empty drink container on its edge in circles on the metallic surface.

Abby nodded. She was not sure how to feel: in a sense, two more fellow humans meant that a double tragedy was now added to that of her and Denny's. Each had a unique and solemn story of woe to tell, and that story now went beyond simple survival and health. On the other hand, she was curious as to whom these two new souls were, what they were like. Heaven forbid they were contentious like Lindsey.

No, that's judgmental, she chastened herself. *Don't go into this with any preconceived notions. Just be ready with a friendly ear, should they desire it.*

"We will first return Miss Maguire, as she desires." Mil was voicing his game plan. "Since we will be outbound, it will be important to move rapidly. It has been my knowledge from others' experiences that transport is when there is the greatest risk of interception."

"So you have never had any run-ins with these slavers?" Dennis probed.

"That is correct, Mr. Webster." Mil showed little, if any, defensiveness from Dennis's earlier testiness. "Others have, though. Some have had unfortunate outcomes. My good fortune, as you might be fond of saying, is in the luck of the draw?"

Mil did not offer any further enlightenment, and for once, Dennis looked a little less motivated to push issues. That sounded like a good idea. Best to let it ride, for the time being.

Risk of interception? Abby repeated through her mind.

She closed her eyes and let the phrase echo a few more times in her head. When Mil said that he had been "lucky" because he had not had any "run-ins" with slavers, he could only have meant that there was a chance of an encounter, one that could very well result in either death or enslavement.

Both were hideous options.

CHAPTER THIRTEEN

Abby contemplated the empty space above a meter wide disk set into the deck between storage lockers. It was a smaller version of the transport platform aboard the ship. The actual event had not yet happened, but already the air was charged, roiling, and vibrating. It looked alive.

Dennis drew up beside her. By his expression, and like her, he was mesmerized by the event about to transpire.

From behind, Mil conversed in his incomprehensible native tongue on a secure, untraceable channel with the one called Thalmond Garr. The conversation sounded casual enough, though there was a slight guardedness to his inflection, in her opinion. Not quite like friends, more than acquaintances.

Not that she was a linguist. But that was okay. Abby's first impression of Thalmond on the visual monitor was, to say the least, questionable. Too much swagger, overconfidence, maybe a con artist of sorts. He was definitely an opportunist. He probably even strutted in his sleep.

A faint cloud of glow condensed in the air and shimmered over the pale metallic disk. For a few seconds, the gathering apparition was more ghost-like than human. But that changed as the arriving form rapidly grew in intensity, concentrating at two or three different points before shifting, pulling together. The unknown person solidified, charged energy congealing to solid matter.

It was a female. Her face was pulled taut in a frozen grimace, her eyes tight lines. There was no question this one was terrified by her experience.

She was slim and about five feet four inches, maybe a tad more. Straight raven-black hair fell below her shoulders and was clipped back, nice and neat. The transport hadn't disturbed it. Her heritage was Asian. Her complexion had a soft olive caste, and she appeared to be in her mid- to late twenties. She wore jeans, a pink pullover turtleneck sweater and, like Abby, sported a modest gold chain necklace and pendant. Instead of a stone setting like hers, however, the newcomer's was a modest gold coin encircled by a crusting of small gold nuggets.

A full five seconds ticked off from the last shimmering of the transport process before the new arrival began to relax facial muscles and open her eyes. When she did it was with deliberate slowness through thin, round, gold-framed wire rim glasses. She looked at Abby first.

"Hello," Abby said slowly, softly.

Despite the fact that Abby and Denny were strangers to her, the arrival relaxed a little. Still, she made no effort to leave the security of the disk. She opened her mouth to speak, but speech failed her.

"My name is Abigail Webster. Please call me Abby," Abby attempted to break the ice. She next indicated Dennis. "And this is my husband, Dennis."

The new arrival nodded ever so slightly. That was an encouraging sign, however minimal.

"I can't say much for the circumstances," Abby smiled, "but it is a pleasure to meet you. And your name is?"

Looks could always be deceiving. In spite of any perceived relaxing, her voice was taut, halting, caught between a whisper and what was adequately audible.

"Lydia...Lydia Chang." Although she was of Asian descent she had no accent.

In a slow steady movement, Abby extended her hand.

Wary at first, Lydia accepted the gesture. The touch of another human hand relaxed her still more.

"It's nice to see another human face, even if we are complete strangers," Lydia now commented.

A half smile was a reply to Abby's, and Lydia slipped from the disk. Drawing up before her hostess, she spent a long moment taking in the station.

Once more the transporter came alive with energy to announce the arrival of still another living, breathing soul.

Abby kept one eye on Lydia in case she needed help. The other focused on who was about to next appear.

The second arrival was a black male.

Even before his catatonic form ceased its energized antics, it was apparent he had an athletic build, trim and muscular. But he was not necessarily a hulking dynamo of power. African-American, a gray-tinged, close-cropped goatee and hair and perhaps a decade more years in age than Lydia lent him an air of smooth sophistication and handsome maturity. The initial apprehension Lydia suffered with was lacking in this one. By all appearances, he could have been reading a book or on a stroll through a park.

Such self-control, Abby judged. *Definitely very suave.*

"This is Marcus Scott," Lydia introduced to all. She made no effort to go beyond a name.

The intelligent, swarthy face looked around, taking in the new surroundings. Abby held her breath, awaiting some kind of reaction. Then he appeared to be satisfied with what he saw. He relinquished the neutral facade and replaced it with a confident, easy grin.

The stranger first focused on Dennis. "You must be..."

"Dennis Webster," Abby heard her husband from behind and to the right.

"And this must be your significant other?"

The man now looked at Abby. So far, her estimation of his character was right on, smooth and sophisticated yet amiable enough. She nodded as Dennis affirmed his query.

"I am Abigail Webster. You can call me Abby. Pleased to meet you."

Marcus nodded. "A very nice, quaint name, if you will permit me." He stepped up and offered his hand. The three traded courtesies. Then, "I must say we do find ourselves in a most unusual situation, do we not?"

"To say the least," Dennis agreed under his breath. Past skepticism wafted through.

Abby nearly giggled aloud at the enormity of Marc's opinion. She turned her lower lip in and bit into it to stifle a childish outburst.

Unusual's putting it mildly.

"I'm sure we will find some way to make the most of it," Marcus said.

"It sounds to me that you have already accepted all of this," Dennis said in a veiled challenge. An encompassing sweep of his left arm gave emphasis to his abiding skepticism.

Abby closed her eyes, shook her head. This was not the place or time to mix it up with their new acquaintances. These two were also survivors and had no need to account for their actions or opinions.

"Maybe, maybe not...uh, Mr. Webster," Marc countered, noncommittal.

Abby turned around to see Dennis purse his own lips. Mr. Scott's tone let it be known a discussion on the matter would not forthcoming for the immediate future.

Mil finished his own discussion and signed off the monitor. He turned his attention to the newcomers. An offer of a meal to Lydia was refused: Marc agreed to a cup of coffee.

"So, may I inquire how you all wound up in this situation with rest of us poor, unfortunate souls?" Dennis asked.

Marc settled in, took a slow sip of the hot liquid and thoughtfully put the plastiform cup down on the table, around which all were crowded in on. He took a breath, perhaps in an effort to figure out a good place from which to launch off. Then, he said, "To begin with, I am an economics professor at the University of Washington."

Abby noted a subtle change in his tone, like he was remorseful. It was the same feeling that she found herself often wrestling with in this still all too new existence. It was going to take weeks, if not months, to acclimate.

"Lydia is an administrator at the same school. We were on a pleasure cruise up around the San Juans the other evening on a friend's sailboat. There was a fuel leak of some kind. A fire broke out."

Marc's voice quivered. His gaze sank heavy to the deck for a few seconds. This was a man whose own terrible burden, for the moment, was too much to bear. It overwhelmed him.

His voice brimmed with regret and lingering pain. "Lydia and I were forward, fortunately. Jim and Megan, they were, uh…"

Marc's voice failed him.

Abby shuddered in sympathy of the vivid mental imagery that had to be assaulting him. Learning of such tragedies was getting to be an all too common event that she was growing to hate. Marc did not have to fill in any more details for her to get pretty much the whole picture.

A moment's respectful silence ensued.

"I'm very sorry, Mr. Scott," she picked up.

His head hung back down chin on his chest, the fingers of his left hand stroking his goatee.

Abby could not see his eyes and the deep emotions she knew to be flooding forth. She did not even want to.

"No, it's alright," Lydia spoke up. "At some point, you have to talk about these things. It can only help." She hesitated to draw in a small measured breath. "The last thing I remember was the fireball rolling toward us. Mr. Garr said the boat was entirely engulfed, even as he rescued us."

"You know," Abby contemplated, "I seem to remember something in the news about your disaster early yesterday. It was the fire that struck me the most. Funny," and she sighed, turning introspective at the enormity of the thought just occurring to her, "the day was also our anniversary."

"I'm…sorry to hear that." Lydia's voice was almost a whisper. She lowered her gaze, as if embarrassed to meet Abby's.

Abby winced.

She did not know what feeling she felt at the moment. Disappointment and loss...that was pretty close. She pushed it down. Now was not the time to burden these newcomers with her own heap of anguish. That would come later.

"Thanks. Anyway, they said two victims were recovered when the boat's remains were towed to shore. Two others were presumed missing."

Marc looked up. "Yours truly." He worked up a brave smile. Abby and the others tried to smile or chuckle but there was no humor to it. She bestowed a sympathetic nod.

Marc was coming across as a gentleman cut from the same material as Mil. And Dennis was, too, when he was not, on those rare occasions, immersed in a spell of obnoxiousness, pigheadedness, or being all self-righteous. Unfortunately, he was still in the middle of one of them and could only wonder how long he would carry on with it. Typically, his spells were short, like a passing shower, but enough to throw some rain on their parade. But their life now was a universe beyond what was typical.

Maybe when everyone had a chance to pick through the pieces of their lives and sort things out they could share their common feelings more in depth. If it was one thing Abby knew about herself, as a strength, it was that she had a desire to take more than just a passing interest in others she came into contact with. She wanted to be a listening ear and the consummate, compassionate soul.

"Perhaps you would tell us something of your story?" a livelier Lydia spoke up.

The query caught Abby off guard, though she could not say it was unexpected. After all, fair was fair.

"By all means, please, Mrs. Webster," Marc urged. He raised his cup to take another sip. "Please forgive me if I appear presumptuous, but I think we shall be getting to know each other very well in the coming days and weeks. The more we become mutually familiar the better and easier will be our lot, don't you think?"

"By no means, Mister Scott, do I think it presumptuous, and yes, I agree wholeheartedly with your wisdom on sharing. Dennis and I would be happy to."

"Oh yes, by all means," her husband agreed. His chilly tone conveyed his feelings on her coercion.

Abby ignored it. "Very well."

Abby smiled and drew in a long breath, using the time to collect her thoughts that still blurred on some points and frayed around the edges on others. She decided to hit the highlights and dispense with the trivial. Future conversation would provide all the details and then some.

"As I said, yesterday was our anniversary…"

*

"It is time for us to depart," Mil broadcast. By now the idle chatter around the table had ebbed, like the last trickle of a stream in a dry summer.

It was good his four guests were conversing, sharing. Only Lindsey Maguire was the recalcitrant holdout. The station monitor doing sentry duty over the ship indicated she was stirring some. He wanted to be well under way for her return by the time she was fully aroused, mostly to avoid another nasty altercation because they were not moving fast enough or some other petty excuse. Miriam had proved a handful in her own right when provoked, but this Lindsey was enough to cower a Vandarian swamp dragon…and put it to flight, to boot.

Well, if Lindsey was that set on returning, then the talk was finished. The infinite Heavens bore witness that all of them had done their level best with their combined repertoire to convince her otherwise. Actually, and with much thanks, it had by default fallen mostly on Mrs. Webster. It was a regrettable task never delegated her. Unlike Abby most people, for a while at least, closed in on themselves or with their significant others and tended to be little islands of aloneness, giving little care for others. Mrs. Webster had definitely been a relief for him.

For that, Mil took a small measure of comfort against the mind-distracting remorse that usually tailed in once a return was accomplished. But it was Lindsey's life, the same right to one of self-determination that he and every freedom-loving Majoran, and some of Earth, cherished. It was a crying shame, but it was for the best.

Yet, it also meant one less problem to deal with on a flight that would be long and arduous. Provided nothing nasty happened along the way.

Miriam tasked herself with gathering some of the needed things for the out journey, while the others cleaned up after their meal. Everything done, Mil made a last round of the station, of this "home away from home," if it could be called that. Everything was in proper order and should stay that way until Thalmond's turn to visit.

In spite of the station's meager comforts and limited space, it was still a small haven on a planet maybe hostile, definitely unsafe. With that in mind, his many years of experience notwithstanding, a momentary shudder of insecurity snaked through him at the thought of leaving.

Homesick? That was an antagonist never quite conquered. And him, Milankaar, a trusting man! Paradoxically, what could be homey about a bland observation station?

Each soul filtered back to the access and up to the ship, leaving Mil the last to leave. It was the captain thing, as he had observed on an Earth transmission. While the ship was powered down and docked, physical movement to and from the ship was the preferred method of transport. The molecular disassembly and subsequent rejuvenation was a complex event in its own right and had inherent risks that went from the almost unnoticeable to the hideous. Though rare enough, there was no point in pushing it for the sake of convenience. Besides, a little exercise never hurt anyone.

Mil powered down life support, leaving what was necessary for monitors and the computer core. He began climbing the ten meters to the ship's keel access, closing and sealing the station below him. He stopped at an exposed keyboard pad set into the shaft tube beside the ladder rungs, the ladder doing double duty as shielding for conduit and cable routes between ship and station. With left hand wrapped around a brace the other deftly typed in a command. He tapped the enter button.

Concealment and ample safeguards were built into the station to discourage detection. So efficient was the design that to date nowhere in Majora's benign contact with and observation throughout the known galaxy had there been a station discovered, inadvertent or otherwise.

At this particular station all Majoran contract and research vessels of his civilization's persuasion had access. Right now it was just he and Thalmond, two lonely sojourners on a very big planet.

Upon docking, the ship's computer communicated its legitimate presence upon interrogation by the station's own computer via a transponder code. A correct match up of those stored in the station's memory core obviated the security standby destruct sequence. Any intruder attempting access to any part of the station without the necessary authorization would not personally suffer injury. On the other hand, every system and circuit contained within would be assailed by a massive power overload, all safety overrides and breakers neutralized. In essence, the station would be fried from within. The electrical conflagration would leave the place a defunct, burned out mystery.

To any of Earth who happened to stumble upon the remains and the fairly common materials with which it was constructed, it could not help but *allude* to the presence of aliens. Proving them was another matter. Some quarters of the planet's population would surely be propelled to a frenzy by rampant speculation of aliens skulking among the populace. But that could not be helped. Alternatives were few, other than to abandon such a successful endeavor altogether.

Satisfied, "We are all set, Miriam," he spoke to the miniature visual monitor and her image. "Give me a minute to get up front."

She nodded as the screen went blank.

Before clearing the access well, he could already sense the surge of energy and life through the very fabric of his ship. It was coming awake, ready to do as bidden. Save for a seasoned spacefarer like Miriam, the others probably would not take notice. As for himself, senses had long since been honed and attuned to the particular "feel" of his ship. It was more than what computers, sensors, and probes sniffed, felt, and relayed. There was objective data, and then there was "feel".

In a sobering thought, he still wished he could get a grip on that cranky number three repulsor. Insight and "feel" eluded him on this one, and he hated it. No way could he feel a sufficient sense of peace about what lay ahead. To be sure, he could not escape the niggling worry that a temper tantrum of some sort in that unit would figure in the business ahead of them.

All he could do was shake his head in concern.

CHAPTER FOURTEEN

Mil ambled into the transport chamber that now did double-duty as a lounge. Abby paid him casual attention while seated on the edge of the platform with Lydia, both conversing in quiet tones. Having been more or less the intellectual misfit, Dennis now found a kindred spirit in Marcus Scott. The two men poked about the many panels and available gadgetry, like two kids exploring the magical environs of a toy store.

Abby paused in her chat to watch the Majoran focus on Lindsey who was seated in the aft, inside corner. As her and Lindsey's eyes met the latter broke off and in a spiteful snit looked away, two like-end magnets pushed together and repulsed.

"You would think she'd be happy to be on her way home," Lydia said. She joined Abby in a double-barreled stare.

Abby nodded. "Yeah, I don't think I have ever had the misfortune of knowing someone who wanted to isolate herself or himself so completely. Such arrogance and contempt, that has to truly be one of a kind."

"Here, here. Me too," Lydia colluded. She embraced herself and shuddered, shifting her gaze to Abby. "I don't know about her myself. I have hardly even talked to her, not like you have, but just being around her gives me the jitters."

"That makes two of us."

"Well, I can't quite put a finger on it. Maybe it's nothing."

"No, not quite."

Abby was tempted to yield to the temptation to give her newfound friend a quick briefing, sotto voce, on some of Lindsey's more distinctive characteristics. Gossiping, though, was a behavior she never really had been comfortable with. It was just as well. Lydia already appeared to have a reasonable grasp on Lindsey already.

Best just to say, "Just watch yourself around her, though. Try not to do or say anything to provoke her. Cobras are best left alone."

"Such as?"

"Such as 'Good morning' or 'Hi, how are you,' for starters."

"Got it."

"Just the same," Abby angled off onto a more reflective note, "I have wondered if she is capable of any feelings even approaching something warm, like affection."

"I wouldn't hold my breath, Abby." Lydia let go a quiet sigh. "It's enough to make a person think there is a genetic predisposition to contention and rudeness."

"Right. Remind me to laugh later, okay?" And she really could have, had it not been for the gravity of a person who was making a bona fide decision to die, actually suicide, and not even appreciating what others were doing in her best interests.

Lindsey remained a prisoner of her seat, which normally would be folded in on itself and then stored in a deck recess. Dennis had earlier joked about them looking like rumble seats from some old classic cars, a term that required a further

164

expansion of Mil's vocabulary. While Lindsey might be an inexhaustible source of anti-social emotions, her unwillingness to socialize gave the impression of latent insecurity in some form or another.

Mil was working his way around the platform, stopping first to say something to Dennis and Marc. He then drew up to the two ladies. Abby assumed he intended to wind up at Lindsey to brief her on her situation.

"Oh, Mil, we were just wondering…"

That stopped the Majoran. "How may I assist you, Mrs. Webster?" His readiness to offer assistance in an instant was welcome and coming to be typical.

"I know you have given us an overview of these slave traders that might be lurking about, but just exactly what are they *really* like?"

Lydia winced, mortified.

Mil curled his lower lip to, gather his thoughts. He crossed his arms and got comfortable leaning on a shoulder against one of the niches. "To begin with, it is kind of like confessing an alter ego, Mrs. Webster. I find it a sort of evil twin I wish could be locked away or rehabilitated, if that were possible."

"You really don't have to, if it's that…" Abby began to say. She came up short as she wondered if maybe she had broached a subject better left untouched.

Mil waved her off. "No, it is a fair question requiring a fair answer and you need to know, anyway. In and of themselves, these other Majorans are not really scoundrels and thugs, criminal types.

"But those who inhabit Majora Prime are of a slightly different moral temperament. They are our kindred and, yet, they do not see personal freedom in the same way as my people do. For them degrees of status and power carry complimentary degrees of privilege. Much of it is centered on the acquiring of wealth and passing it on to the offspring.

"Several of your centuries ago a faction, which were my people's forebears, were uncomfortable with that nepotistic concept and the unfeeling coldness that went with it. Unable to change their larger society's entrenched beliefs, they banded together and moved to the world we now call home. There they created a culture more in keeping with their ideals.

"It may seem idealistic, but my ancestors took a world much less blessed with resources than Prime and shaped it into what it is now. With hard work, and a fair amount of good fortune, the corporate whole now enjoys the payoff of that earlier toil. And it was done without the sellout of our moral integrity: no slave labor, no profit exploitation at the expense of those who have no power, and no widening disparity among the social classes."

"It sounds like Eden, Mil. Perfect," Abby commented, a little awkward. It was hard to believe such a utopia existed in a universe that was turning out to be filled more and more with questionable practices, evil.

"Far from perfect, Mrs. Webster. No society ever quite attains that to which it aspires. That is the price of individuality." Mil's tone took on a different quality, more sober and a little stiffer. "But I must get back to your question: you will not find many Majorans slave running, though there are a few that I have heard of. Our main concern is always who and *what* they hire to do their dirty work. And just for your information, Miriam and I are considered criminals in some of the more nefarious quarters. From what I have been told, I have a bounty of ten talents on my head, dead or alive."

Abby gawked. She had no idea how much a talent was worth, let alone ten, but it had to be considerable, as a bounty. Hedging her bet, "That must make you pretty significant somewhere?"

"A talent would pay off the remaining contract requirements for both Thalmond and I this time around," he told her. "I could either buy a ship outright and provision it or retire to a life of ease for some years to come."

"Wow!" Abby breathed, impressed. While it was not good news in one sense it did mean Mil had to have had enough impact on his maladjusted kin's financial health that they wanted him shut down…permanently.

"You said 'who and *what*'," Lydia probed, assertive. Abby stole a sideways glance and saw that the expression on her new friend's attractive face was stained with distaste. It looked like an unpalatable morsel had violated her lips.

"I most certainly did, did I not?" Mil confirmed.

"And please tell me they aren't monsters and ogres," Abby ventured. Her comment was more an attempt at dark humor than a seeking of fact.

Lydia shuddered. Abby's impulsive comment had not been the wisest of utterances. It would be her dumb misfortune to have scared her new friend half to death, though adults would normally be beyond monsters and ogres. But that *was* another place, another life.

"Put bluntly, yes," Mil replied evenly. "Slave traders are almost always off-worlders. A good description, to use a term you would be familiar with, is that of hired guns?"

"You weren't…one of them, were you?" Lydia wanted to know, now timid.

Mil chuckled, shook his head. If anything, Abby thought he might have been just a little embarrassed by the question.

"I may have been many things in my life, Miss Chang, but I can assure you a trader was never one of them or a criminal, for that matter." He turned downcast. "That profession, if you will allow me to use the term, requires a creature devoid of soul or compassion. Only personal gain would drive them."

"So why have they not resorted to plain ol' abduction?" Abby next asked, Lindsey's plight on her mind.

"They very easily could, if they so desired." Mil tapped a finger against his chin, thinking. "There may be cases, especially ones that might involve disappearances that crop up from time to time; however, I personally am not aware of any on record. So I would have to say it is an infrequent occurrence, if at all. On the other hand, it would be a significant turn of events and very unwelcome, if I may say.

"Their method, the same basic covert strategy we employ, is still the best way to operate. It raises no undue suspicion, in spite of certain complications, like timing constraints. What it boils down to is this: why compromise a method that has a proven history of solid profitability?"

"You make it sound so business-like explaining it the way you do, Mil," Lydia harped.

Mil had not time enough to respond when another voice cut in. The force of it shoved aside Lydia's weaker delivery.

"You claim that you aren't one of those so-called traders or slavers," Lindsey snapped. "For all I know, and am willing to bet, is that this is all a cleverly concocted ruse to dupe us for reasons that are as yet unclear. I, for one, am definitely not taken in by it. All we really have is your story, and it's a gem, if there ever was one!"

Abby went wide-eyed with surprise at the diatribe. "I didn't think you were listening from over there, Lindsey."

Lindsey turned from Mil to her with all the spirit of a fighter finishing off one opponent and now targeting a second. "You only get to the top of the heap by being attentive to what goes on around you, lady," she snapped. "Fools and idiots do not, if you've ever noticed. They're lucky if they even rise to anything above mediocrity."

Lindsey added a hard stare that bore right through Abby, searing the words of her caustic accusation onto her soul.

Abby stiffened, stung and stung hard. She'd had a pretty good idea of what Lindsey was about and the mental fuel that drove her ego. There was every confidence the others did too. Still, in front of them, the innuendo of being thought an idiot hit solid way below the belt.

But that all paled in light of the fact Lindsey's stubbornness was buying her a one-way ticket to the grave, once she left the safe confines of the ship. There would be, what, three days to ponder the consequences of her choice? Then it would not matter.

Marc and Dennis drew surreptitiously closer, taking an interest in the goings on. Having finished with Abby, Lindsey now turned to Mil. It was the latter who spoke up first.

"Miss Maguire, the fact you are about to be returned stands as proof of my sincerity," he countered in earnest. "That remains a guarantee I cannot voluntarily violate, even against my better judgment."

On an impulse an upbeat Lindsey blurted, "If it's secrecy you wish to keep…"

"I believe secrecy, especially of what you have witnessed, is an alien concept, considering your particular character qualities."

Now it was Lindsey's turn to be put in her place. She recoiled ever so slightly. Abby was sure it was more a statement of opinion rather than sniping barb. Either way, it was an accurate opinion. Lindsey shook it off.

"But I have no fear. There are other considerations, however, that do concern me, some of which you have already been made aware of."

Lindsey stared unblinking for a few seconds longer, already in a mental contest over this final appeal. The conflict, though, was a fleeting wisp of vapor from a warm breath on a frosty morning as personal desire won out. "It's all still a big fabrication, storyteller," she smirked.

A brief frown swept across Mil's face. Then it too was gone. "You will relay tales of 'alien abduction' to anyone and everyone, all the while in the process of dying from infections too numerous for your people's medical science to contend with. You will find yourself both ridiculed and pitied, both a curiosity and a mystery. And yours will be a demise drawn out in a most ignoble manner, Miss Maguire. Most pitiable, is that it will be a needless shame, especially being one blessed with your physical and character qualities."

"I can handle that, alien." Her words dripped venom.

"Then prepare to transport, Miss Maguire." Mil turned all business with an air of finality. "I will set you down close to an area of multiple habitations. I believe you refer to it as a hamlet."

Abby and the others found their seats. She was not quite sure how to feel about events very soon to transpire. Would anyone really miss her? One thing was for sure: in spite of Lindsey's obnoxious pathological temperament there was no joy in her leaving.

"Thank you," Lindsey smirked.

TRANSIT

CHAPTER FIFTEEN

"Ten minutes to transport, Miss Maguire."

Abby quietly studied Mil as he scanned across the transport instrument display. One hand braced his frame against the periodic rolling of the ship while Miriam guided them to their destination from the bridge. He looked like an oceangoing mariner, swaying as he was, in tune with his ship as it rode the swells of a sea. In some ways, an atmospheric sea was not too much different than a more typical one. It had such a natural look to it that his other hand was little affected as it worked here, moved there.

"Do you have to make me bloody airsick before we get there?" groused Lindsey. Her grip on the armrests of her seat forced the blood from her fingers until they were deathly white, which was also a pretty close approximation to her complexion.

Abby had to repress a grin. Pity. There was little to doubt Lindsey's love for flight, now with a little turbulence or maneuvering thrown in. It no doubt extended about as far as the nearest toilet or waste receptacle. Call it an initiation. Later she would feel bad about it. Maybe.

"Sorry, Miss Maguire," Mil deadpanned in a polite apology. "A lot of our local navigation follows road courses and landmarks, much in the same way as your auto-piloted air vehicles do."

"Terrific! That's all I need now, a course on aeronautics."

"Bear with me for a few more minutes."

"Not if I die from heaving my guts out!" A hand went to clutch her stomach, the other her mouth.

In Abby's quick estimation, Lindsey looked like five miles of bad road. She muttered a few words under her hand-stifled breath, but Abby entertained no desire to ask for a repeat. An inaudible uttered epithet was better than another well understood tongue-lashing.

*

"Three minutes to destination," Mil voiced in a general broadcast. "Your set down point will be near a cluster of approximately six dwellings one half kilometer to the northwest. Any closer and we risk detection with your materialization."

Mil let an air of finality bleed through on his last statement to forestall any argument on Lindsey's part. Lindsey opened her mouth and almost, but not quite, uttered what was no doubt another biting commentary on his and Miriam's flying skills. After a brief hesitation, she instead gulped her words, released the seat restraints, and pushed up on unsteady legs. Lindsey was not the first, nor would she be the last, to critique his qualifications. Such was one of the lesser curses of his profession.

Just then something felt wrong. Just what, he could not tell.

A violent shock from very close by reverberated through the ship's structure. Reality turned upside down.

An insane chorus of alarms blared impatiently from everywhere. They crowded in on the already tense air. Screams, cries, and the strained whine of tortured engines melded into a singular, deafening cacophony.

Lindsey yelped as she was hurled back into her seat by violent forces assaulting her. Unfettered by restraints, she wrapped both arms around the armrests and clamped on for dear life. The seat was now a life preserver.

"Somebody better tell me what's going on!" she wailed.

"For heaven's sake, what's the matter!" Abby beat out on top of it.

"Incoming ship!" was all Mil had time for. He was already jabbering unintelligible commands over the comm monitor to Miriam.

Another healthy jolt, not quite so bad, made for an instant replay on the heels of the previous one.

"Miriam! Get us out of here before they knock us down!" Mil barked, now in plain English. "Head out, evasive course, maximum boost on all thrusters. Push her as hard as she will take it!"

"Now you just wait a minute!" Lindsey demanded. "What about me?"

Mil was all over his instruments, punching at switches and buttons to access what limited information he was able to glean on his ship's condition. For now, Lindsey's request went unheeded. It was just one more distraction among a million others to be ignored.

"Mil?" Lindsey insisted. She was up now and not letting the ship's writhing dissuade her from stalking toward him, drunken gait notwithstanding. Another twist of the deck's attitude, though, forced an unceremonious retreat with all due urgency.

After a couple seconds and much too busy to be intimidated… "Currently impossible! We are presently under assault, should you have failed to notice."

"I think we should vote on this!" a now desperate Lindsey bellowed for the benefit of all. All symptoms of stomach distress were forgotten.

*

How idiotic, was the first thought that came to Abby's mind. They were about to die and now the insufferable Lindsey wanted to be all democratic. Somehow it struck her as odd, considering Lindsey's general pig-headedness.

Lindsey scanned to each face in rapid order, expecting from somewhere, everywhere, to find support.

She was all alone.

"Well?"

More silence.

"I don't believe…" Lindsey muttered under her breath. The next words were wholly inaudible.

"A slaver?" Marc chimed in from the background. It muted her plea.

"Logical. That would be the winning bet," Mil tossed back, preoccupied.

"But how?" now Abby's turn.

"Chance encounter…most likely."

*

A brief silence held sway with only the protests of a ship maneuvering strenuously in flight encompassing them. Sandwiched between pressing concerns, Mil tried to guess what the odds were of something like this coming about. It had to be astronomical. But it had happened here, now. At least he was appreciative of the respite from his guests. Now he could

174

concentrate on his limited perspective of possible damage sustained.

So far, they and his ship looked none the worse for wear. The fact they were in a controlled, yet evasive, flight profile was a relief…for however long. Still, that number three unit remained uppermost in his mind, like an abiding sense of dread that refused to go away.

For the time being satisfied with their situation, "In any event, they will most likely try to disable us, either slowing us down to overtake us or else running us to ground. Then once having abducted all of you, they will either commandeer this ship or tractor it somewhere convenient for disposal, such as the bottom of an ocean."

"You're kidding!" exclaimed Dennis.

The others were in similar states of befuddlement. Lindsey sank back to her seat.

Mil ignored him. Later they could rationalize this all they wanted…should there be a later.

"Miriam," Mil hailed, holding relentlessly onto the console. The mention of her name initiated a programmed flashing prompt on her panel to snag her attention. The picture he had was again a slightly oblique wide-angled view from forward. Her left hand nursed the throttle while the right worked a small joystick. She glanced to him. "Have the sensors and computer punched through that other ship's cloak and identified it yet?"

Hers was the usual silent reply.

"I wish you had better news than that."

The ship lurched and shook once more. It was as violent as the first one, maybe a little more. By now, Miss Maguire was livid, but at least she had the good sense to remain seated.

The rocking and rolling on their invisible roller coaster ride intensified accordingly, as Miriam tossed them through a kaleidoscope of evasive maneuvers. Joints, fittings, and bulkheads registered their impatient complaints. The carryings on of the others kept the racket at a raucous level.

Unexpectedly, the deck pitched up, like a boat catching a wave head on, while still rolling from side to side. Normally subtle background noise, the repulsors rumbled and growled upon shoving the ship's bulk up in an abrupt, contrary direction.

Mil let go of the console after a quick aim for the vacant seat extended in place behind him. It was a bad guess. Without warning, the ship contorted around him before he landed. A leg collided hard with one of the unyielding armrests. In an explosion of pain, he tumbled into the seat and struggled for the proper posture to get the restraints hurriedly in place and secured.

"Hold tight!" he grimaced in warning. "It could get rough from here on out."

"Then what d'ya call this?" howled Lindsey.

Again, she was met by silence from her companions.

*

Abby latched onto Dennis for a brace…and security. He was doing likewise to his seat.

The sudden threat of extinction was bad enough, but in him she sensed, felt a current of calmness. He had endured a stint of daredevil aerobatic flying after flight lessons but had never made it an enduring hobby. Lucky him. That experience had instilled that which was necessary to quell much of the inherent terror, compounded by the immediacy of their predicament. The others, Abby included, did not enjoy that luxury.

Dennis turned to look her way. Abby saw fear in his eyes, but her assessment had been correct: he was keeping it under control, at least on the surface.

She should do so well.

"I love you, Denny," Abby whispered. She tried to mean it, but it came out so mechanical, habit-like. He gave her a little nod, then closed his eyes and tilted his head back against the headrest to continue riding out the wild gyrations.

The positive angle increased to a stomach-twisting, precipitous attitude. In a moment, it mellowed out to something barely resembling level flight.

Mil's ship had to have some kind of exotic inertial dampening capability, from what she knew of the basic science of motion. It was either that or else others besides Lindsey would be in varying and deepening shades of green. It was still early, and such would be a ratio depending on how long this craziness lasted. It was a good bet there was also an artificial gravity field that kept things in place while in flight mode. The ship, so far, had just about everything she could imagine. Or not imagine.

The jolting amplified. Added to that, Abby now felt an increasing leaden sensation to her left. They were accelerating. She could only wonder what their airspeed was, their altitude.

Then again, maybe she didn't want to know. The latter had to be considerable, since her head felt full, her ears stuffed with cotton. She swallowed hard a couple times to clear plugged ears.

Thankfully there were no more of those nerve-numbing detonations. At least they had abated for now. Either pursuit was still a grim reality or else a very strong possibility. Miriam was evidently not taking any chances.

"Mr. Webster," Mil beckoned, "I understand you have some flight experience?"

"You should know, Mil," Dennis replied. "Tell me you remember what we were doing when you just happened to be going our way?"

"That will suffice. We may need it." To the others he announced over the din, "It will be best if everyone else remains securely seated. I am certain we are still being pursued. As such, our evasive maneuvers will continue for the time being."

"Oh, spare me," Lindsey grimaced. "Why don't you just blow them off and leave 'em behind?"

"I fully intend to."

"Somehow, I don't like the sound of that."

"Just deal with it," Abby overheard Dennis grumble.

Lindsey did not appear to have heard the snipe.

"No doubt they intend to shadow this ship until such time as we stand down. I would expect at that point an immediate renewal of their assault upon us."

"How can you be so sure of that?" Lindsey sniffed.

"Because I would." Again there was an ominous finality to Mil's voice that chilled Abby's blood. "And I can assure you, that given another chance, they will not be so inept as to miss again."

Abby let her eyelids close. This whole thing had a surreal movie-like quality to it. A dread fascination of whom or what that sought their demise crowded in a rush upon her mind. None were human, and she didn't have to put any effort into conjuring up those monsters and ogres. The ones that were bred out of the darkest recesses of her imagination were of a certainty nowhere near correct. Then again, the only models she had to draw upon were numerous sci-fi movies, both silly and believable and, of course, Mil.

One thing was very certain: she could only expect the unexpected.

Lindsey stewed on slow boil across the chamber. An occasional epithet or slur sounded over the more common noises, human and otherwise. And since this was getting to be typical no one gave her any attention.

Abby confessed no particular feelings one way or the other over Lindsey's failure to return home. If she had to make a choice, she was relieved fate had lent a hand in stymieing her companion's return, doing their collective job of pleading one last time with her for them. Now if only she did not come to regret it.

But Lindsey would live. Not only that, she needed a good dose of humility, whether she acknowledged it or not. She *was* no better and no worse off, maybe, than the rest of them. Most important they were all on an equal footing, where each having escaped with their lives was concerned.

For a couple moments, the ship maintained level flight. A slight shudder rippled underfoot, detectable through the seat. The ride felt a little different, smoother. Perhaps it was the gravitational enhancement and/or inertial dampening fields Abby had imagined. For now maintaining a semblance of a stable flight attitude without any dramatic stunts gave the sensation of normal airliner turbulence, or one of Dennis's more notable jaunts.

Abby would have to ask Mil about those engineering marvels sometime, though she could by no means qualify herself as technically inclined enough to understand.

Speaking of Mil, he brought himself out of his seat with that same sailor's balance necessary to get around on a ship at sea. In wordless motion, he limped his way around the chamber and out.

Abby was half tempted to follow him.

*

Miriam yielded the pilot's seat to Mil but he hesitated.

The ship was on autopilot with a programmed sequence of random, dissimilar maneuvers, one to follow another, in place for the duration of their transfer. Unpredictable spans of no more than a few seconds elapsed between each one. Pursuit by this bunch and long spells of straight and level flight were not conducive to long, healthy lives.

"Good job, Miriam," Mil acknowledged. He gave her a proud smile.

Her sweat-beaded face relayed her struggles with their earlier evasive flight. She stared in anticipation into his eyes, awaiting instruction, one arm wrapped around the seat headrest for balance.

"If we make it through this I am going to recommend you to the Council for your master's certification…Oh, you are not interested in having a ship of your own?" he repeated of her silent statement. He feigned a hurt look at the refusal of his magnanimous gesture, but it lasted for only a pair of moments. "Well, no matter. I would miss you, anyway."

He winked and sent Miriam another smile, this time a coy one.

Mil maneuvered into the seat. She leaned around from behind and wrapped him in a one-armed hug, to which he took the time to stroke it with his right hand. She pulled back to let him lock the seat restraints into place. For an instant, he rubbed the painful telltale knot on his right knee that even now had to be developing into a healthy bruise. He then grasped the throttle and joystick. The action disengaged the autopilot.

Turning his head and making sure she could see his face, "Please take the monitors and keep a close watch behind us. Let me know if you catch a hint of anything, even a ghost or an anomaly. *Anything.* I know they are still there. They are not going to quit so easy, even should they remain sensor quiet.

"I intend on doing a dirt-close flyby of Earth's moon. Such a close perspective should draw them out and level the…uh, playing field. Yes that is it, level the playing field. It will also give us a chance to throw them off and perhaps make good on an escape."

At least it was a plan.

Mil began to manipulate controls as he continued to glance up and sideways into his confidant's cherubic face. Miriam mouthed a concern.

"No, I would prefer you be on the monitors, Miriam. That repulsor is behaving for now. Each of us can keep a partial watch on it from our respective stations. Should it act up I intend on calling Mr. Webster forward to take over for you."

Still, another soundless concern came from her mouth.

"No, Miriam, I think he will be able to figure it out with a minimum of instruction. Mrs. Webster managed well enough, and she is not as technically endowed as he is."

Miriam put in a silent commentary.

"I know there are many facets to intelligence besides academic. Insight and common sense make her his equal in any plebian arena."

She nodded thoughtful agreement and took up the sensor station aft. She would watch the space behind them with all the vigilance of a Cinerin Swifthawk.

Unless the slaver de-cloaked or did something uncharacteristic, such as unleash a continuous volley of disrupter fire, she most likely was not going to see much of anything. They could be tailgating right up their exhaust ports and neither of them would be any the wiser.

Which brought to mind another concern: how could he, Miriam, and the others have been discovered in the first place?

Earth was an average planet, as far as size went. It was large enough with a complex layout of topography and abundant vegetation. They should have been all but lost to medium and long-range look down sensor scanning, even had they been uncloaked.

Exhaust trail…

He had heard of such a vague possibility. The more he pondered it in the brief time he had the more sense it made. It was either that or something much more sinister, like the ability to penetrate their cloak. The latter would be the worst case scenario…and an insurmountable disaster. The implications were unfathomable. The first and foremost would be his and Miriam's demise. That forced a wish that it was their exhaust, bad as that was, too.

Was that it? Mil tried to assure himself. *It had to be!*

It could not have been anything else but their exhaust trail. That meant detection had to be at very short-range, no more than a few short kilometers. Such made the occurrence the wildest stroke of coincidence he'd had the misfortune of enduring.

Earth's atmosphere, with its myriad constituent gases, pollutants, and the convoluted wind patterns that stirred it all up, was supposed to have dissipated any ion trail in moments, at least enough to make detection and tracking difficult. Probably only the immediate ionized exhaust plume was painted on the other's sensors. Though otherwise safely cloaked in invisibility from normal modes of detection, it was the only logical way that came to mind to explain their discovery here, in the middle of what humans called nowhere, or out in the dingleberries. That was the working theory then that gave focused direction to his immediate plan of action…which was doing what they were doing now.

Unfortunately, this whole mess had to happen here, and it had to be now.

Mil had not been specifically scanning for exhaust trails. Only a handful of previous missions that he knew of anywhere had the dubious distinction of going head-to-head with slavers while encountering the same target acquisition. There were just so many select victims of tragic events to garner survivors that the chances were incalculable. Just on Earth thousands perished each day that 'qualified' for extraction, which indeed meant such potential meetings were very rare occurrences indeed.

Tied in with that, the history of undetected activity made it easy to slip into the insidious and disarming habit of allowing one's guard to slip. Of a truth, no high degree of readiness could be maintained forever, though certain practices could be incorporated as routine duty. Maybe this particular slaver or bounty hunter had been vigilant, *very* vigilant.

Should they work their way clear of this fiasco, he promised himself to rethink some attitudes.

If the slaver would tail them in a sweeping turn, especially in the non-hindering vacuum of space, they just might catch a glimpse of the other's ion trail. That would neatly settle the question of continuing pursuit and the subsequent need for evasive flight. A little electronic wizardry and he might even be able to identify the vessel type and, hence, who their assailants were. As least it would confirm what he felt deep in his bones.

He had told Miriam to keep an eye out, and that was exactly what she would do, until directed otherwise. The slavers were experts at what they did, which now no doubt included ion detection. They could be counted on to do their utmost to keep their noses sniffing and dogging his ship's exhaust stream.

*

Miriam's full attention was glued to the sensor monitor, while her hands worked through rapid, deft movements across her keyboard and numerous instruments.

She focused the rear scanners for narrow-band sweeps, sniffing for ion emissions different from their own. Once found she would then be able to track and measure, then hopefully identify, the strongest source. That would pinpoint their nemesis' most approximate position. With any luck, she might not only be able to maintain the contact but also run a profile and match it against the propulsion specs of known ships. Gleaning the most knowledge available, she then just might be able to create at least a few options for dealing with this threat.

Miriam brought the display to maximum resolution. The haze of background ionization of Earth's tenuous upper atmosphere, excited by the Sun's powerful radiation, made the screen glow with a faint, roiling, jade-green wash. It would almost entirely disappear upon gaining true space, even more so the more distance they put between them and the Sun.

She rubbed an eye with the back of one hand and squinted, moved closer to the display to better see any changes. The briefest blip, the faintest shadow, might be all there was to see. She dared not blink.

The screen started to swim. Her eyes ached. She pawed at the other eye and beat back an urge to yawn.

The ship exited one of Mil's periodic, irregular maneuvers. He then skewed into a bank to port, leveled, swung *Starlight Mistress* into a starboard yaw.

Miriam's eyes strained to keep track of the portrayed objects, all the while maintaining awareness of anything that might move in among them.

She had to blink and hazarded it.

It was not quite a flash, more like a rapid brightening the size of a fingernail.

The fuzzy blot lingered for a heartbeat. It then faded only slightly slower than it had appeared. In that brief moment, the slaver had allowed itself to be seen before correcting.

That was all she needed.

Miriam decided to type in her report. Keying it in, she sent it in a print display with a message prompt. Several seconds later, her comm display above the sensor monitor flicked to life. Her companion's grinning expression steadied and focused, framed squarely within.

"Just as I expected," he stated with a small degree of triumph. "They are still on us, shadowing us. Was it their exhaust plume you saw?"

Miriam nodded.

"Good. Then I am going to assume, at least for the time being, that they are ignorant of our awareness; otherwise, they would have renewed their assault or maneuvered more aggressively to hide their track. Keep watching and let me know if anything else arises."

He flashed a playful wink her way then let his consideration travel back to his flying.

Through the space between her console and the cluster of instruments and panels affixed to the ceiling Miriam glimpsed part of the vast curve of Earth's horizon. Distant, dreamy, sun-lit islands of towering cumulus and feathery cirrus dappled the distant surface. They combined with the hazy ring of life-sustaining atmosphere to keep that line separating the black depths of cold space and the rich earth-tone hues of a living, breathing world from being sharp, distinct.

It was a panorama she never wearied of. It was all the more stunning, and humbling, considering her minority status of being among those privileged on any world to witness the aesthetic appeal of such a vista.

In this respect, it was reassuring to know that Earth, both Majoran worlds, and dozens of others were identical from this perspective, where landmarks and outlines tended to blur into a collage of indistinct pastels. There was blue water, green plant life, gray and brown landmasses. Then there was the pristine white for clouds, ice caps, and snowfields.

There were also the barren, lifeless chunks of ice or rock, like Earth's moon and a majority of the other members of this solar system, populating the vast galactic ocean they were in the midst of. Then there were the great swirling gas giants, cousins of Jupiter and Saturn, which looked like the grandest, variegated celestial marbles.

Then there were the in between ones, the exotics and misfits. A prime example was that not too distant desert world of Primar Maunda. It was one of the oddest that came to mind. Sun-scorched, wind-blown, shifting sand seas could in a matter of a day bury any disabled ship unfortunate enough to alight on its eternally unstable surface. But that was during its closest approach to its modest, yellow-orange star in its highly elliptical orbit. At apogee its atmosphere simply precipitated out, freezing as surface snow and ice for centuries until its next fall toward perihelion.

At the opposite end of the spectrum of marginally habitable worlds was the bog world of Sordes and their first destination. It was a steamy, fetid globe of muck and ooze orbiting a golden gem of a star by the attractive Earthen name of Tau Ceti. How such a pristine luminary, that was only a little smaller and cooler than Earth's parent sun, gave birth to such a hideous offspring was anyone's guess.

And their first contact, one Dyman Predish, fit perfectly. An oily, slippery character, he was generally trustworthy in his dealings with Mil and her in the running of their charges over the months and years. The same went for a number of their other contacts that ran the network that Mil, Thalmond, and others had developed over time.

As the view without swept along the arc of distant horizon, the moon climbed into sight. Its full, glorious presence ballooned into a glistening orb that sought in relentless effort to free itself of Earth's intervening disk. It was being birthed for her and Mil to witness. Miriam knew that even in his preoccupation Mil would take notice. As it continued to rise, a slight course correction for a couple moments brought it to bull's-eyed center through the forward view port.

At any other time, she would have loved nothing better than to be able to luxuriate in the breathtaking scenery. Here was a celestial mother and child, the intricate symmetry of Earth's surface scrolling past far below, the silent, still, eternal stars scattered on an ebony canvas that gave witness to it all. It was a waste not to be able to enjoy it when the opportunity presented itself.

Miriam caught herself, annoyed for lapsing into an idle daydream. Now of all times! Maybe later there would be time to revisit it. It was the monitor that required tending.

Maybe.

She dredged herself back to the task at hand.

Very shortly a troubling thought came to mind to fill what she had just pushed out. It was one of those flashes of all too familiar foresight that came when someone or something was going to be in trouble at some point in the near future.

It always started this way, an unsettling impression, like the appearance of a dark cloud on the horizon of a clear day. It was vague, formless, this time indecipherable. It was almost, but not quite, a hallucination.

She reached out with her mind, tried to grasp the incorporeal presence in order to pull it closer to see, to analyze, to know its meaning, all while trying to stay focused on her flying.

Then it vanished.

It was like awakening from the surreal dreaming of a night's sleep. And just like that it took a moment for reality to crystallize around her. Everything was as it should be.

It will happen, Miriam, now worried, told herself in no uncertain terms. An uncontrollable tremor coursed through her. For some unknown reason this particular one was vague, nothing more than formless shadows, no faces.

That did nothing to alleviate how unsettling it was. All the others had been clear, easily interpreted, able to lead Mil and her right to the source. Perhaps, just maybe, this vision's vagueness and the lack of attendant distress, this time, meant distance, both in time and space. The circumstances were certainly different.

How she hated the knowing of the bare central fact and precious little of the surrounding details.

At some point when this pursuit was over...and it had to be successful...Miriam promised herself to dissect and sort out every aspect of this occurrence to glean the last dregs of meaning, information, insight. It was only then that she could do something about this premonition. Until then it promised to be a burden on her mind that would tempt her to dangerous preoccupation.

CHAPTER SIXTEEN

Once clear of the Earth's atmosphere, Mil nudged the throttle.

I feel you accelerating, Miriam relayed in type. *Think you can fool them?*

"An abrupt velocity change might, but I doubt it," Mil said when she was looking. "Such a trick is pretty standard. They will be expecting it. But doing anything that puts even a few seconds on them is…uh, money in the bank, as our human guests might say."

Sounds good, Mil. Push it harder, if you can. She'll take it.

"The ship is not the one I am worried about."

There also had to be balance. He did not want to do anything rash. The last thing he needed was to work through a maneuver that might spook the slavers into a drastic action on a par with blasting them out of the sky. That was guaranteed to ruin everyone's day.

They could not boost to a velocity near star flight in this mode, even for a micro-jump. They were still too deep in Earth's gravity well, not to mention the distance tolerances being too narrow, with even light photons taking only a couple insane brief seconds to make the round trip from Earth to the Moon and back. The latter took time to figure out exact calculations, time and effort they were currently unable to invest in. Of a certainty, they would either overshoot the natural satellite or else plow a new crater on its tortured surface before he could react. *As if the pockmarked satellite needed another one,* Mil mused. Much depended on the slaver's determination.

And those ne'er-do-wells would be behind him all the way.

Less than three minutes present course and speed would get them to the Moon and among the stark tumult of craters, mountains, and rifts. Upon planet fall, he was going to have to chop speed to a fraction of what it was now to begin maneuvering.

The slaver would not be so easily fooled. Their captain, savvy to what his prey was up to, could be counted on going all out in bringing them to heel. Mrs. Webster and the others would be so much profit; he and Miriam, competition to their business interests, would be dealt with accordingly as bounty payment.

Mil's tension was climbing in congruence with their velocity. At any moment renewed salvos of disrupter fire would again bracket them. It held all the more terror, considering his planned crazy race on the deck through a lunar obstacle course that offered no visual relief to judge size and distance. If the slaver was anywhere near the ability he feared then the Moon was their best and only chance for a successful evasion. All he needed was a dozen seconds to make a break for star flight.

And those dozen seconds were an unobtainable treasure, under present circumstances.

…What about turning on them with the holdout ion pulse cannon while we have a small distance advantage? another typed message appeared on his monitor.

"Article seven, clause 'four' of the contract, Miriam," he reminded her. "But that does not mean I am not tempted. Had it been just you and I on a trade run, I would almost welcome the opportunity to butt heads, one-on-one."

It would be a true test of flying skills.

"True. But indulging in gunplay is a regrettable contradiction, if it means endangering those we are supposed to be saving."

Even as a last resort? Miriam tested him.

"I think you know my answer, Miriam. I will do what needs to be done."

Miriam let it go at that with a knowing nod. The contract was specific: *No lethal preemptive actions, offensive or defensive, unless all other measures have been employed to alleviate immediate loss of life.*

That was all there was to it. There was to be no pretext for retaliation of any sort that might lead to armed conflict, even war.

The latter part certainly fit, but Mil was far from exhausting his options, realized or otherwise. He just had a problem sometimes with creativity. Besides, personal integrity and his promise overrode any feelings he had to the contrary, regardless of how noble or righteous.

On the periphery of Mils mental preoccupation, he wondered how long it *had* been since he last engaged in some stunt flying. He knew it to be at least a few years. And that time, his last, had been his closest to a lapse in his law-abiding citizenship.

It was an approach to L-Brianna. A nosy security patroller decided he had nothing better to do than to run an import/export tariff record check on *Starlight Mistress*. Mil was running empty at the time as a cargo hauler before his contract work, and the pending cargo assignment that was to be shipped by him was nearly a break-even prospect. In reality, it was more of a favor to an acquaintance.

Upon finding himself the immediate object of interest and on a whim, he had pulled out and made a run for open space. The convenient story line to his customer was an abrupt call to an emergency shipment in another system. Of course, it was a farce and had cost him six month's trading privileges in that lucrative system.

It had not really affected...

WHUMP!

"Right on time!" Mil chortled into the air. Shaking off the last shred of his mental lapse, he poked a finger at the visual display. Miriam's expression was fixed askance. When she shifted to face him, "Did you get a fix on their weapons discharge?" he asked.

An energetic nod left no room for doubt. Another brace of detonations kicked at the ship in rapid succession. A storage compartment panel at the rear of the flight deck popped open spewing a shower of emergency survival items. Miriam typed in a one-handed response with a rapidity that matched a spoken comment.

Position is directly astern at slightly less than six thousand meters. Variation in point of fire between rounds would indicate a closing rate of about nine hundred meters per minute.

"Which is about what I expected," Mil muttered. Miriam sent him a puzzled look. "No, it was not important. Stick around, though. It shall be very busy shortly."

By now the moon's brilliant, mottled orb filled the entire view port, flooding the deck with ghostly white light. Smaller features, like mountains, craters, and writhing fractures, now started to resolve with the diminishing distance and each breath. It was so fast that it was dizzying in its incomprehension. Soon they would appear close enough to almost reach out and touch.

Nice thought, Mil wedged in a sentiment.

Mil steeled his nerve. Once their forward velocity was cut any laughable distance advantage would vanish in less than a wink. At that point a few hundred meters would matter very little.

What would be a phrase our guests would find appropriate? Ahh, they would be breathing down our necks.

It was a good bet the slaver pilot would anticipate Mil's move. The former, too, would have to reduce velocity in a real big hurry to prevent a grinding collision with Mil's exhaust ports or, at the least, avoid their searing breath.

On the other hand, another storm of well-placed disrupter fire would greet him at the pullout, relaying those slugs' unequivocal displeasure over this whole affair. And they were notoriously predictable in employing every trick of intercept known. That included ramming and clipping flight control surfaces and other external hull fixtures. There was nothing cordial or fair about this bunch.

Mil snatched a quick glance to the surface/object distance indicator on his main panel. Less than twelve hundred kilometers remained to the surface. The close-range instrument LED readout was little more than fuzzy blue blur.

More angry energy bursts shoved the ship first this way, then that. He corrected with the slightest play of the joystick, plus a little extra to evade.

Fortunately, from what Mil was privy to of slavers, their ships were designed more like customized freighters rather than fighters, cutters, and gunboats. Just like *Starlight Mistress.* They were similar to the *Mistress,* but it was safe to assume they were of necessity modified with heavier weaponry and holding cages. Had

Mil been facing an upgraded vessel built for pursuit and/or combat, on the other hand, all of them would be nothing more than vaporized metal and debris.

Ahead and hurtling at them at an obscene angle the Montes Alpenninus Range burgeoned insanely, ready to explode. Perspective made them little more than a jumble of dusty hillocks on a rippled, crater-pocked wall rather than a collection of soaring mountains the equal of what he knew existed on Earth.

At the last possible moment, Mil brought the throttle back, twisted, and pulled back the control some more. Circuits engaged. Vertical thrusters normally of use for landing/liftoff snapped to just several degrees shy of their angle of attack. With the loss of thrust and the addition of maneuvering thrusters slaved to the right-hand joystick forward momentum bled off.

Thus shoved, the ship angled away from its inward plunge. The distance indicator slowed its blur from the insane to the merely hyperactive. It now loitered around two hundred meters: *Mistress* was inserted nice and neat along the down slope of a hulking lunar mount. It had been that close, just as intended.

And Mil was that good. Fortune was indeed smiling on them, so far.

"About time," he said to himself.

The anticipated onslaught of renewed weapons fire once more harassed them, an intimidation meant to dissuade further evasion. He tried to ignore the distraction.

"They do not seem to like putting a little fun into flying," Mil quipped, more to relieve the tension. The rush of adrenaline both knotted his stomach and excited him. There was no denying some small part of him felt good to be back in his old element.

He leveled out on a stretch of flat surface but only briefly.

In a beat, he slewed the ship in a snaking course along desolate valleys and around squat mountains. Devoid of relief provided by trees and structures depth perception was an elusive luxury. This kind of knife-edged flying required the coolest of nerves and keenest of experience, to employ an appropriate Earth metaphor. To the neophyte it was lethal. An object appearing a couple kilometers away might be a dozen and one a dozen just a few. Such distances at the velocities they were rocketing along at mattered little.

The slaver's at five hundred fifty meters and holding steady, Miriam relayed across the screen.

More detonations swatted the ship, jarring open still more cabinets and storage nooks.

Mil had deliberately set his sights on this particular mountain group. The lunar Apennines happened to be familiar territory. More appropriately, it was the northern reaches. That was the site of the old Apollo Fifteen lunar exploration mission. This western side ran in almost a straight line to the northwest. It was along here that in a past flight he had searched for and examined the remains of that modest baby-step, space-faring effort.

Since slavers were not noted for general curiosity or intellect, he planned to put some of that topographical familiarity to good use. If still a little distance could be gained, he might be able to temporarily shake them and gain the breathing space needed to jump to star flight, his tail clear. But this was a tenacious bunch, not likely to be fooled by a fake turn or a double back.

In the stark distance ahead a symmetrical dome-shaped mountain loomed at the end of the valley they were negotiating. The easiest course would be to just fly over it; instead, a break to either the right or left meant a fifty-fifty chance of both ships splitting to either side. In that good bit of fortune contact would be lost, even for a fraction of a second. That small span of time could then mature into a loss of contact for good.

And he would take what he could get.

That is, if they are gambling on an over-the-top ploy, Mil hoped.

Mil pushed from his mind any deliberate decision as to right or left. He did not have the time for that, and he, in particular, did not want to risk advertising his intentions with some innocuous twitch or wobble. It needed to be that spontaneous. Miriam and the others like her were the closest the living came to mind reading, but personally, he did not believe in that talent. Still, there was no point in pushing his fortunes.

Slavers and their ilk had never been the sort of group he had a mind to associate with, and he would be the first to admit ignorance of their more mysterious traits. There were assuredly slaves or confederates among the crew behind them, those who were sensitive to the very immediate future that allowed them to do what he did by way of Miriam's ability.

On an impulse he broke right.

The maneuver put them in a tight sweep around the uprising's dusty, gently rolling flank. A fraction of a second later a disrupter blast hammered the space just vacated by them at the point of the turn. Reflexes kicked in, and Mil worked throttle and yoke to counter the blast wave's shove.

He juked in a roll the other way. Boulders and small craters careened in an indistinct, absurd blur just meters away to the left. The detour complete he leveled out just in time to crest a small rise.

Mil was treated to distressing flat terrain that stretched to the horizon.

He kicked the ship into a tortuous right turn then settled into a semblance of a normal flight attitude. But it was only long enough to re-orient after the first part of their wild ride. It was all he would risk.

For now, Mil intended on hugging the rises and falls of the scrolling foothills on this side of the range. Soon enough even these would bid good-bye, tempting him to double back for refuge. To the north was another island of rumpled topography: the Montes Alpes. They, too, were also reasonably familiar.

In a heartbeat, Mil decided on a flat-out run.

Those piloting the flying bug trap behind them knew their stuff. This crazy race was not going to play out indefinitely. He had no doubt as to his own abilities, but, sooner or later, one of them had to make a mistake. That would be the end. Mil just needed to make sure it was not him. A high-speed race with a spontaneous jink or quick flick of the controls thrown in held reasonable promise. He needed time to think of alternatives without having to worry about maneuvers, mountains, and crater walls.

They have decloaked and I have them visually, another message appeared on his monitor. *They are still tight on us, but the range is holding steady.*

"Understandable."

That little tidbit of news had only one meaning. He had thought of it himself, once clear of the mountains now receding behind. Now the sluggards were doing it themselves.

"They are trading visibility for extra power to thrusters and weapons…probably the latter. They will just dog us and bring us to heel at their own leisure. Let us not disappoint them."

His left thumb moved a couple centimeters and pushed on a recessed rocker switch inset on the side of the throttle grip. A gentle shudder rolled underfoot. A brief hazing of eyesight could have passed for a teary-eyed interlude between blinks. Reality firmed.

Mistress, too, was uncloaked.

Mil shifted in his seat, re-grasping both controls. The last vestiges of what had been a good-sized range of obstacles now diminished to nothing more than an indistinct unevenness far behind. Ahead lay only a flat, sprawling expanse of nothing. They were all but naked.

Too late to change minds now.

The finality of that fact did nothing to ease that nakedness and Mil's ultimate anxiety. Sweat trickled under his suit in spite of the air's ambient coolness.

The slaver has fallen back to five hundred meters, Mil read at the bottom of his monitor.

He raised a brow, first in perplexity, then in acceptance. Maybe this was that mistake. With that thought, he would count it a ray of good fortune. The explosions still punctuating space around them on occasion told otherwise. Either they were truly pulling away or, more likely, the slaver was hanging back on purpose, harassing them in the arrogant knowledge their quarry was all but in the bag. Haste made waste.

The latter was the most logical explanation and the one he would exploit. Having settled that in his mind, he felt a little more at ease and more prepared for any nasty surprises the folks behind might toss their way.

"I am of a mind they are playing with us," he relayed his appraisal to Miriam. "Stay on them, though. I would like you to slave your sensors over to my monitor and magnify. It would be nice to know who it is trying to vaporize us."

Miriam complied. She wasted no time expediting a rearview panorama of the diminishing Apennines that replaced her face. A pair of perpendicular red lines divided the screen into quadrants, while an in-falling targeting square shrunk and zeroed onto the point of intersection. That point disappeared inside the geometric shape that stopped to form a two-by-three centimeter box. Framed within was an object. Speed, altitude, distance, and target data decorated the view in the upper right corner.

It was the slaver.

The targeting circle then rebounded to fill half the monitor. The expansion pulled their nemesis into easy, naked eye discernment.

It had a distinct reptilian flavor to it, one he had seen some time ago but brought back to ready remembrance. He had never encountered one, personally. What he knew came from perusing data on a Majoran trade registry. Still, it was enough to chill his blood.

"I am afraid these are Chelonites," he spoke up.

Miriam blinked once, her eyes relaying comprehension. Any worry was buried beneath a veneer of cool professionalism.

These soulless vermin were spawned on a world not too dissimilar from Sordes, their hoped for destination. They were technologically advanced enough to learn spaceflight technique, yet that did little to improve their proclivity for being morally stunted as a civilization. What might pass for rudimentary virtues long ago born of more primitive human and Majoran clan cultures and since refined had been arrested at an early age with this group. The best guess Majoran sociologists could come up with was that the Chelonite culture was highly adaptable, a product of their harsh environment. Some past sustained contact with an alien culture or recovery of a derelict spacecraft or two was the most logical explanation for their now being on his tail…or anyone's tail, for that matter.

Being described as animalistic in nature was a fair description, both figuratively and literally. It was a reputation they were purported to be proud of. That fueled their macabre effort to custom modify or design their own starships to mimic their less than endearing qualities. Shady at best and terror-inspiring at the other extreme, they were the optimal choice for their Majoran overlords. Intimidation had its place.

It allowed for one bright spot, if it could be called that: he, Miriam, and their charges were more likely to survive an encounter by these highly profit-motivated lizards, since living cargo was worth a considerable sum more than a trashed one. Had they instead been confronting bounty hunters only proof of identification and destruction was all that was needed to collect. Capture was just an add-on and not necessarily lucrative. Had that been the case, they would have long ago met their demise when all this craziness began.

Either way, Mil had already made his choice if it came to hard choices. The Websters and the others would never know what hit them: a merciful high-speed collision would spare them a fate worse than the death each had earlier stared in the face. It would be that fast. Even Miriam had committed to never being taken alive.

A green haze enveloped the slave ship.

As he watched, the phenomenon migrated to and concentrated on either side of the snakehead-shaped forward section of the ship. Small flashes ensued.

In the next instant, he felt the detonations close overhead.

An immediate burst of starboard and keel thrusters nudged them left and up several meters. He figured the Chelonites expected him to duck out of the way and were already leading him. Instead, he put the *Starlight Mistress* back where the slavers had aimed.

The swamp crawlers were applying only partial strength to their weapons, instead of a higher dose garnered from shielding down. It was adequate to disable, not necessarily destroy. The popular theory was that a forced landing on the dust-covered surface would then lead to an underhanded exchange of cargo and crew. A final pass at full disrupters would then destroy most evidence of their transgression, should it go that far.

They were indeed so far fortunate.

The abrupt sound of a voice from directly behind caught him off guard.

"Are we really going as fast as I think we are?" a stupefied Dennis gawked, peering forward and out. Hands to either side purchased bracing wherever available.

Craters, boulders, and other surface irregularities appeared on the horizon for a moment as insignificant features, only to leap at them at an incomprehensible pace. They then melded into a homogenous gray/white blur upon streaking past.

"Ah, Mr. Webster!" Mil greeted in hurried acknowledgment. "It is certainly faster than you are presently thinking. You coming forward is most convenient." He paused long enough to juke to starboard, straighten briefly, then side slipped up and to port even farther. "I presume you have come to assist?"

"As per your request," Dennis deadpanned, "and to let you know everyone in back just happens to be thoroughly terrified. They all think we're gonna die."

"And what do you think, Mr. Webster?" Mil found time to ask. He took care to maintain an air of calm.

"Hard to say, present circumstances considered."

At the same time, Mil swung around the blasted wall of a kilometer-wide crater. It crested unevenly a hundred meters to port and maybe another ten above *Mistress*. The pristine flank that had never known the major forces of erosion beyond the more gentle combination of eternal and extreme temperature variations, micrometeoroids, the solar wind, and deep space radiation rolled out below them at a jumbled forty-five degree angle onto the nearly flat plain they were traversing.

From this perspective, boulders and slide paths gave indication the ancient meteorite strike was anything other than an impact point. It looked benign rather than a creation of violence, like any other lunar hillock. And minus the weathering of rain and wind it could have been a couple thousand years old or a couple million.

A disrupter round hit dust-covered rock some distance ahead. An insane geyser erupted a curtain of thick gray debris. The billowing cloud, some of it molten, fell heavily back to the airless surface. There were no wind currents to suspend aloft the smaller, nearly weightless dust particles.

Mil got only a glimpse, more by chance than by deliberate observation, of the blasted gouge. It was already refilling with stuff loosened up higher on the hill and sliding down.

He arched a brow. An idea was forming in the back of his head. Logging it for future reference, he got back to the business at hand. That future might very well be in mere minutes or seconds from now.

"What?" Dennis wanted to know.

"Maybe nothing, Mr. Webster. Then again, maybe it is everything. Just an observation and a thought."

That was all Dennis needed to know for now. Survival demanded flexibility, the glimmer of a plan requiring the right setup. Chances were excellent it would be stillborn, anyway.

"But in an expansion to my query…" Mil added.

The strain of bracing against Mil's seat was taking its toll on Dennis by the sound of his voice. "I guess I would have to agree with them about the death thing, Mil. As for myself…personally, this is pretty close to some stunt…"

He had to pause as Mil pitched the ship up, down, then back to level for a second. He topped it off with a half roll, first one way then a reverse the other. He repeated the pattern, changing the time spans in each to give the whole series an unpredictable, serpentine course. His seat swayed unnaturally from the extra mass clinging desperately to it.

"As I was saying, I had some stunt flying experience…under my belt some years ago."

Mil detected an odd enthusiasm flavoring his guest's tone between the stifled groans and grunts. It was no doubt a reliving of old memories from some past experience. There was no denying a certain energizing thrill to this. Too bad it was not for fun, rather than the principle ingredient to their survival.

"As for the others, Lindsey's thoroughly sick…again. It's definitely worse than before. Since she didn't eat earlier with the rest of us that was probably a good thing." Dennis paused, used an arm to clutch his stomach. "Started in again right after you entered that first series of turns."

"I suppose I will hear about this, too."

"My sentiment exactly," Dennis agreed, unsympathetic. "I feel for you but, fortunately, it won't be my problem."

"I doubt you will find denial much use when the storm breaks, Mr. Webster."

Dennis humphed. "You definitely have a quirky way of building up someone's confidence, you know, Mil."

Mountains and crater walls were predictable obstacles; Lindsey Maguire was also getting to be that way.

Abandoning the useless bantering, "In the meantime, may I ask that you replace Miriam at the sensor suite?" Mil requested. "I need her at engineering." Dennis opened his mouth to utter something, but before a word came forth Mil cut him off. "If I need something of you, I will explain the procedure as I am able."

Mil glanced up and back. He was in time to see Mr. Webster snatch a glance outside and shake his head in bewilderment, despite his pervasive skepticism.

That tended to happen a lot. Fact was, no human, other than Earth astronauts, had come anywhere close to this kind of velocity in a terrestrial setting, except in an old test program referred to as the X-15 project. Those who did were never privileged to share quite this perspective.

Mil scanned past the comm monitor while Mr. Webster shuffled back to his assigned area. The Chelonite slaver once again had that all-too-familiar aura about it as it powered up for yet another weapons discharge.

By chance, at just that moment, Mil had the ship in a level attitude. A twist of the controls and he had them slinking into another starboard quarter roll, just like a few seconds before.

The ship responded with instant obedience, which was none too shabby, considering her age in spite of its mass. A flash and corresponding concussion wave swatted them.

This time, however, it was different…too different.

CHAPTER SEVENTEEN

An ominous jolt emanated from somewhere behind, port side. A second collateral one hustled in behind it. Neither was on the flight deck.

Mil squirmed around for a quick glance and was just in time to see a fountain of fiery sparks gush out at Mr. Webster. More of the energetic particles cascaded from seams, vents, and any access in several overhead panels, a glittering argent pyrotechnic display. Spindly tendrils of turquoise static discharge followed, snaking, arcing, and probing along metal conduit and framing.

Dennis yelped in exasperation, recoiling back from the searing assault. Gouts of orange and teal flame feasted on the ambient oxygen, lashing at him like an angry beast from the instruments clustered before him. Serious though it was, Mil had his own critical problems confronting him.

"We have been hit!" Mil broadcast of the obvious. "We are losing atmospheric pressure port side!"

That was all he got out.

Thankfully, the breach was in an unoccupied space. The *Mistress's* damage control system would already be dealing with the damage, sealing the wound from the infinite blackness of space and the vacuum that would suck the life from ship and crew. Still, in spite of the built-in protections, he had to gulp hard against the slight pressure difference, even up here.

The keening whine of alarms and prompts added a deafening fury to the lingering shock of the detonations and violence in the ship's frame. In a hyperkinetic flurry of movement, Mr. Webster had rid himself of restraints he had only just tried to don and bodily flung himself to the animated deck. Hands and arms flailed at the flames consuming his jacket as he rolled about in the limited space.

Writhing deck notwithstanding, Miriam was up and over him. She braced herself against the side of the disintegrating sensor suit and began to douse him and the area with a handheld fire extinguisher.

Opaque, acrid smoke billowed through the flight deck. Miriam hacked and wheezed in the poisoned air but managed to get the upper hand on the flames. Soon the conflagration was extinguished. Satisfied after a couple moments a flare up was not in the offing, she let the empty canister clang to the metal deck.

Dennis was not slack to bound back up and shrug off the smoking apparel. Miriam offered a hand, but he waved it off. Instead, "Thanks Miriam," he gasped. He then plopped heavily back into his seat. He patted and massaged in a search for injuries and came up empty.

Miriam never heard it. She was back at her station, working frantically to bring some kind of order out of the tangled chaos of warning lights, alarms, and psychotic indicators.

Mil joined in on the chorus of spasmodic wheezing and coughing. To make matters worse, the suffocating miasma of smoke and extinguisher compound wafting in front of his face was hindering his flying. Anyplace else it would have been dangerous enough: at a hundred meters above an uneven lunar surface at the velocity with which they were rocketing was squarely in the realm of the mere suicidal.

He was tempted by a powerful urge to just pull up and away…and certainly right into the Chelonite's gun sights.

Mil really could have used a facemask right about now with its emergency supply of oxygen but decided to cope long enough until life support came to the rescue. Keeping his concentration cemented ahead, he tilted his chin, sucked in a chest full of marginally clear air, and guided his left hand from the throttle to a small auxiliary panel off to the side beyond it. Another coughing fit made him retract it.

He strained to beat it down to keep from flinching on the control grip. Just a small, sudden jerk would be his last mistake in this existence. He tried for the controls again when the coughing subsided enough. A couple finger strokes on switches brought the first hint of much needed relief.

A breath of cool, fresh air blew past his face. In a moment, the recirculation ventilator was well into dissipating the noxious cloud and the vexing respiratory distress. Soon, Miriam would have the environmental system stretched to the limit, purging the flight deck of smoke.

*

Indeed she was doing just that.

In the mess confronting her, Miriam brought up a diagnostic code and tried by sheer force of will to hurry it through its routine of diagnosing and cataloging *Mistress's* various and sundry injuries. When the prompt indicated ready, she made a quick scan of ship's functions, as systems and subsystem scrolled past.

Everything was more or less intact, though several of those systems were tagged with warning cues. Most significant, they were not indicative of an immediate disintegration in an all-consuming explosion or failed structural component. But that all depended on Mil avoiding any more hits. *Starlight Mistress* might be as solid as a planet but disrupters and solid matter made for poor companions.

The main corridor and transport chamber was reading *good* on atmosphere and pressure. Miriam restrained a cough and wiped at teary eyes. A hint of a smile turned up one corner of her petite mouth. It was the best possible news that the latter area's integrity remained intact.

Conversely, she had no desire to take a stroll back to see how things were going. It did not take an idiot to comprehend Lindsey Maguire's emotional state right about now.

I would be surprised if she wasn't *contemplating homicide…multiple ones,* she speculated in a passing sanguine mental image.

For some reason, the thought struck her momentarily funny, and she grew a wryer smile, current grave predicament notwithstanding. She gave it a final, silent chuckle, then got busy again.

"Mr. Webster, are you alright?" Mil got out between stifled coughs.

His immediate reply was a spasm of hacking. Then, "I have been worse," Dennis choked out. Another cough and a raspy inhale filled the pause. "A little singed…but that's the worst of it. I'm pretty much useless here, Mil, so I'm going back…to see to Abby and the others."

"My thought exactly. Please report over the comm link if you find anything more than bumps and bruises."

"Will do."

With that, Dennis pushed up and helped himself out on unsteady legs.

From what was becoming more and more apparent as Miriam studied, correlated, and double-checked data, was that they had sustained a hit on the port side, in the compartment across from the transport chamber and aft of their stateroom. The second explosion and ensuing ear-popping sensation was the subsequent hull breaching and violent hemorrhage of normal air pressure into the near perfect vacuum of space.

The hull was designed with self-sealing capabilities that mended minor leaks created by small debris impacts that managed to get through their navigational repulsor field. *As of now, I am still reading a failure on the life support panel to regain equilibrium in the damaged compartment,* she typed in a prompt to Mil. *Unless a mend occurs that means someone, either you or me, is going to have to suit up, break the compartment's pressure seal, and perform a manual inspection and repair, if possible.*

When Mil could spare the moment to read the message, "Understood Miriam. More information would be useful."

We have obvious damage to the sensors and probably the attendant subsystems and wiring.

"So noted."

The energy release generated from the hit had to play out somewhere. The sensor group was bad enough but better that than some of the other systems that came to mind, ones they could ill afford to do without.

Grim thoughts of that feedback storm victimizing propulsion, maneuvering, the computer, or the environmental systems spawned only terrifying outcomes. While they were flying they had a fighting chance of making it through this.

Thank the Creator of all things, she offered up in a quick, silent prayer.

The Chelonite's reduced power output on weapons did almost as Mil had predicted, disable not destroy. Next order of business was to put order to the myriad visual and complimentary audio prompts she could not hear. Then she would have her work cut out for her bringing some kind of life to the defunct sensor group.

*

Mil was just relieved *Starlight Mistress* had lost none of her power or agility. If he was not mistaken, the disrupter barrage had diminished to sporadic fire. Without the rear sensors, though, they were all but blind. The Chelonites had to be holding back, assessing their handiwork. In that case, the respite would not last long.

But long enough, Mil hoped. In about half a minute they would be careening into the Montes Alpes Range now spreading across the forward field of view.

One particular feature, a bisecting rift called the Valles Alpes, was where he intended on renewing some more fancy flying. It would have to be good. No doubt would remain in those Luvian slimeworms' minds that his ship was still functional and up to the task. More bothersome was that at some point they might just get tired of this game and decide a lesser death bounty was still a good deal.

A full disrupter round would definitely solve everyone's problems.

*

WHUMP!

The ship flinched around him, like it feared a renewed assault.

Mil mourned the loss of his sensors. Right about now, he would give his trade rights to the Markab fire gem mines on Theredor just to get another glimpse and fix on that flying sewage tank still latched onto their tail.

"If they are not wise to the true nature of our condition they soon will be," he mouthed to no one in particular. It was certainly not to Miriam. Even had she noticed, he knew she was way too busy to indulge in idle distracting chitchat. Too bad. She loved to "talk."

He had about three seconds to react as the entrance to the Valles Alpes screamed toward them. The mountains exploded in size, the gap betraying its presence like a missing tooth in a mouth full of dentition.

A fear began to nudge its way into his brain: were the Chelonites aware of his plan to cut and run the canyon? He strongly doubted it. At this point, it really did not matter.

Melding throttle, attitude, and braking with all the experience of the seasoned space jockey he was, he cranked into a snap with a complete roll. The slide into the lunar rift was perfect. Several detonations lashed their exhaust trail in punishment.

"So they know," he affirmed when he caught Miriam looking. "Thus go great plans. The way I figure it, this canyon is our last best hope to put some distance on that bucket behind us."

It had better materialize soon, she now mouthed.

"Painfully right, I am afraid." They were much too close to the gravity well of this body to attempt a safe jump to star flight. Also this evasive weaving back and forth was not going to last forever.

For once, a kernel of hopelessness began to germinate in his mind. It threatened to blossom into full-blown desperation with the realization that things could very soon go from bad to worse. Something needed to happen and happen fast!

But without the comforting watchful eye of the sensors covering their tail…

A wave of inspiration rolled over his budding hopelessness. That thought tucked away earlier came back into clear focus, evolving into a plan with hardly any conscious effort. It was both a realization and a plan, the obvious. Those Chelonites had been flying through a continuous mistake, and there was no reason to believe that had changed. He just had not realized it until now. It had cost them dearly.

Another blast rattled his *Mistress* as he knew what had to be done.

If only for the sensors…

Mil sank to the canyon floor as close as his instincts dared…then a notch more. With all his hope, he pictured the slavers laughing at what they would undoubtedly perceive as desperation, gloating at victory now within their spindly-fingered grasp.

He nudged down still more…

Without sensors he could not trust his altimeter to confirm their altitude. Currently it read twenty-five meters. He intimately knew the dimensions of his ship, knew her at the same level he knew Miriam. He just hoped there were no big boulders… He pushed more.

A sharp jolt slapped *Mistress's* underside. Another batch of alarms spouted off.

They had struck something…and still they were flying! Those in the transport chamber had better be belted in all snug.

Mil jammed the throttle forward just enough to brake, then back to full power. In that instant, the repulsors and everything else that drove *Mistress* obeyed him.

The insane violation of momentum overwhelmed the inertial dampers for a pair of moments. Instantly, invisible forces slammed him against his seat restraints, forcing belts to cut painfully across chest, shoulders, and abdomen. His breath gushed out as lungs constricted in on themselves. Ribs and muscles would pay dearly for it tomorrow.

Eyesight hazed, blurred. In spite of the debilitating forces warring against Mil's body, he managed to hold his precarious course. The Chelonites would be mere meters from *Mistress'* tail, breathing hot, ionized exhaust.

Deep in his gut the time was now! Commanding all his strength and will, he shoved the thrusters straight down.

Now Mil had the impression an invisible leviathan had dropped atop him, squashing him deep into his seat. Another kick walloped *Mistress's* underside. His eyesight continued to suffer from the violent stresses heaped upon him.

He eased off the upward thrust. Thankfully his vision started to untangle. It was hard to tell but he might have caught a glimpse of a flash on the shadowy aspect of one crest before it slipped past and below. He could not be sure. The gush of rock and dust thrown up by the thruster exhaust *had* to have worked.

If only for the sensors...

It *had* to be what he'd hoped for. Just to be safe, he re-grasped the controls for another round of insanity.

It never came.

It was a long moment before Mil dared level off. He did not bother wiping the sweat trickling down his face, off his brow. He glanced to the altimeter. In mere seconds, they had purchased seventy-three kilometers above the rumpled lunar landscape, again if the reading was correct. From this perspective it had ceased its nauseating, helter-skelter blur.

No better time to get us out of here.

Mil hauled back on the joystick. *Mistress* went vertical to the receding lunar surface and clawed for altitude in an accelerating climb.

The prudent thing would be to give the drive motivator, inertial dampers, fuel converters, and any and every one of a hundred related parts a good inspection to make sure their escape from this system did not go awry. The stars forbid they should lose that number three repulsor or slag a main drive unit right now. But since slavers were purported to have the irksome habit of working in nothing less than loosely coordinated pairs, but pairs, nonetheless, there was every likelihood another one was spooking around closer than he cared for, to make good on a failed claim.

Mil brought up the visual monitor and keyed the prompt to get Miriam. Almost unnoticed, Kikki crawled up his left leg, coiled on his lap. The little beast's tail looped around his belt restraint in apparent understanding of what they were about to do. A soft, feline-like purr emanated from its throat.

Miriam glanced to him, preoccupation exuding from her expression. Plugging in the requisite commands into the star-drive panel on the right side of the main panel cluster, "I am priming us to leave here, Miriam," he relayed. "Give me a reason not to."

She hurried through a propulsion check. In a moment, a shake of her head confirmed what he wanted to know.

"Thanks love. See you on the other side."

Miriam nodded, smiled. A twinkle in her eye conveyed no small relief at being away from this mess and doing what they were supposed to.

Mil sat back, drew in a breath, eased the throttle back. A release stud under his thumb allowed it to drop further, engaging the star drives.

There was a click felt in the shaft of it, then a slight hesitation. Around them the star-dusted backdrop of space exploded in a flash of dazzling blue light and elongated star lines.

Mil opened his eyes and breathed. They were on their way.

STARFLIGHT

CHAPTER EIGHTEEN

"Just what do you think you were trying to do back there, kill us?" Lindsey laid into Mil.

At the sight of him entering into the chamber a simmering Lindsey exploded, like smoldering embers finding renewed fuel and oxygen.

Abby braced herself for another round as the tempest burst forth in a flurry of rage-driven motion. Lindsey stormed about the dais and halted only when she was toe to toe with the Majoran.

Barely. Whatever size difference Mil enjoyed…most of a head… it was negated by the sheer energy of the other's fury. In spite of the melodrama playing out, it struck Abby as peculiar Lindsey's choice of pronouns, the expansive "us" instead of the more arrogant "I" that had come to so typify her.

Abby was regaining a healthy portion of her wits back, not to mention her stomach. Dennis was doing just fine, looking like all was well. Marc and Lydia, well, time would tell.

As the tête-à-tête played out between host and guest, Abby had to wonder if there was any challenge too great for Lindsey.

Such could accomplish either great good and mutual benefit or just the opposite, personal selfish ambition and self-aggrandizement at the expense of everyone around her. This was a soul who did big things, not necessarily great things.

Abby could only imagine what this obnoxious blonde had going for her, what she had accomplished. Personal experience in the hours they had so far had together did not instill much cause for hope.

The two opponents were engaged in a mutual stare down. It was Mil who finally blinked. He turned away to check on his other charges, rather than continue suffering the other's onslaught.

"Now you just wait a minute, flyboy!" Lindsey demanded. "I'm not finished with you yet."

Her hand shot out and grabbed a wad of sleeve. She reeled Mil in and twisted, to bring him back around.

Abby cringed. Mil appeared to offer no resistance, though in a test of physical strength Lindsey was way outclassed.

"I told you I wanted to go back, did I not?"

"As you are well aware of, Miss Maguire, I was quite prepared to do so," he explained. His tone was free of any defensiveness or hostility that might goad his nemesis even more.

"That's not good enough!" Lindsey planted both hands on her hips and leaned a menacing centimeter closer. "What's wrong with now? You wouldn't be here now if things were not under some kind of control."

Mil hesitated, eyes searching. Then they went to anywhere but on those belonging to his antagonist.

"Well?"

"Miss Maguire," he began anew, more careful, "it is not quite as easy as you may think."

Abby sank down into her seat, growing misgiving at what the answer would be and for the impending nuclear blast that would result. The proverbial fuse was lit and burning fast.

"I'm all ears. Tell me a good story."

Mil folded his arms, but it was anything but a provocative stance. He was putting emphasis to what would very soon be uttered.

"To begin with, Miss Maguire, you were correct: had we not been successful in evading our pursuit neither you nor I would be standing here discussing this."

Chalk one up for Majoran wisdom.

Abby forced back a smile at that much deserved parry, deciding that the better part of valor was to keep mouth closed and remain neutral. If they were ever to have any chance of cordiality on all sides there was nothing to be gained by insult, verbal or otherwise. Not that the chances of even a polite interaction rated long odds.

Lindsey nodded. "Okay?"

"Second, and what is the most practical reason, our current position is not where you think it is."

"Really? Lemme guess. You have us flying rings around...uh, what's it called, Antares, right?"

Lindsey now crossed her arms and began to stalk about in slow, deliberate circles in front of Mil. At least she was not venting scalding steam, at the moment. But then again, dormant volcanoes were not dead, just sleeping.

"Not exactly that far," Mil drew out slowly.

Lindsey stopped, giving all appearances of being toyed with. She spun around and speared him with a hot stare, one brow arched in irritated confusion.

Dennis turned part way around in his seat to Abby, one hand over his mouth. "That's putting it mildly," he whispered.

Abby gave him a curt nod but did not encourage him with a query or an inquiring sideways glance. She instead used the tense pause to firm up her wits for the impending shock. If she was going to believe in Mil, she was going to have to get used to an appetite of surprises.

"To put it in succinct terms, we are currently, oh, about two light-days from Earth and slowly accelerating."

Lindsey drew back and smirked

"Come again, alien, 'two light-days'?" She closed her eyes, shook her head in simmering annoyance then began massaging her forehead with the fingers of her right hand. "What's that supposed to mean?"

"It is as I have said," Mil affirmed. His candidness balanced Lindsey's skepticism. Though no genius, even Abby grasped that concept. "We are currently traveling several times faster than the speed of light, in a reference familiar to you."

"So what you are telling me…"

"Is that home, as you know it, is very far away."

"You know, I would have been better off dead back there," she blew off under her breath in an impulse.

"Believe it when I say there are many things worse than death, Miss Maguire."

"What could possibly be worse than this…this insane piracy?" She threw both hands up in the air and let them drop in a loud, dramatic slap to her side.

Abby was thankful Lindsey, the quintessential example of contentiousness, was at least not escalating. It was difficult to perpetuate an argument, or worse, when only one side indulged.

"Hardly piracy."

"This is living proof here, billions of kilometers from where I call home," she grated. Now a deceptively delicate finger speared toward the deck. "There must be *some* chance of going back?"

Mil closed his eyes in apparent regret and shook his head. "Slavers, Miss Maguire," he explained carefully, "the same sort we just successfully, and barely, eluded."

For once, Lindsey looked to have spent much of her energy. An eerie quiet settled in for several seconds. Even hurricanes had to blow out sometime.

"I've gotta sit down," she muttered, wringing a hand in front of her. She shuffled to her seat and plopped down. When she looked up weariness and confusion had gained equal footing with the anger staining her expression.

"Let me share with you a grave concern, Miss Maguire…"

"Oh please, Mil, stop calling me that. It sounds so patronizing. I do have a first name, you know."

As if she knew an iota about dignity…or cared, Abby told herself.

"Of course…uh, well, let me just say that slavers are not generally known to work alone," he explained. "I think you would understand the term 'lone wolf'?"

"That is really quaint, Mil. Keep it up."

Mil nodded, now walked over to and behind the transport console. Leaning casually forward on it, "There is every likelihood another was lurking close by where the first one latched onto us, just in case their compatriots missed bagging us."

"Oh swell! You make it sound like a grab bag proposition."

"Please forgive me, but I do not quite understand that phrase."

"Oh forget it. I take it you dumped your friends that caused us all the grief?" she interrogated.

"Correct. But suffice it to say the other one probably knows more about us now than I would dare to estimate and is ready to make their own bid on us. Since we destroyed the one chasing us, I would suspect that other one is also entertaining some rather strong thoughts on dealing with us in ways that do not include capture."

Abby found herself shaking her head in disbelief. Mil had already explained slavers, but to put it in such blunt terms with such stark conviction...

"Which leads me to another very important point."

"And that is?"

"We are also damaged. It is serious and perhaps beyond our ability to repair adequately, without the services of a facility capable of major repairs or refit. Our external sensor array is down, and I cannot predict when it can be brought back on line. Or if.

"That leaves us almost blind to the universe around us, except what we can see directly before us. Essentially, we have to rely solely on our computer for navigation among the known interstellar bodies, phenomenon, and hazards. And I emphasize, 'known'. We also currently lack our cloaking ability, which makes a return back to your planet a venture in complete folly."

"How about some good news," a disgruntled Lindsey countered.

"We have also suffered a hull rupture in the compartment across from this one. *And* I should also add we have sustained at least one stationary surface collision. Until Miriam and I have had a chance to inspect both it is theoretically possible enough structural integrity was compromised that a high-velocity trans-atmospheric entry could elicit a major structural failure."

"I said some *good* news, not our obituaries."

Mil paused from his detailed assessment. Though it was directed toward Lindsey it was for the benefit of all present. "We are still alive," he said, contemplative.

Lindsey rolled her eyes in exasperation.

Abby felt queasy. At least the subject of plane collisions now gave her a new appreciation for Mil's predicament. Twice in as many days most of them had survived as many disasters. How often did that happen to anyone, and how long would it continue? Three times was a charm.

"I do not think you would relish the prospect of your being scattered across a large segment of your nation," he tagged on with thoughtful consideration, ignoring her unspoken complaint. "Atmospheric breakups are nasty affairs."

Abby shifted her gaze to Lindsey, making every effort to appear not to be staring. Mil's appraisal had gone far to douse her rage back to smoldering embers. If expressions were any indicator, however, then Lindsey's relayed an obstinate belief that all she had been told remained a huge fairy tale. It was solidified when an oily, calculating grin spread across her mouth. Maybe verbal and physical tirades were no longer on the menu, at least for the time being. But that did not necessarily bode any good. She would merely exhibit her insistence in more subtle, devious ways.

"Okay, *Milankaar*," she conceded. She put particular snide emphasis on the name. "I will do it your way, for now. But I want to make this *very* clear." She paused to convey a spiteful gaze around the chamber to each and every one present. "You know exactly where I stand. Clear?"

"Very clear," was Mil's terse reply.

"So, Mil, exactly what happened to whoever it was that was giving us fits?" Marcus asked in a change of topic. The tenor of their interactions changed noticeably.

Abby settled in to listen to the running account, relieved with the godsend. While it was interesting, she was more grateful for the diversion from the knife-edged tension Lindsey so competently brought into any gathering. At least, for once, the other appeared to be accepting her situation for the way it was.

For how long was anyone's guess.

*

Seeing that none of his charges were the worse for wear, Mil made his way toward and out the transport chamber exit.

Abby pushed up from her seat…and collapsed back from the effort. She tried again, found her legs, and wasted no time in a test of balance. Since returning from the flight deck Dennis had all but ignored her. Her queries had been met with either impatient head gestures or the fewest words possible.

Well, if he saw her as little more than a pest right now she was not going to be where she was not wanted. Few things hurt or repulsed so much as a cold shoulder. Against her better judgment of wanting to patiently reason with him, and running afoul of his moodiness, she would leave him alone. At least Mil would accord her the courtesy of some straight answers, even friendliness.

In her rush, she met the exit portal, just as it started to solidify back into place. The mechanisms sensed her presence and in obedience did a double take.

"Mrs. Webster." Mil stopped and gave her a friendly smile. "How may I help you?"

The door closed. For the time being, they had the corridor to themselves. Only the life-pulse of the ship droned around them.

She ran a hand through tousled hair that was in desperate need of some attention.

Folding her arms across her chest, "Please forgive me for being curious, Mil," Abby responded. "Dennis hasn't been the greatest source of information lately, if you know what I mean."

"I understand well enough. And?"

"Well, is there really any chance for Lindsey to be returned?" she probed.

Abby was quite aware of Mil's earlier explanation and just wanted to make sure. It was a temptation to harbor thoughts of indifference at best and a desire at worst to be rid of this nuisance, once and for all. It warred with her nobler sensibilities. She willed her decision for good: Lindsey was a fellow victim in all of this, and she, Abby, would from now on never advocate "getting rid" of her, however much she might be tempted.

For several seconds, Mil stared into her gaze and returned the passive gesture. Something else was brewing there. Was it concern?

Whatever it was, Abby did not fear it. In their short acquaintance, she just knew he would do nothing cruel to her or any of them, physically or mentally.

"Please, let us take this to more private surroundings." He ushered her to his and Miriam's stateroom.

About the size of a modest bedroom, it was furnished with a relatively standard bed, a bare table, two gray, thinly padded movable chairs, wall shelving, and a workstation. Another door, closed, probably led to the Majoran equivalent of a bathroom. Mil directed Abby to one of the seats, then slipped over to the head end of the bunk and leaned back against the bulkhead. Abby nodded her comfort.

Continuing the conversation, "I would hope you would allow me to be so bold as to first inquire something of you?" Mil started off.

Something was indeed up. Abby held the breath she had already drawn in but forced casualness of expression. If Mil went to all that effort to be candid with her, then she at least owed it to him to match it. He deserved that much.

"Feel free, Mil." She relayed an easy, friendly smile. She rested her right arm on the table surface and idly began tracing invisible circles with her forefinger on the cool, smooth surface.

"Of course, Mrs.....uh, Abby." His gaze meandered about in a display of awkwardness over the question he felt he needed to ask. When he focused back on her, "I would just like to ask if your difficulties with Dennis are more complicated...uh, than what might be expected by our current circumstances?"

So it really showed that much?

Abby thought she had braced herself for any and everything she had given permission to, that no secret existed that could interest him. This query, though, caught her off guard. The heat of a blush of embarrassment rose in her cheeks. Interpersonal problems wore like an ill cobbled together wardrobe.

"I hope it hasn't caused any problems for the others, Mil," she chose to instead answer. "I mean, with Marc and Lydia and you and Miriam…"

Mil waved her concern off. "None that I am aware of. Everything is still so new to them that they are too preoccupied to really notice. But, otherwise, one would have to be blind to not see that your relationship is particularly strained, at the present time."

"Hmm…" Without realizing it, a tear coursed its way from the corner of her eye down the side of her nose. She dabbed at it with the back of her hand. In respectful silence, Mil gave her the time she needed to gather herself.

"Mrs. Webster, please forgive me if I have in any way embarrassed you by my impulsiveness…"

Now it was Abby's turn to be gracious. "No, Mil, it's okay." She worked through a sniffle. "I love Dennis dearly, would do anything for him."

She came up short for several seconds when the significant reason for their incongruity surfaced to confront her. It was more of an admission of something she had been aware of for some months, rather than an earth-shaking epiphany. It now stood on the verge of gushing out.

"It's just that…his business," and she shook her head in mild distaste, "seems to have robbed us of some of the affections we used to have for each other. Maybe I'm just being a pessimist, but sometimes I think we've had to sacrifice time and energy between us just to keep his career on the fast track."

"In other words, his priorities shifted?" he clarified.

"Shifted? It's like they have always been slightly askew." Abby had to laugh. It was a little spasmodic titter that broke the drama of the moment. For that little bit of her own impulsiveness she was thankful. "I do believe you missed your calling as a psychologist."

"Believe me when I say it comes from plenty of experience." Mil directed a glance around the chamber, his tone giving plenty of emphasis to the obvious many he'd had to deal with over the months and untold trillions of kilometers. Then he turned sober once more. "Still, Abby, I hope once more I did not shame you by prying into your personal affairs with my brazen curiosity."

Abby closed her eyes, shook her head. "No. No you have not, not in the least bit." She brought her other arm up to lay her left hand atop her right, wedding ring set showing. For a long moment, she stared at it and wondered. Then softly, thoughtfully, "In actuality, I think it helps to discuss such things with caring individuals, other than those you are close to, to confront our fears, to air the laundry, as they say."

"Ahh. You enlighten me with a new metaphor." Mil chuckled. "I take it that it means to bring things out in the open that might be less than pleasant?"

"You are a scholar and a fast learner," Abby smiled. There was a thoughtful pause. "But only among those we trust, Mil. Sometimes we risk much in sharing our deepest feelings, hurts, and wants with those in whom we place our confidence. Fortunately, it looks like I am in just such a position with you."

Here she was, going all introspective. But it did feel good to unload a burden much needing unloading.

"I am in much agreement, Abby."

"It is all the more remarkable after less than what, two days? But most of all, Mil, I appreciate it. I really do. None of the others I know well enough yet to take the risk."

"Funny thing trust. Comes with familiarity, getting to know those who are close to us and then measuring how much to confide in each. With some it is much; others it is just a little."

Out of the mouths of aliens...

"I am finding Majoran wisdom to be quite commendable. It sounds like we connect on a similar, complimentary level. My compliments."

Others might have exuded an air of self-importance after such a gushing ego stroking. If anything, Mil glowed with a gentle appreciation to be held in such esteem by another and being able to share some of his insights. If anything, he was maybe a shade awkward.

Now it was Abby's turn to demure when Mil delayed a response.

"Oh, Mil, I hope I haven't embarrassed you," she said. She could have kicked herself. "Give me half a chance to run off with the mouth…"

"Please, no apology, Abby." There was still an uncertainty to the inflection on her name, but at least he was making the effort at the easy familiarity acquaintanceship wanted. "Let me just say, I would like to reciprocate the high regard you hold for me and, I hope, for Miriam."

"Of course, Mil.

Mil nodded once.

"I just don't know about Dennis," she shifted back on track. Perplexity played on her words. She allowed herself to slump a little in her seat, the stress of her and Dennis's conflict weighing like a ton on her shoulders. "He just goes from day to day, thinking the good ol' world will keep spinning away and everything else around it, that excluding him, all will be as it has always been."

"At the risk of being presumptuous, you mean self-centered?"

Abby had to reluctantly nod at that appraisal. She didn't want to say that, really did not even think it, but there it was, up close and personal, brutal and correct. "As I said," she shook her head, but taming it down, "that goes for everything and everybody but himself. But what can I say about his profession, his rising star?"

"Which comes back to your relationship. Maybe Dennis is not even aware that he has put his career ahead of the two of you."

Abby stiffened inside. Again, it was something felt but not quite cognizant of, not until it was a plain truth confronting her. Though an innocent assessment, it hit the bull's-eye dead on. "Perhaps. Dennis just doesn't take it seriously like I believe he should. In some ways, it's like the two of us have landed on a plateau...maybe even become stagnant."

The self-admitted truth brought another tear to her eyes, and it was all she could do to keep from wiping at it. Trust or not, she did not want to appear to be a weak-kneed crybaby.

Well...maybe just one wipe would do.

Was it possible that their relationship, among the most important in the universe, was in danger of being left behind on the traveled road of life? God forbid. Now having confronted that, she found a strange resolve from deep inside to do whatever it took to mend her bridges with Denny, to make their gears connect to produce that which was useful, enduring between them. To that she committed herself.

Mil nodded comprehension.

"Sort of tests those eternal vows that some so easily throw around like cheap jewelry."

"Please, enlighten me."

Abby sank a little deeper, now acutely aware she had placed their conversation on a much deeper level, aware of a growing sense of insecurity. But what was done was done.

"Oh, to love, cherish and honor," she explained in a dreamy tone. "Vows each of us makes when we commit to each other." She was rattling off the facets of their love for each other, ones she had pondered on occasion. Such was the deep, unfathomable mystery any relationship did and should instill, the *for better or for worse, riches and want, health and sickness, till death do us part* thing. How could love be measured or explained, especially to one from an alien culture? "At least for me they are among the most solemn that can be made."

Mil comprehended and now was captivated. A soul of contemplation, he came across as one never to weary of learning some new fact. "Some might see them as idealistic," he offered. He then slid down to sitting on his bunk.

"Some things in this universe have to be idealistic, Mil. There is enough change the way it is. I just believe there need to be some constants that do not change, things that we can cling to and draw strength from."

"You have no argument with me on that that, Abby. Such were some of the foundational stones our initial colonizing effort was built on and continues to this time. For you and yours it too has provided you with a firm foundation, given you direction and strength in the path you must travel in your destiny."

"Yeah, but it seems sort of hollow at times, doesn't it?" She humphed, letting a thread of despondency drift in.

"Quite to the contrary. Among my people such sacrificial commitments are also held in the highest regard. It can only come about that when, as in Dennis and your case, each works together can the whole then stand a chance succeeding. But yes there are, unfortunately, some in my acquaintance who know a lesser level of integrity. How do you say it, they pay lip service?"

"Hypocrites."

"I had not thought of it that way. Perhaps...yes."

"I would not go quite that far," Abby backed off. She was now acutely aware she might have passed judgment on the most important person in her life.

"Oh?" a puzzled Mil turned up a brow.

"Dennis does care, really," she explained. She pushed up from slouching but still tried to remain on a casual level. "I think sometimes, though, the commitments we make get lost in the occasional upheavals life at times tosses our way. Maybe it's just the plain old routine of going from day to day that makes things...sort of rusty."

"That would be true and most unfortunate," Mil frowned.

The misgiving he attached to his statement sounded almost like an indictment against her and Dennis, though she knew it was not particularly meant that way. For some reason, it just touched a nerve.

Now for a much needed change of topic. This line was pretty much all played out, like an orange squeezed for its last drop of juice.

"Mil, a short while ago you said we were some two light-days from Earth…"

"Which has changed considerably since we began our conversation," he interjected. He changed conversation tracks with the ease of a change of clothes.

Abby came up short and went wide-eyed in bewilderment. "You're kidding! It's only been several minutes."

"You need to change your frame of reference, Mrs. Web…Abby," advised Mil. He adjusted to leaning over to rest both elbows on their respective knees. "Movement among the stars, for all practical purposes, will be an alien concept for you and your companions. Such travel requires velocities, distances, and compressed spans of time that will take some getting used to. But I suspect you will have little trouble making such an adjustment."

Mil smiled that patient, amiable smile of his. It was one she guessed never wearied at what had to sound like the naïve queries of a six year old…and not just from her but from all Earthlings he came into contact with.

Briefly her stomach quivered. She raised her right arm and rested her head on her hand. "I don't know, Mil…"

"Once we have made adequate repairs," he changed topics again, "I would like to have the pleasure of giving you and your companions a more thorough inspection of *Starlight Mistress*. It is equipped with four navigational astrodomes, which I think you will find will give you a somewhat new perspective on the universe. And I have no doubt you will find it of considerable interest to see what you sun looks like from this distance."

Abby glanced to the solid bulkhead and the unseen door of the transport chamber across the corridor, imagining Dennis inside, doing his thing. It hurt a deep abiding ache of the heart that she wondered would ever go away. She could not remember a time when she had felt so cold and confused in her soul. With their personal universe all but collapsed around them, it would have been nice to have shared Mil's generous offer, arm in arm with her husband.

"Thanks Mil," she replied. "I think I would enjoy that very much."

"Good. Then that is settled."

A prompt sounded, indicating someone desired entry. Mil stood and in a moment activated the entry command. When the portal opened there stood Dennis, bigger than life. Even though he had to have expected her to be here, he still shot her a puzzled glance. He then gave her a look that was unreadable.

Mil cut off any interaction. He paid a polite acknowledgement to Dennis with a tip of his head.

"Mr. Webster, I took the liberty of inviting you, your wife, and the others to engage me later in an inspection of my ship."

Dennis did not verbalize a reply but put on a look of roused interest.

"As for you, Mr. Webster," Mil went on, "might I ask for your assistance in making needed repairs?"

"To be honest, that's what I came here for. As an engineer that would be right up my line."

"My thoughts exactly."

Dennis shifted a glance back to Abby, who nodded her silent approval. At least it would give him something constructive to do and take his mind off his lingering grievances.

In a moment, they left her in the main corridor, excusing themselves to their appointed mission and engaged in their own conversation. Just for a few seconds, she envied the easy camaraderie the two men had slipped into. How much she wished she could say the same for her and Dennis, the way it used to be when they were first married. There was no reason it could not be that way again.

Or, could it?

CHAPTER NINETEEN

The environmental suit was a bit bulky, like some childish Halloween costume Dennis had garbed himself in years ago. With the ship's enhanced gravity field it was also clumsy and heavy. Not that he had any prior experience with space suits. Still, Mil made it look like it was an everyday occurrence of dressing in work clothes for another day on the job.

They were not unlike NASA units he had both read about and seen in pictures, though they lacked the familiar boxy life-support packs. But that familiarity went no further. There were attachments in the storage locker that contained maneuvering thrusters for external work outside *Starlight's* secure environs. Then there were implements and equipment modules stowed in the space, the use of which Dennis could only speculate at. Such appeared to be the progress of Majoran miniaturization technology.

Dennis stood passive in the glum, sterile surroundings of the propulsion bay and engineering, fully suited with Mil's help. Now he watched through his open faceplate as the Majoran sealed his own helmet over the collar lock ring. He gave it a twist, locking it into place, as he had helped Dennis do with his own.

"I think we are all set, Mr. Webster," relayed Mil.

"As if I would know. Pardon the pun, but this is all so alien to me."

Mil appeared to have missed the humor in it, replying with a straight-faced, "Of course." Then, "Please press the green button on the top of your left wrist."

Dennis brought both wrists up and glanced from one to the other. A strip panel, each with five separate colored buttons, adorned the top of each cuff. He guided a gloved finger toward the one indicated.

"That is your comm link between us," Mil said. "I will explain the others as we proceed and have need. That way you will not have to struggle remembering details. When you are ready, you may pull your face visor down into place. It will automatically lock into place, seal, and initiate suit pressurization."

"Understood chief." Both hands reached up and fumbled with the tinted but transparent bubble-shaped helmet face shield.

True as said, when the faceplate slipped down into place a whiff of air brushed past his face. A musty redolence soon faded, no doubt from infrequent use. Something else came with the helmet closure, something unexpected: a claustrophobic sense of containment. Actually, it was more like entrapment, entombment.

Dennis's closest and most drastic experience with this same emotion was that powerful mixture of terror and ecstasy that had threatened to overwhelm him during his first solo flight. This time, however, his trepidation settled to nothing as his senses came to accept the confines of the Majoran suit and that his feet were not leaving the solid deck underfoot.

Must be a slightly elevated oxygen level, Dennis surmised. It dawned on him how loud his breathing sounded.

Mil reached into the storage compartment where two more identical suits hung, like props in a studio room. From what Mil had explained, each chamber and the flight deck were equipped with similar storage points and more suits for ready accessibility, in the event of compartmental depressurization. Of a more realistic nature, they were meant for movement through an airless main corridor or one of the chambers. They were of a certainty also meant for extra-vehicular use. Only in the transport chamber was there an abundance of suits for all on board, plus a few extras.

There was one sobering prospect, however: those souls in an occupied compartment would be long unconscious or dead before they'd had a chance to suit up. Dennis's own inexperience confirmed that sad fact.

Mil withdrew a black briefcase-like container from a recess and closed the access panel. Turning to Dennis, "Mr. Webster, can you hear me?"

Dennis nodded.

"With the button and verbally, please, Mr. Webster."

"That's a loud and clear, Mil."

"Thank you. Let us get to work then."

Mil strode past. The motion of walking was almost comical, about midway between a normal gait and a slow, stiff shuffle.

"Hey look at me, the Mummy," Dennis joked. He exaggerated his stiff-legged gait as he put motion to his own feet.

"The suit will feel awkward at first, Mr. Webster. The gravity generators will still be functional in that chamber."

"You mean I won't just float away?" Dennis had to ask.

Mil twisted around enough to send Dennis an amused look. "I believe I have already replied to that," he said. Now normal, "I would urge you to take it slow, at first."

"I gathered that, Mil. I can see how it could be a problem in a trip and fall."

"True in that regard. But there are plenty of solid handholds round about to either steady one's self or to get back up, except in the main corridor. Therefore, while a real threat it is not much of one. It would depend on how clumsy the one is."

"Hey, I grew out of that stage a long time ago, Mil." Dennis could feel himself go just a little red-faced.

"No such insinuation was intended."

"And you are not an accomplished liar."

Mil nodded and let it go at that. "We will enter the compartment from the main corridor, which will necessarily be purged of atmosphere first. The other areas will be temporarily rendered inaccessible and sealed until the corridor pressurized again."

He followed Mil out of the propulsion bay.

In the main corridor, the access door materialized behind them as usual. According to Mil, once the propulsion bay or main corridor reached space-normal vacuum the barrier was solid like any other bulkhead on the ship and just as impenetrable.

The whole concept was unreal. Dennis tagged along on Mil's heels. Shortly this innocent more and more familiar environment was going to be no more hospitable than the flooded corridor of a passenger liner resting on the ocean floor a couple thousand meters down, or perhaps the surface of one of the Saturnian moons. No doubt Mil had visited them all on some weird vacation getaway trip. The fact that such a forbidding environment would be scant centimeters from his face made it just a little thought provoking.

Mil reached a square panel access on the corridor's port side beyond the damaged compartment's access. He set the case down at his feet. Dennis watched while he poked at a stud and lifted the intervening plate out of the way. A maze of instrumentation presented itself.

Work had only just started when a dull honking ruckus penetrated Dennis's helmet. A pair of brilliant flashing strobes, one at each end of the corridor, pulsed their urgent, synchronous rhythm. There was a shudder, not much, but with his out of kilter center of gravity brought on by the suit Mil's advice rebounded back to mind. A vertical conduit of unknown purpose came in handy.

"Just think, Mr. Webster," Mil spoke up, still working the gadgetry, "you are now basically an astronaut…and without the months and years of preparation your people put into the process. More significantly, you are *beating* them to the stars."

"Gee, I never thought of it that way," Dennis said.

"Quite normal," Mil replied.

"You know, I always had a fantasy of wanting to be an astronaut, the adventure and prestige, but the competition was, and is, always very stiff. I guess I shied away, not that I really had a chance. The intellectual reservoirs I would have been up against made me feel, well, a little inadequate."

Just then he realized he had let a pall of dejection tint his words. The mere mention of the subject transported him back across time and space to resurrect a long dead and buried dream. Now it withered and died all over again. Truth be known, becoming a pilot was his one way of being "up there" and away from terra firma, compensation for part of the dream.

"I had to lower my sights to something less glamorous and more mundane," he went on to explain. Still a ray of brightness pushed through. "But I guess dreams can still come true, even in a weird sort of way, thanks to you."

"Perhaps your ambition should have been of the caliber of Miss Maguire?"

Dennis snorted. "You mean, like her?"

"Only in determination, not character," Mil amended.

"Good. For a minute there, I thought you were insulting me."

"Never my intent."

"Thanks. Just know I consider her and I as different as night and day, as hurricane and gentle breeze."

"Really, Mr. Webster?"

There was something peculiar about his comment Dennis could not quite figure out. He hesitated a moment but decided to ignore it. "Well, there's something twisted about that one, something that makes me want to avoid her like a boil."

"I understand your point, Mr. Webster. Hers is a *very* strong personality, backed up with what are, shall I say, some unique character traits?"

"Yeah, the personality of a tiger with the ethics of a serpent. A real snake in the grass, that one is."

"Serpent?" Mil asked. Puzzlement came through loud and clear.

"It's a long story, Mil. Maybe later."

Mil let out a quick chuckle and backed away from the panel. "I will hold you to that, Mr. Webster." A pause, then, "There, we have zero pressure and override access to that compartment." He turned to face Dennis and smiled a sentimental sort of one. "Your fantasies on career options are not that unusual. On Majora, I think you will find you would be in good company."

240

Mil retrieved his case and shuffled toward the chamber.

Dennis figured trying to be relaxed was the best way not look so inexperienced and perhaps a little "cool". He was getting better at it, but he wondered what zero gravity would be like, the ultimate space experience. It could have been the sensation of weight that caused that earlier feeling of entrapment, restraint. The usual sensations of normalcy…gravity, a normal corridor…would likely conflict with his senses. Floating around in the dark depths of interstellar space would, on the other hand, give his brain a very different perspective.

The entry to the port side compartment remained closed before them. With his left hand, Mil tapped three buttons on his right wrist. The barrier went translucent, vanished.

What greeted Dennis was an almost black void. Like a sepulcher of the dead it was spooky enough to cause a good case of the willies. An emergency alert was the only illumination, flashing its dim warning in its struggle to not be overwhelmed by the gloom. Mil had said this was a storage area, for the most part and, more important, where the lifeboat compliment was located. That meant there was no reason to keep it lit when it was not inhabited. And just to be safe, power was cut off anyway, save that to keep the lifeboats functioning on standby mode.

The Majoran took three tentative steps inside, stopped. Dennis followed suit. In moments, his eyesight adjusted downward to the lower light level.

From spare initial appearances, Dennis guessed the compartment was roughly the same dimensions and size of the now familiar transport chamber. Already he was looking about for the cause of the depressurization but, understandably, it eluded him. Even with the pulsation of background illumination there was none of the violence he had envisioned, either from an explosion and subsequent fire or the sudden violent expulsion of atmosphere. That was best explained by the numerous containers and canisters secured in place with tie down straps and brackets and no debris underfoot. At least any that had not been deep-sixed through the breech.

Mil tapped another button, this time on the left wrist. A pair of bright beams of light from helmet-mounted lamps exploded forth with focused rays onto the opposite wall. Splattered light reflected round about. He continued to hold down the button. While Dennis watched, the width of each light source widened to less intrusive area illumination lamps. He explained the procedure to Dennis, who in turn brought his own lamps up and running.

"Well, that is something to be thankful for," Mil uttered to no one in particular. He moved his upper body in a panning motion, searching.

"I take it you mean the amount of damage?" Dennis presumed.

"Indeed. I had expected more devastation." Now Mil was on the move, stalking about, searching. "What it does mean is that most of it must be external. Without a remote visual feed it is difficult to tell. Therefore," and he bent as far as the suit would allow him to search a dark cranny under an auxiliary power relay node, "we do a visual search."

"You mean a spacewalk?"

"A contradiction in terms, Mr. Webster, but essentially correct, should it be needed."

"Thanks for the reproof." Just as usual, Mil either missed his sarcasm or ignored it. This was someone who would be no fun in a duel for the title of most obnoxiously witty in a group.

"Just trying to help, Mr. Webster."

In the lead, Mil came erect and began to work his way around the compartment, first along the sloped outer bulkhead. A pair of large, dull, brass-colored domes occupied the center of the space. In the garish lighting, each of the matching structures was chest high, flat on top, and graced with what looked like a fairly standard access hatch.

They briefly caught Dennis's attention. A couple of steps closer and he could make out some printed stenciling. One thing was obvious: like all the other written script on this ship it was alien and pretty much a safe bet Majoran, whatever that looked like.

"Were these storage bins at one time?" Dennis inquired. He knew *Starlight Mistress* had once been a freighter in a former incarnation. He stroked the closest one with his right hand.

"No. Those have always been the emergency lifeboats and their housings," Mil replied. "We are equipped with two of them. Each is equipped and provisioned for six passengers apiece." He paused to push into, then extract himself from, a recess between two containers, moved left to the next space. As he continued his inspection up and down, in and around, "They are fully rated for re-entry, which makes them most useful near a planetary system or in orbit.

"Unfortunately, their minimal thrusting capability makes them less suitable for a deep space stranding, unless ejected near a shipping lane or a deep space port facility to have any chance of a timely recovery. But being equipped with comm and beacon equipment we would not be completely helpless in the event of such a remote stranding."

"You don't know how much that thrills me, the prospect of being marooned billions of kilometers from anywhere," Dennis mumbled.

"Light years," Mil corrected.

"Excuse me my shortsightedness. Light years."

Mil pulled and grunted at something Dennis could not, for the moment, see. Still struggling with the recalcitrant object, "Believe it when I say, Mr. Webster…there are some planetary systems of my acquaintance that would make an interstellar stranding look like a vacation."

"Yeah, deep space, a great place to get away from it all," Dennis smirked. "I would beg to differ with you, though."

"For instance…wait one minute."

Dennis fell silent as Mil squirmed some more into the tight space he was examining, attention redirected. "You found it, Mil?" he said, moving closer.

After a moment longer Mil retreated. "Correct. See for yourself." He backed up some more out of the way.

Dennis moved in. The second part of a two-person huddle, he followed his host's outstretched arm and pointed finger.

There, lit by his own helmet lamps but partially hidden by a hull frame and a tubing bundle, was the source of their anxiety. It appeared to be an oblong, football-sized hole. Wisps and arcs of crimson energy continued to spark and coil along the fringe of the injury, like a bizarre, hungry aurora gnawing on the ship.

At one extreme, Dennis had expected something more jagged; at the other there might be a clean-cut violation. Instead, what he saw looked more like it had melted though. No, that was not quite right, either. There was no puddle of slag or congealed metal that would be expected with a melt in a gravity field, no discoloration or deformation. Then again, the decompression could have sucked it all out. There was just the hole.

"Typical disrupter damage," Mil explained, "and probably at or near full power."

"That being the case, I would think there would've been much more destruction…like total."

Mil crossed his arms. Even in the suit it did not look clumsy. "Which ordinarily would be the case. However, there is, or was, an external sensor probe assembly right about at that point that is usually extended during space flight. I am thinking it intercepted a near miss, relaying an energy surge along part of the grid passing through there. The result is that it burned out nearly the entire sensor system. A portion of that energy load transferred to the hull, with the result of what you now see."

Dennis was agape at the frank explanation. "That must be some weapon, Mil, like a movie version of a death ray."

The comparison of weapons produced a dry chuckle from Mil. "Let me assure you it is *most* effective," he said, now sober. "Had it hit us directly and with more power, neither of us would be discussing this now.

"The energy package creates a traveling wave of complete molecular disruption through most kinds of solid, crystalline matrices. It does not really cause matter to explode so much as to simply fall apart and evaporate as atoms and molecules lose their cohesiveness with each other. Fuel cells and containment devices, particularly those under pressure or stress, would provide impetus for an explosion and/or fire.

"A direct hit would have disrupted half this wall, along with structural supports and at least one primary control channel." He then sent a look of grave concern to Dennis, an expression that found its compliment in his voice. "Quite simply, Mr. Webster, we came very close to becoming another crater back there."

That was enough to chill Dennis's blood. With his lingering attitude, though, this whole affair still had a flavor of the preposterous running through it. Never mind that conflagration in his lap forward on the flight deck. He did not know how but it was still possible this was all a charade, props and all.

Dennis got his mouth working. "So, how do you go about fixing this?"

"In most cases I would not," Mil responded.

"Come again? You would just leave it like this?"

"If you were to understand Majoran design techniques, Mr. Webster."

Mil kneeled, laid his case flat, and opened it to reveal just what Dennis suspected, a tool case. Mil withdrew a tubular device, most like a socket wrench extender. At the end a small ruby red light winked on. He then moved back into the recess and began probing about the void's periphery.

"Normally, even a breach this large should reseal on its own," he began to explain.

Dennis arched a brow and only just stifled a chuckle. What he found surprising was that his visual field was unhindered by his helmet faceplate, being nearly as wide as without it. "That's a trick some of our people are only beginning to envision, Mil. It's the nanotechnology concept, if you know what I'm talking about."

"A concept I am familiar with, Mr. Webster. I believe we have used micro-machines for many years for numerous reasons. Not being an engineer, such as yourself, however, leaves me at a loss to discuss this on any kind of an intelligent level."

"Well, Mil, rest easy. That makes two of us. I have only read about it in tech articles and science fiction books."

There was a pause before the Majoran picked up anew, tracking back onto the original topic. "The hull is designed to conduct a small electrical charge employing a woven network of microscopic conduit. When that network is disturbed by a breach or some other physical disruption a high-density corridium plastiseal compound imbedded in the hull alloy is activated. It melts out, oozes into the disruption, and hardens. The process continues until the system senses closure and neutralizes the process.

"As you may have perhaps gathered by now, it is modeled on a humanoid body's physiology and the ability it has to mend itself following external injury. Unfortunately, I had forgotten disrupter weaponry neutralizes this particular type of damage control…which has now brought it back to full recall."

Mil paused as they both stared transfixed at the gaping wound. Dennis bent closer, hoping to spy any indication of this hull regeneration he had become privy to. It looked like it wanted to, but to his disappointment he saw no evidence of regeneration, no closure.

"Our next option," Mil went on, "will be a magnetic pressure seal."

"You mean a patch?" Dennis wanted clarification. He moved in still closer for a better look. Through the unnatural void distant lines of starlight drifted past, like some kind of odd film reel. It was truly an ethereal sight.

"An exact description. Once we accomplish our task we will be able to use this compartment again. However," and the gravity Mil attached to his last word made Dennis stiffen, "I am afraid we have a new problem."

"As if we don't have enough already to deal with."

"Until I have had a chance to assess exterior damage, we might find ourselves unable to pass into trans-atmospheric flight. That will depend on if the repairs we can make will suffice and what kind are needed. More importantly, if it comes to that, we may need the services of an orbital docking facility. Another consideration, and one just as grave, is that cloaking is presently impossible."

"So what else is new?" Dennis deadpanned.

In a flash of acute regret, Dennis now wished more than ever he had heeded Abby's trepidation when they'd departed the restaurant for their fateful flight. That accounted for another reason he was off center with her. He did not like being shown up and proven wrong, not so much by others but, well, by her.

A wave of anger began to boil up, hustling the first emotion out of the way. The plane idea might have been his idea, but it was Abby who had insisted on such a late hour for din din. None of this probably would have happened had their reservations had been, maybe, half an hour earlier.

Now it had all gone insane, and he could only wonder how much more so it would.

Indeed how much worse?

CHAPTER TWENTY

Abby drew back from her perusal of the patch job. She was never one to hide her feelings to any extent around Dennis, and now was no exception with her uncertainty.

"I don't know, Denny," she said slowly, adding a small headshake. "Do you think it will hold?"

All casual and with arms crossed and leaning against the forward lifeboat housing, Dennis watched her investigation. "That's what I asked Mil," he answered. Pride in his having been instrumental in fixing the damage carried through on his tone. "He let me do any and everything I could to dislodge it, short of messing with the controls. I pushed, twisted, even used another magnet to disrupt it. I tried to pry it off but could not so much as get a tool tip between it and the wall."

In a final gesture of curiosity, Abby kicked the toe of her boot at the three-quarter meter diameter disk. She paused before turning, still studying the object, arms wrapped around her mid-section, countenance sunken in mourning. She shuffled toward him.

"Gee, Abby, who died?" he teased.

Abby raised her face, eyes filled with the turmoil of emotions grappling with emotions. The repair was fine, would probably last indefinitely. No, her earlier talk with Mil had once more stirred up her simmering hurt, and it was high time to clear the air and settle matters. If she did not the disgruntlement between them would only fester and do them both in. She didn't know about Dennis, but she was miserable to the bone.

"Denny, we are alone now and need to talk."

Dennis frowned. "Oh no, this looks like a serious discussion. What's the matter now?"

His cavalier attitude only served to heighten Abby's frustration. She hated it when he was like this, when he used this tactic to brush off a concern she might have that he did not want to deal with.

"Dennis please. This isn't just about you or me. It's about us. Ever since all this began, even before, I have tried to…"

"You're still miffed at me, aren't you?" he cut her off. A silly smirk was pretty much an open taunt and still conveyed a lack of sobriety the situation demanded.

For a moment, her hazel eyes were a projection of the accumulated hurt and present incredulity heaped upon her. It was bad enough the preponderance of it had to be by way of Lindsey Maguire. Worst of all, and of all people, Dennis had to be unloading his own share, that one person she was supposed to be closest to. Together they should have been sharing and dealing with all that had been foisted upon them.

So far, she thought she had managed well enough….or the most part. But now, here, it was all she could do to keep from losing it and bawling her eyes out, with all the complimentary visual and audio affects. And she might have, had it not been for the fear of how he might respond in his present mood.

More insult upon insult upon injury.

"If you want to think of it that way," she drew out. "But, Denny, I don't want to be, not here, not now."

Abby knew she sounded a bit more firm than intended, but it was more an effort to maintain self-control than a confrontational stance. Hopefully, he did not take it as a verbal slap…not that a good physical one to instill some sense of normalcy had not crossed her mind.

The ensuing silence was uncomfortable in its intrusiveness. Once again, the distant drone of the ship's pulse kept it from being unbearable. The mutual test of wills she was engaged in through their locked stares held until Dennis yielded. He glanced away then back, expelled a sigh of flustered resignation.

"Okay, Abby." Then he added an audible huff. "Let's hear it. What's on your mind?"

Abby forced steadiness. She blinked a couple of times and tried to ease off the harshness. "Denny, all I am asking is that you give me…this whole situation we are in…a chance. I don't pretend to know everything that is going on around us, but I had hoped you would have accepted my being able to take all this for what it is. After all, I am entitled to an opinion, just like everyone else."

"Ahh, so we are back to what started this little tiff between us," he sniffed.

That was not quite the way she remembered it, at least from her angle. It did not matter. A self-righteous attitude was no more likely to see the other side of any difference than a sinner could comprehend a saint. Her spirit sagged.

"Can we put this behind us?" she urged instead. "This is something both of us are in together, and I don't see that as changing anytime soon, no matter what you, or I, or anyone else may think."

A stiff pause filled the air.

"I just want your understanding. Is it so hard for you to come to grips with this mess?" Abby invested an expansive look around, trying to take in the sum of their universe.

"I would be stupid to not at least take things at face value," he relented just a little. "Maybe this *is* some kind of weird practical joke, a big celestial one."

"And folks back home are probably penning our obituaries now," she tossed out innocent enough.

Abby had not meant it, but that *did* get a reaction she had not intended. Dennis shot bolt upright and laid into her with a fierce glare that could have ignited a bonfire.

She cringed.

"What I find so hard to deal with is how easily you fell for Mil's explanation." He stabbed a finger in her direction like a flaming spear. "It's like you were seduced and all too ready to go along with destroying everything we…I…had built up."

"As I said, this is not just about you, Denny, and no, I was not seduced. It was my decision and my opinion."

"Personally, Abby, the jury's still out on his convincing me Mil is unable to take us back. A person…excuse me, I mean an alien…who can do the things he does, with a vehicle like this, should be capable of doing a great many things.

"Then there's his sincerity. I still can't get it out of the back of my mind that this is still some grand hoax. I personally never did like practical jokes."

"You know, you're beginning to sound just a little bit like Lindsey," Abby bit out on an impulse, "except that she still has the forthrightness to deny all this. That makes it difficult for me to understand why you have been so agreeable toward Mil lately. If that isn't…"

"It isn't necessary that I have to defend myself, Abby. And you have the self-righteous audacity to claim I am hypocritical?"

"I never said that, Dennis."

"Of course you didn't. I don't know which is worse, being hypocritical or gullible."

Now the wood was on the fire.

She really had no stomach for this kind of jousting, which was in serious danger of escalating into something very ugly. Atypical, her hurt had allowed her mouth to get way ahead of her brain this time, tearing down the restraining inhibition bolstered by her reserved nature. Already she was feeling the first bitter twinges of deep regret.

But now she was committed. A point needed to be made. To back down now would only serve to make the situation between them even more intolerable. If now she could only keep from venting raw emotion from the anguish that was knotting her soul…

She shrugged.

"Then you *must* think me a hypocrite?" Dennis challenged. It was obvious he was stung by her refusal to clarify. His temper rose on a par with the flush tinting his cheeks.

"I refuse to go there, Dennis."

Abby held up a firm front, but behind it alarm bells were going off in her head in a deafening cacophony. Inside she was already cowering.

Dennis's chest swelled and his glare blazed with kindled contempt. Like a coiled spring released, he was in motion…just as Abby's reflexes screamed retreat.

In a sweeping arc, he flung his left arm out with the impatience of brushing aside a curtain of annoying cobwebs. And connected.

"Get out of my way!" he snarled. In the next motion, he stomped off for the exit.

Abby yelped.

Not meant as an intended blow the impulsive gesture had the same effect. Landing on her left shoulder, the force of it sent her reeling sideways off balance.

Abby shot both hands out for something...anything...with which to stay her fall. Instead, her effort produced only empty air. She collapsed to the cool metal deck as Dennis disappeared out of the chamber.

Never, *never* before had he laid a hand on her!

Even before righting herself on hands and knees, anguished sobs wracked her body. Through tear-blurred eyes and tangled strands of dark brown hair, she could see the exit portal had re-solidified. She shifted around to sitting.

She wiped a sleeve across her eyes, against the hot tears cascading forth as she wailed into the sepulcher silence of the chamber. Drawing her knees up, she buried her face atop them in the same arm.

A horrible realization cascaded over her. Something had snapped between them. For once, she was all alone in the universe, a universe cold, dark, impersonal. And all too lonely.

After long moments, Abby sat back against a cold, gray container. Dejected, she had to will effort into her hand to push the hair out of her face and then smear the moist droplets at her chin along her jaw. Her mind stunned to numbness, the only identifiable feelings amid the tangled wreckage were that of crushing loneliness and the unbearable hurt. It choked her breath and mind.

No, not quite. Both were all wrapped up in an acute sense of overwhelming hopelessness. Never had a night looked so dark or a day so bleak.

For once, she wondered if death in their plane might not have been the more preferable fate than this mess.

*

Dennis was miserable. And that was putting it mildly.

Upon storming out of the storage/lifeboat compartment he had stalked forward to the flight deck and plopped down into the seat at the burned out sensor station. Charred electronics and whatever material that had housed it still gave the air a sickening sweet bite, but he was much too caught up in his turmoil to care or even notice.

It was a good thing no one had seen him. He had purposely steered clear of the transport area and his other marooned companions, since he was not up for explanations of his foul mood, much less concocting a story, to cover it. Such a venture was about as welcome as a gas pain. Where could one go on such a cramped tramp steamer to be alone and brood in silence?

He pretended to study the defunct instrumentation and idly let his hands play around the dead board. It was more for something to do than anything else. He just needed to take his mind off the remnants of the adrenalin-fueled, anxious jitters still working over his body from his nasty spat with Abigail.

But dog gone it, she had it coming, he fumed in a flush of self-justified heat.

His right hand balled into a fist. It came up and in the same instant slammed down on the console housing. How he longed to escape to somewhere remote! Just to be alone and distant, to kick something, to sort out this whole tangled mess…from Abby, from Mil, from this blasted ship!

Frack! Blast it all!

With his left elbow planted on the edge, Dennis rested his forehead on his hand and began to massage it with his fingers. Lost in the quagmire of emotions, he at first failed to notice Mil and Miriam's presence on the bridge. Only when they were right behind and Mil said something to her did he snap to. Once again he tried to look occupied.

"I think you will find that station is all but useless at the present time, Mr. Webster," Mil pointed out, all helpful.

Surely this was not his attempt at humor, because if it was, it was the lamest effort in recent memory.

"Uh…yeah, Mil, right," Dennis muttered. He now felt just a little idiotic. "I was just messing around."

"I see, just messing around. Unfortunately, it is pretty well 'fried', as you might say. It will be some time before we can bring it back on line or else replace it all together."

That much was obvious. Not wanting to come across more ignorant than he already must have appeared, nor desiring an entanglement in a protracted discussion on Majoran electronic wizardry, he mumbled a lackluster, "I think I already had that figured out for myself."

"For your information, my inspection of external damage was as I feared."

Here it comes.

"Sounds swell, Mil," Dennis responded, absent-minded. He glanced up and back to see a puzzled expression coming down from his nosy host. Miriam's gaze, as usual, was fixed on Mil's lips in anticipation of continued speech.

Mil instead shook his head, appearing to throw off the absurdity of his statement.

"What it means is an extra wrinkle in our plans," the Majoran instead elaborated. "We will still make Sordes, but there was a coolant leak, which I managed to fix for now. Should the temporary seal rupture, we will be forced to remain in orbit and await help from the surface. Fortunately, I have contacts that make a side living off the occasional repair job that comes their way. More than a few owe me at least one favor."

"I'm glad to hear that," Dennis said in a tepid tone. "Did you happen to find anything else out there?"

Instead of an immediate answer there was a heavy pause, until, "Is there something wrong, Mr. Webster?" came the drawn out query.

In his own stewing anger, the two faces staring down upon him were unwanted intrusions, rather than caring souls showing concern. Some part of him knew that.

"Yes…no. I mean…" The words knotted in his mouth until they came out in a perturbed gush. "With everything that has happened who wouldn't be upset?" Dennis had every expectation that Mil would have shrunk back, even a little, from his brief tirade. Instead, the Majoran maintained the same maddening, implacable, and unmoving presence that had come to typify him. That in itself was unnerving and an unexpected reaction, or lack thereof.

Doesn't anything rattle this guy?

"Very well, Mr. Webster," Mil relented. "Should you require anything…"

"I will certainly let you know. Thank you."

Mil looked to Miriam, who exchanged shrugs and confusion. They then split up, her to the engineering suite and Mil to take

257

over for the autopilot, which had overseen the flight during his external inspection. Miriam had backed him up inside.

Dennis toyed several seconds longer. There was one indisputable fact he could not ignore with being all keyed up: it was near impossible to set his mind to a productive train of thought or activity for much more than a few seconds. If he did it just derailed. Then he wearied of the facade, got up, and moped off the flight deck.

He paused at the transport chamber. It sensed his presence and opened in silent mindless obedience. Inside, everyone was bunked down. From all appearances all were asleep among their individual niches. That was no big surprise. None of them, himself included, had managed any real sleep over the last couple days.

Come to think of it, he could feel the lack of it in each and every one of his weary bones and muscles. His mind was another story. With its hyperactive flip-flopping of tangled emotions there was no way he was going to doze off, not without the help of a pill or whatever it was Majorans injected, tossed down their throats, or sniffed to deal with insomnia. Maybe they just stuffed it in their ears. Never mind he suffered exhaustion in every fiber of his being.

His gaze fell upon Abby. She was curled up in the original niche she had first found herself in, in her new life that she had so easily fallen into. Her back was toward the chamber and him. He imagined her no less afflicted by insomnia than he was and faking slumber.

He was tempted to enter and steal quietly into his own space. An impulse even to crawl in next to her stroked his mind for a second, like the faintest of cooling breezes on a hot day. She looked so alone, so pitiful.

The bitter sting of her incrimination and what he took to be her insinuation came back with a hot vengeance. A fresh flash of contempt bore into him. The way he felt now, he had no desire to see her, much less be around her.

Stepping back, the access sensor field lost its contact with him and disengaged power circuits that kept the door open. Once more he was alone. Maybe there was solace in the emptiness of the lifeboat compartment with Mil and Miriam forward. For how long he could enjoy some privacy before an unwanted intrusion occurred was an unknown variable, but he would take what he could get.

For once, his feelings began the slow drift to things other than his anger. It was surprising Abby did not cross his mind to any degree. Maybe that was good. That and the awareness he was cooling off to something less caustic. There was even room for another more pleasant emotion or two.

Like curiosity.

No one could say he did not like to explore. That was certainly the boy in him, bolstered by an engineer's inquisitiveness. Knowledge sated curiosity…but just as certain it created additional hunger for still more. It was one of the eternal quests of mankind, to seek, to know.

With that in mind, and the undiminished hope of somehow returning back to Earth and all he knew, Dennis promised himself to gain maximum insight and savvy into this ship and anything else of use. The world might mock and scorn a story of alien skullduggery into the realm of the grandiose and delusional, but there was no reason why he could not benefit in a number of ways from the technology he had within reach of his fingers. He just needed to employ the appropriate subtlety. This was all pretty good stuff, even if it turned out to be trickery.

Just the thought of accruing a monetary windfall from some of this, in spite of the mess his life was in, did send a shudder of giddiness flashing through his mind. Certainly in this entire universe most civilizations had some kind of means of buying and selling, of dealing with financial transactions. Though it might look different, money had to be money.

He only wondered what form it took.

*

Abby could only run.

How long she had been doing so she had no idea. All she knew was that *it* was chasing her again, that she was ready to drop from exhaustion as her lungs threatened to explode with many more breaths. Yet against her will her legs continued to drive her along, controlled and driven by a force she felt outside of herself.

Once again, she glimpsed the odd, hazed over sky overhead, a star-filled, day-lit canopy. There, too, was the washed out sun and its attendant host eyeing her every move in detached, cold silence. Just as with her legs and the lack of volition there so, too, her mind dwelled hard on the meaning of the conundrum, surprisingly free of oxygen-starved exhaustion that came with exertion.

She hazarded a glance back over her left shoulder. That she could control. *It* was there, evil and malevolent, somewhere in the swirling mists that gathered behind her in her passing: the heavy, plodding footfall, the deep growls and snorts. She should have seen it; it was that close, breathing down her neck. Yet only that maddening mist gave witness to the beast ready to fall upon her from behind.

And that was the ultimate terror: the unknown, the undecipherable, the stifling malevolence, that which crowded in on her but refused to reveal itself.

Was this a nightmare? Or was it some sort of insane vision, present or future?

There was no time to decipher that mystery. For now all Abby could do was run…

*

Inside the repaired chamber, Dennis stopped at the first bell-shaped lifeboat housing. For a brief moment, he could almost feel an afterglow of negative energy still permeating the sterile air from his earlier conflict. This time it was easier to brush off this dark creation of his imagination.

He hefted himself halfway up for a better look at the construct's top. A recessed hatch crowned it, with attendant maintenance panels, conduit, and visual displays surrounding it.

I must be missing something, he just knew. *There has to be an easier access than this.*

He slid back down. A meter around to his right, he found a vague seam line that could have been a panel joint, except that it ran vertical from the deck to the first angle leading to the top. Ten centimeters to the left at the top was a nondescript square button.

Might as well go for broke.

He pressed it, stepped back, and awaited the chain of events perhaps very soon to come to play out.

A strip panel separated itself, inched forward, then pivoted out of the way. Now clear was a set of dark foot rungs of an access ladder.

"Now that's more like it," he chimed in relief into the cool air. He rubbed his hands together in success.

Like an open gate to a walled city, the way up beckoned to him. Dennis shuttled part way up, then laid his upper body across the flattened, cone-shaped upper housing. In front of his face was the hatch and to the right within easy reach a T-bar handle latched into place amid a cluster of switches and readouts.

That had to be what he was looking for. He grasped it, hesitated, then pulled it up and back. It resisted him, like it was holding back on a secret.

There was a spate of mechanical taps and clicks. A sigh emanated from the hatch. Within a pair of seconds, it raised enough to clear the housing and began sliding back out of the way on parallel tracks.

"Now we're cooking with gas!" he congratulated himself. "Definitely batting a thousand today." Dennis inched closer to the open maw and with due care peered over the edge.

It was about four meters to the bottom and from initial appearances looked about like he had imagined it. The space was as Spartan as most of the rest of *Starlight Mistress* had proven to be. For a lifeboat, however, that was understandable. Little room could be spared, beyond that which was absolutely necessary. That meant its compliment of souls and their requisite survival supplies.

True to Mil's explanation, it appeared to be capable of conveying six people in a cramped ring to safety. If any were much bigger than Dennis's own five-foot, ten-inch frame and medium build it would be a tad more intimate than he cared for. The presence of Mil and Marcus would pretty much tilt the scale to that of crowded.

Lindsey's presence…well, he would just as soon not deal with that potential debacle.

Overhead, above the seats, ran a ring of compartments, undoubtedly survival supply storage. There were two gaps in the ring, one for the descent ladder that ran down right below his eyes.

Occupying the other gap, folded up against the circular wall, was an odd contraption that had to be a control unit, since there was no other means of piloting the boat that was apparent. Mil or Miriam would in all likelihood sit there, if things ever got that desperate. There was also no reason to doubt an identical setup graced the other lifeboat. It was also a sure bet there was more storage under the seats since space would be at a premium. His gaze traveled to the deck and a circular ring inscribed on it. A handle and locking mechanism belied another hatch. He could only guess its purpose.

Dennis hefted himself up and through the hatch. He climbed down into the emergency craft's confines and in a moment was on the deck. A number of lights here and there blinked on peaceful, idle standby. Several strategically spaced glow panels yielded sufficient illumination.

As he panned about examining various details, he could only wonder how long it would take being sealed up here, with others and minimal room to stretch, before someone went stark-raving insane. How would Mil and Miriam handle a psycho case all cooped up and crowded? And the prospect of drifting off into the endless cosmos with what had to be limited propulsion and life support…well, it made for a cold shudder in the pit of his stomach.

Best to just pop the hatch and get it over with. Out of the frying pan into the fire…or the deep freeze.

It was a dismal prospect that he just knew was not that far removed from a nightmare. He maneuvered into the nearest seat. In an odd way, it was comforting to be secreted away down here, detached from the rest of the ship proper. The solitude was near complete and the best that could be hoped for.

For now, he just let his feelings run unrestrained. And, for once, he just relaxed.

CHAPTER TWENTY-ONE

"I thought I might find you here, Mr. Webster."

Dennis winced at the unexpected presence. Lost in thought, he had failed to notice the Majoran's unflinching upbeat presence filling the hatchway above. He wondered for a moment as Mil clambered down if even the solitude of a morgue was immune from his cavalier intrusions.

Two intrusions in less than an hour Dennis groaned. *Mil must have a secret desire to inflict torture on his extractions.*

Dennis looked up and forced a polite smile, wishing not to have to bear up with any kind of a dialogue with an unwanted guest. Even less desirable was the interrogation he just knew was coming. It was sort of like mom's well-meant inquisitiveness when he'd had an off day at school and really wanted nothing more than to be left alone. Any put off was an exercise in awkwardness and amounted, usually, to a litany of barely believable white lies that life was just dandy and school peachy keen.

"I'm sorry," Dennis alibied. "I must have lost track of time. The peace and quiet here is most enjoyable."

Come on, Mil, take the hint.

Mil gave him an understanding nod. "May I join you?"

Tell me he didn't notice!

Dennis compelled himself again to politeness, in spite of an audible groan, and managed a gesture just short of curt to a seat opposite him.

"Thank you." Down and seated, "You know, Mr. Webster, you would not be the first we have extracted that found one of the lifeboats, or a few other locations aboard the *Mistress*, a haven to think and meditate. To get away from it all, I believe is a phrase your people sometimes use."

"Really?" Dennis played up in thinly feigned interest.

"Really…which is the reason I sought you out."

"Uh-huh."

Mil rested both hands on his knees, now good and settled in. As feared, peace and solitude were just stowed away.

"I know you said there was nothing wrong back on the flight deck; however, I also suspect there is some kind of friction between you and your wife."

A sudden burst of irritation jabbed at Dennis that must have reddened his complexion by at least three shades. The only indication Mil might have noticed was his inquisitive expression.

Was nothing sacred anymore?

"She told you?" he queried, all suspicious. Chagrin began to leak through.

Mil let silence be his answer for a couple moments. He then leaned forward and clasped his hands, interlacing the fingers. "Miriam did."

Dennis now blanched, not quite convinced. Abby could talk up a storm when she had a mind to. But rather than drag this down to an odious, drawn out level, "You're kidding?"

"Her foresight ability also gives her a sense into the strong emotional bursts of those around her. And with your race's greater propensity for emotional energy amid such extremes it is fairly easy for her."

"You mean she can read thoughts?"

Mil snorted. "By no means, Mr. Webster. She can only 'feel' them. I suppose the closest comparison would be like the feel of a breath of wind. You can interpret the direction and whether it is warm or cool and, with some practice, its strength. She can distinguish, to an extent, and even interpret some."

Dennis regarded the Majoran now with slightly warmer interest. There was something obscene about being able to invade another's thought processes, but now that the substance of the tiff between he and Abby remained safe out of reach he relaxed some. From that perspective, perhaps it was safe to venture a little conversation into a topic that would take the focus off his self.

"I guess that sort of flexibility makes Miriam even more useful, doesn't it?"

"As I have said, none of this would be possible without her." Mil rolled his eyes and head in an upward arc to give emphasis to the ship and, by implication, its mission.

"So, for all practical purposes, she was responsible for your coming to our assistance." That much he had known, but the depth of reality Mil's emphasis put on it gave it a new, more sober meaning. "Sort of the key, in other words."

"Otherwise, you and Mrs. Webster would be at the bottom of your Puget Sound. All of your hopes, your dreams, ambitions, triumphs, and sorrows, everything that is created and treasured in life, would be buried with you. It would be a needless and utterly tragic demise. Most tragic."

That, too, struck a chord, a glum one. "Which is about what it is now, Mil," Dennis summed up. "We pretty much have lost everything. Everything."

Mil's eyes narrowed in a look of wise disagreement. "Mr. Webster, you operate from a wrong premise, you do. Life is much too precious a gift to be squandered or measured by what or how much a person has possession of or accomplishes, on a personal level. Truly it is no small tragedy to suffer loss. To lose life and all its opportunity, though, especially needlessly when the chance for survival exists, that is the greatest loss and so permanent.

"If you were to look at it on that basis, you will find you really have not lost everything. Setback certainly. Loss? Hardly. Temporary? Yes."

"For an alien, you have an eloquent way of stating things, Mil."

There followed a studious pause. Mil appeared to be gauging the effect of his well-placed hit of wisdom. With a degree of trepidation, Dennis now wondered if it would be his dumb luck if Mil did not launch headlong into a psychoanalytic head probe of his problems with Abby. Instead, came a variation of it a more subtle, backdoor approach.

"You must understand the relationship you enjoy between yourself and Mrs. Webster is a priceless treasure, a much desired commodity," Mil said.

"No kidding, Mil."

"I think you will find it a most valuable resource in surviving the uncertain future all of you face, which is also true for Miriam and I. It will be that critical. And I am also of the opinion that that truth would hold whether the two of you had suffered your aircraft collision or not, instead going on to lead a long, healthy life together back home. It will take the two of you to prosper, especially with your present circumstances."

"Well now, aren't you the philosopher! Words of wisdom are always easy to come by from the other side of the fence. You really ought to live life on the other side."

Mil smiled all confident. He appeared to have a ready answer for everything, which was about the most galling trait he could at the moment think of. At any other time, and maybe in someone else, it might have been a respectable character quality. Now, here, it was an annoyance, no arguing or contradiction, no defensiveness, just an impenetrable shield of reasoning and patience.

"Observation, Mr…"

"Puleeze, Mil. It's Dennis. Just D-E-N-N-I-S…Dennis, okay?"

Mil straightened as a timid grin turned up one side of his mouth. "I think you will find I am not as naïve as you might believe, Dennis. As I was saying, observation, plus personal experience, goes a long way. Also, you will find our cultures share a number of similarities."

Dennis rolled his eyes, wondering how much longer he had to suffer with this torture veiled as a well-intended lecture.

"Among them is the value of enduring relationships," Mil charged on. "Your people have a saying about it, especially in dealing with inherent difficulties that living out a life brings. I seem to remember it as the concept that 'two are better than one'? And just as obvious the more harmonious the relationship the better."

Now sermons! That was all he needed to hear.

"That comes from what we call the Bible, Mil," Dennis highlighted. He shook his head and let impatience bleed onto his tone. "It is a text many on Earth hold as the Word of God, divinely inspired scripture given to those of us who are believers in a faith called Christianity."

"Indeed!" Mil nodded in growing fascination. "I have copies of many of your race's writings, books, letters, and so forth, stored in the computer. Your Bible I have read much of. It is most fascinating, intriguing even. That is where I found that gem of wisdom."

Dennis nodded, smiled weakly.

"I would like very much to discuss this with you more in greater detail, Mr. Webster."

"Dennis, remember? But later, okay?"

Then Dennis realized he was beginning to squirm. He imagined it was like a neophyte criminal going through an interrogation and being confronted with the blunt truth of his act. It either made one think or else squirm.

Well, if Mil wanted to play mind games, then maybe taking on the role of devil's advocate might divert some of the stress. Besides, a good argument might provide some much needed entertainment.

"But, going back to what you said earlier, even you have to admit that on Majora many among your citizenry do not get along, assuming they are probably as quirky as we can be," he took up the cause. "Believe me, a bad relationship can be pure hell, as opposed to no relationship at all."

There, that felt good.

Dennis studied the opposite's expression, exulting at the well-placed verbal punch and hoping to see a complimentary effect.

After a moment, Mil displayed none of the anticipated fallout. If anything, he was all the more curious. "Of course, you are completely correct," he admitted. "But it is here, though, that occur the greatest differences between your people and mine."

Dennis straightened, crooked up one eyebrow.

"You will find that we are a people of considerable feeling and commitment. We attach much value on justice, fairness, and compassion, qualities your people hold in the same high regard and nobly strive for. But so often you fall so very short of in attaining. I do not mean it as a boast or an insult upon you to make out Majorans of my persuasion as having succeeded in them, to a greater degree. We have just had more time to practice them."

"Well, Mil, I hate to rain on your parade but that is exactly what it sounds like, bragging."

"Then please accept my apologies for my brashness."

"You, brash? I haven't seen you angry once, and that is an insult. Considering what we've been through, it's not normal. And I, for one, would really hate to be around when you do blow off."

"Do tell, Dennis."

A thought occurred to Dennis. Seizing on it, like a choice weapon in this battle of wits, "Well…putting off the anger bit, tell me this."

"Of course."

"Why did you run Lindsey's abductor off that cliff? Why didn't you just transport him aboard and play with his head to make him a decent and fit member of this elite little tribe?"

Mil held his peace.

"Instead, you put yourself in the position of judge, jury, and executioner, Mil. Sort of makes you out to be God, if I am not mistaken."

Mil now shook his head in thoughtful denial.

"And kind of hypocritical to me and definitely unethical, from a civilized point of view," Dennis tacked on for good measure.

Mil raised a brow but otherwise remained silent, taking it in. There was no anger, hostility, defensiveness, or anything else. The alien was taking his best shots, and, for all intents and purposes, his feelings appeared to be shielded by the armor of battleships.

When Mil did not answer after a long minute, "Well?"

Mil drew in a breath and expelled it in a silent sigh. For once, through his own passion, Dennis thought he saw an emotion that could have passed for guilt.

"Dennis, I did not say we were perfect," he admitted. "On the contrary, we are more human than you might think."

"Boy, that's a switch, Mil. A minute ago you were extolling your race's virtues. Now you're lowering yourselves a couple notches in the direction of humbleness. At least when I get the chance, maybe I can sleep more peacefully."

"Then that is a start on your successful assimilation," Mil commented, missing the sarcasm. "But please, let me return to your question."

"Oh by all means. This I want to hear."

Mil braced him with an earnest look. "Even in your own society this man would have been branded a dangerous, unscrupulous menace, am I not correct?"

"I can't argue against that."

"He had, for all intents and purposes, committed abduction and assault, even capital murder, as you call it. All were his intent and are horrendous crimes against humanity. I merely established the circumstances whereby he received his just reward for such heinous acts."

There was a contemplative pause, one in which he could feel Mil peer deep into his soul.

"Would you have not done likewise, Dennis?"

A hint of a headache began to make its presence known, just behind his left eye. In as absurd way, Mil was right. But to play God, as he had said? No one had that right.

Try as he might to rationalize the morality of the contrary stance he had chosen, Dennis could not escape the niggling grain of a brutal truth that had not Mil and Miriam interceded a tremendous injustice might very well have gone unpunished, maybe even undetected. It did not matter what his sentiments were toward Lindsey, regardless of her more detestable, recalcitrant qualities.

Throw in the knowledge that some other poor soul, or souls, might run afoul of this monster in the future reluctantly gave growing legitimacy to Mil's deed. But outright, it was still vigilante justice through and through. That made the whole thing an ethical conflict he would need a lot of time to sort through.

"I think I see your point, Mil," he had to admit. "But that means understanding, not wholehearted agreement. Not yet. Americans have been wrestling for a long time between our various rights and liberties and the need for responsibility, like the right to privacy and due process, versus the responsibility for justice and fair play. We just don't go out and punish people on our own like might happen in the old Wild West. We have laws, police, courts."

"Then let me clarify this by saying this was only a special circumstance, not a regular practice. I would not have had a clear conscience if I had had the means to stop him and then let him go, to either face no consequences for his actions or else to prey on other innocents."

"I think we can let that rest there then," Dennis agreed. The topic had been hashed out for all it was worth for the time being.

Mil nodded. Then for a spell, the Majoran continued to stare at him, a questioning sort of look growing more disconcerting with each second.

"You have something else you wanted to say?" Dennis wondered.

"I was only concerned for the sake of you and that of Mrs. Webster, if the two of you will be okay?" he asked.

A knot tightened uncomfortably in the pit of Dennis's stomach. He let slip a sentimental chuckle, nodded. Mil *was* concerned about him and Abby, and not just out of lip service. Perhaps…just maybe…he had been unreasonable with Abby all along. She was too gullible, as he had crowed about, but, come to think of it, he himself could be just a little closed-minded at times. How many times had that been the basis for a tit-for-tat exchange? In the balance, Abby was Abby. Being narrow-minded really did serve no good purpose and, in an odd way, sort of cut across his training as an engineer, to figure out ways to do things using *all* means available.

Then also Dennis had to admit that Abby was the common sense one, the one who quickly made up her mind about something and then called it as she saw it. No indecision or dallying there, other than necessary flexibility. Decisive. And then there was her long-suffering character that really did put up with a lot. Allied to that was an innate desire to reconcile when things tended to head south between them. She just did not carry on an argument for long, even when right.

That knot, tied in steel bands of guilt, continued to tighten to the point of being suffocating. Any gumption to continue the jousting with Mil slipped beneath under water and was headed for the realm of the terminally stupid. He was on a slippery slope of skewed reasoning and self-righteousness heading down and gaining momentum. Best to just cut it off while he was this far behind.

The ball had passed to Mil's court. The Majoran could have just slammed it back and nailed the lid on his egotistic coffin with an equally arrogant, *I know, Dennis,* or, *I thought you might come around.* Instead, the Majoran graciously, and maybe mercifully, held his peace.

Through his sagging countenance, Dennis levered up his gaze to steady it on his host. There was some much needed self-examination to indulge in and that was going to take some sorting time.

"I guess thanks are in order for the talk, Mil," he had to admit. "So thanks."

"No need, Dennis."

"Thanks anyway. Now I was wondering if I could have some time alone, to work things out?"

"Of course."

And with that, Mil was gone.

*

Abby decided not to wait for Mil to carry through on his promise for the grand tour of the ship. She had tried to get some sleep but found it elusive, like water in a desert. Slipping out into the main corridor, Mil was just leaving the lifeboat chamber.

"Hi Mil," she struck up.

"Good evening, Abby." He gave her a small deferential nod. "I must apologize for the lack of comfortable accommodations, but I do hope you rested well."

"Rested maybe. Sleep?" Abby shook her head. "No, the niche is comfortable enough, especially for someone overcome with exhaustion. I've just got a lot on my mind. Maybe later when a couple blankets and a bare spot on the deck might do."

"Understood. May I help you with something then?"

"Dennis is okay?" she first inquired.

"Deep in contemplation, if I might say. We had a…conversation."

"Kind of a continuation of our own conversation, huh?" she slowly drew out.

Mil replied with a hopeful grin, nodded.

Abby sighed in a quick flush of embarrassment. She had gleaned what she'd needed and now decided to get to what she desired to know. "Actually, I wanted to know about those navigation domes, or whatever they are, that you mentioned."

Mil bit. "Of course. I would like to show you, but I think you would probably prefer some solitude, same as your husband."

"Thanks Mil. You are most astute."

The Majoran nodded once in acknowledgment. "Proceed on into the engineering compartment," and he nodded aft to the sealed door at the end of the corridor. "It will open at your approach. Continue on back. The passage winds around, but you will want to pass the first ladder you come to and go on until you come to a second one. You can either go down or up. It does not matter. Again, both hatches will open at your presence.

"Should you prefer down be aware the gravitational enhancement is neutral, once inside. Though it will be rather clumsy to be floating around you can simply maneuver yourself into the seat. On a console in front of you, you will notice a scarlet luminary. Press it once you are seated, truly seated and settled. The gravity field generator will activate, though your position will be reversed, relative to the rest of the ship."

Maybe this wasn't such a good idea, Abby began to wonder. "Just as long as no one is watching," she grinned, rather sheepish.

"Only you will be there, Abby. Your first inclination will be to panic, as your senses initially make you believe you are upside down. I would suggest you move slowly and take your time. As I said, do not activate the field until you are set."

There was a brief pause, which she took to be the end of the initiation. "I think I have it, Mil. Thanks."

"You will do just fine. I will contact you should you need to be aware of anything that might arise."

"Sounds good. Thanks again."

They separated.

Abby followed the directions, deciding to lead off with the ol' head. Perhaps for the experience or the challenge...or just plain idiocy...she decided to take the down ladder access. Soon enough, she found herself at a sealed hatch that opened at her approach, just as explained. It disappeared into a very dim lit recess.

She climbed in and, as expected, found herself adrift. To her mild surprise, a momentary twinge of topsy-turvy confusion gave way to clumsiness. That she could deal with, as opposed to anything like the two bouts of airsickness that tormented her on a pair of Denny's more notable, longer flights that she had indulged in.

The small, dome-topped, clear-paneled chamber lent the familiar impression of an observatory. The hatch slid back into place with a solid, quiet thud of metal on metal. Only the dull thrum of the *Mistress's* pulse provided an umbilical between the vast unknown universe spread out before her and that which was warm, alive, familiar...or at least newly so.

Squirming, twisting, a few bumps, groping, and a couple convenient handholds and she had herself seated and belted into the comfortable, padded seat. The greatest thing to be thankful for was the lack of an audience to witness her antics. Maybe a couple more times at this and her efforts might be a thing of grace, rather than a source of community amusement.

Now that she could relax, she decided for the time being to forgo the gravity enhancement and just take in the immensity of it all. With the liability of a limited imagination regarding such things, this must be about as close to being an astronaut as one could come. She swiveled the seat forward.

Ahead and slightly lower was the dark gray, more or less streamlined keel of *Mistress* and then the bridge section. Farther ahead and impossibly distant, for only a few moments, a lazy meteor shower of subtly multi-hued firefly dots of illumination stretched into elongating lines in slow motion toward her. In silence they slipped past, some into invisibility. Abby imagined she could just reach out through the view panel and touch them.

She moved her gaze to a more perpendicular attitude. Other star lines, bright and dim, had to be much more distant, their lines being shorter, slower moving. Still others, as a matter of fact a majority, were little affected by their passage through the galactic medium.

Whether a couple moments or a couple minutes, she just reveled in the impossible wonder that surrounded her. How Mil or Miriam could ever get used to such a grand spectacle to the point of taking it for granted…well, she just shook her head. But, then again, it was told pilots who flew for a living went through the same metamorphosis. They got to the point where they looked upon the miracle of flight, and the different perspective of the universe it provided, as no more different than a drive to the supermarket.

That was truly a shame.

Then she remembered the reason for being here. She needed to think, to sort things out between her old and new realities, her and Denny, Lindsey's insufferable intractability.

She reached for and stroked the indicated control. With relentless progress, her arms, legs, the vertical length of her frame, sensed the growing heaviness of weight. In seconds it stabilized.

It felt comforting, reassuring. At the same time, a flood of the same tangled, crushing emotions crashed in anew to beset her: grief, humiliation, anger, perplexity. Despair...

Agony.

A broken leg or some other injury and its associated torture would have been better than this. Those who suffered such were truly the lucky ones. Any illusions, any shred of hope, of things returning to a semblance of normality evaporated like smoke from a fire.

Without realizing it, she simply lost it.

Abby's fingers dug into the lightly padded armrests. Hot tears streamed through her grimace to burn down her cheeks as sobs choked the breath in her throat. It made her body rattle.

"This is so unfair!" she managed to stammer into the cool, dry air. "I loved my life and I loved you, Denny, with all that I had. How on earth could you have been so cruel, do this to me? What did I ever do to hurt you, huh? Huh?"

Her torment swamped the small chamber.

"I love you so much, Denny," it now came out in a halting whimper, "but you hurt me bad. So bad! I honestly could survive anything...but to lose your love, your affection... You! That would truly be the end for me. I would do anything..."

Her words trailed off in an anguished moan.

Once again, the thought occurred to her that maybe the kindest thing Mil could do would be to return her to Earth and just dump her where he'd found her. The frigid waters would soon enough put a kindly end to her torment, as they buried her from not just life but from everything.

She released the restraints and buried her face in her hands as it all came out.

RECONCILLIATION

CHAPTER TWENTY-TWO

Dennis had remained in the lifeboat for some time, lost in thought. Instead of frustration and anger with a universe that had foisted misfortune upon him so unfairly, and Abby's issues, he was swamped in unadulterated shame. And he felt about the size of a microbe. Mil's chat had been needed medicine, very unpleasant but the necessary cure. Well, he was just going to have to man up and deal with his self-inflicted injury. The true question was Abby: how would she respond with a heartfelt confession?

Despite his physique and stamina it took no small effort to put motion to his body and will himself out of the lifeboat and to find Abby. Part of him dreaded a face to face meeting with her. *You made your nasty nest, friend. Now you have to live in it.* Humility could sure be a bitter pill to swallow.

He passed through the now open portal to the chamber and...

"Abby!"

Abby stopped upon passing through the exit from engineering. The opening closed behind her. She levered weary eyes to his. Her reply was a raised brow that gave the appearance of requiring equal effort to undertake as his had been a minute before to climb up and out to that passageway.

"You look awful, like about five miles of bad road," Dennis tried to cajole.

The humor failed to register; instead, Abby turned up one corner of her mouth in a stillborn smile. She crossed her arms in front of her in a self-embrace. She'd had a terrible crying spell, and Dennis winced at a sudden stab of guilt that he had been the epicenter of her grief.

For a silent pause, he considered her. For once since all this had started, he knew he was being civil with her. More remarkable, he could now admit with all honesty to himself that his anger toward her had petered out, evaporated. That he could not explain. It had to be his talk with Mil and it being a much needed catharsis that forced him to his senses.

And true love.

In the mental space, though, some sort of leaden weight remained, one that must have readily shown.

"What?" Abby asked. It was little more than a raspy whisper. In spite of her own turmoil a shadow of concern passed across her expression.

"Not here in public," he gently put off, sotto voce. Turning his chin back to where he had come from, "Inside the lifeboat chamber. We need to talk." His made sure his words were soft, disarming.

Reluctantly she nodded.

*

With a gentle hand on her back, he herded her into the chamber and its solitude. Gently, he maneuvered her to leaning back against the second of the two lifeboat housings. She did not resist. He took up his own position against the one he had done his soul searching in and did likewise.

This was going to so hard, but it was tempered with an overwhelming need to get started with his solemn duty to reconcile with Abby. Actually, he was terrified. He had apologized before…lots of times. It was just that this time things were…well, so different. He had never done it on a spaceship before with possible wreck and ruin…and potential death…staring them in the face every minute since this whole escapade had begun and still a threat.

It was also how Abby would respond. She was not one to hold a grudge, yet he had hurt her and hurt her bad…brutalized her, when it came right down to it. Did that change anything?

He hoped not.

Lindsey suffered no such compulsion. She did not particularly strike him as one to easily exercise the forgive-and-forget concept for even an innocuous slight. Not like Abby. The two of them were so different, well, the like the Andromeda galaxy and the Milky Way. Lindsey probably even remembered them all on an itemized, alphabetized list. His guess was that she even loathed those who kissed and made up. Weaklings, she would no doubt brand them.

"Well?" Abby now said, weary.

In spite of the softness of her prompt it sounded like a rifle shot. He had taken to staring absentmindedly at his hands while playing with his fingers.

He gulped and forced his eyes up. It was time to face the music.

"Abby…" he started. He half-coughed, covered his mouth in an awkward effort to stall another second.

She waited with divine patience, though weariness made for coolness and distance on her expression. It both added to his uncertainty and, yet, goaded him to get this matter settled, once and for all.

This is going to be sooo *hard,* he gulped again like a schoolboy about to fess up to some wrong. *I launched into this, so here's to looking stupid. Wouldn't be the first time…and definitely won't be the last. Let's just keep this short and sweet.*

"Abby, it's like this," he pushed off in his heart-felt confession. It was only a minute, but he had packed everything into it that he needed. And it was as torrent.

"So, to put it bluntly, Abby, I have been a complete idiot and a stupid man," he summed up. It was with all the sincerity he could muster. "And not just since all of this started. I have been for some time."

The flood continued.

"I'm not perfect, and I don't want to pretend to be. I just hope you can find it within yourself to forgive me for my idiotyncrasies and my…uh, that stupidity. I'm still having a hard time completely accepting all of this, but I guess that is really immaterial for right now. We need to move on from here and deal with this whole mess, if we stand any kind of a chance of making it through this, you and I."

For once a small, fragile blossom of a smile began to push through the torment on Abby's lips. Then, she inched closer, reached for, and clutched his hands with her delicate fingers. He drew her still closer till centimeters separated them. His gaze was a fount of earnest searching, pleading…humility.

*

Warmth flooded Abby's soul to its core.

It was *something* of an occasion for Dennis to swallow his pride when it came to error-admitting…and not just the occasional rubs that were common in any relationship. Normally, he would just pass off any irritability or testiness to some site problem or a deadline glitch. Just as typical, they were just excuses, now that she thought about it.

Something must have *really* tweaked his better sensibilities. This was most odd but indeed promising.

"So why the change?" she wanted to know. She was careful not to sound accusing.

"Let's just say it took an alien to bring me back down to Earth," Dennis quipped.

"Oh?"

"Yeah, like a little tête-à-tête down in this lifeboat where I was sulking." His chin turned needlessly to it while he patted the housing with his left hand. "Pretty much a friendly pep talk is what it boiled down to, if you know what I mean. Mil seems to have this overwhelming urge," and he took the moment to role his eyes in mock exasperation, "to be the helpful sort. And, wouldn't you know, he does it at the most opportune, or inopportune, times, just like we've grown to know him since our timely introduction."

Abby only just stifled a much needed giggle. She moved closer, chest to chest, and pulled a hand free to course it back around his neck. "Bull's-eye on that one, Denny, but, yes," and now with quiet, warm affection, "you know I forgive you. Always have and always will. It's because I love you," and her voice trailed off to a, "so much."

Even in the bland glow of the interior lighting, she could see relief roll off on his expression, see the earnestness and old affection spark in his eyes. That in itself spoke ten thousand words.

"And I hope you will do the same for me."

Now perplexity washed over his gaze. "No, Abby," he insisted, shaking his head. "The whole stink between us was my own shortsightedness and unthinking brashness...arrogance. You were just trying to hold the line in a universe collapsing all around us, trying to keep some tiny fragment of an even keel, when everything else was threatening to capsize and sink. And, if I might say so, you did and are doing a most splendid job at it." He was all nods.

Abby indulged in a pause to assimilate the compliment. It was like a miracle antibiotic to a deathly ill patient. "Thanks Denny. You don't know how much that means to me. It really means everything."

"I meant it that way." Her other arm now curved up and around in an embrace. "And I just want to say, too, how much I love you."

A load peeled off her own shoulders as their easy familiarity re-entrenched itself. He chuckled, no doubt exhilarating in the same renewal and incalculable relief she now luxuriated in. She added her own joy to the feast in the temporary intimacy of their enclosed space.

CHAPTER TWENTY-THREE

For long minutes, Abby and Dennis just took each other in, savoring the solitude, the revival. Then she moved back to lean against the lifeboat housing behind her.

There was an abrupt shudder that traveled through the frame of *Mistress*. For a moment, Abby's balance was just a little off, then it settled down as inertial compensators found equilibrium. A voice speared through the air on the tail end of it.

"Attention…everyone. For your information, we have reverted temporarily back to real space. Miriam and I need to make a couple checks and recalibrations. All critical systems are presently functional and there are no problems."

"Well, that's a load off," Dennis quipped. "A deep space stranding's not my idea of getting away from it all."

"Ditto," Abby tossed in. Her giggle filled the chamber.

Abby came erect. She drew in a deep breath and let it out in a satisfied sigh. She had something in mind, and it was time to get to it. Not that they had anything better to do. Besides, she would rather beat Denny to the punch before he got the crazy idea to tinker around all the encompassing gadgetry with their hosts.

"Hey, I have something to show you," she offered.

"And that would be?"

She giggled in anticipation. "You're not going to see it lounging around in here."

She grabbed for his right hand and led him out like a child in tow. In a moment, they were in engineering and making for one of the astro-navigation domes.

"You're heading for one of those domes Mil mentioned?" Dennis guessed easy enough.

"You're gonna love this, Denny. It's absolutely breathtaking. Even the astronauts *never* had a perspective like this."

Instead of the "down" one, she opted to steer for the above one. This time, she led the way up and into the small confined space. Dennis was right on her heels. Once up and in, she closed the access and waited for the gravity enhancement to settle down. They were, for all intents and purposes, alone in the vast universe.

She turned to face her husband who, in turn, had started surveying the encompassing heavens with childlike wonder. "Wow," he mouthed.

"And I only saw it when we were under way," she said, not trying to hide her own awe. "This time it's absolutely the best, sitting still as we are."

Then his gaze came around to meet hers. There was only the thinnest of ambient illumination from the few instruments on the seat's control panel, but in his eyes she could see a gleam the equal of any of the silent stars and nebulae that witnessed the interlude.

"What?" she asked into the tenderness of the moment.

"You. Through all that we have been through, I just wanted to say, again…well, how much I love you. I know I have been a disappointment of recent, but I want to change that. If everything around us collapses, if everyone around us should fail us, I want you to know that I will be there for you, that I've got your back. It's you and me."

"And I want you to remember that happens to be a two way street, Denny."

"Together forever, through thick and thin."

"Well, if I may say, this is about as thin as it gets. Sort of like when we were just starting out with next to nothing."

Hmm… Never thought of it that way. But most appropriate."

Silently, together, they reached for each other's hand, turned to take in the spectacle. For long, silent minutes the enchanted vista worked its magic.

Abby was mesmerized by a particular orange star that reigned over its own small part of the vast star cloud that back-dropped it. It was for no apparent reason. For a moment, she wondered what constellation it might be part of back home on Earth. Most of them she knew. Then quite unexpected, a little off to the right of it, a pinprick of light swelled in brightness, from insignificance to significance.

"Hey, do you see that?" Abby announced, pointing.

"Got it," Dennis acknowledged of the still brightening presence. "How 'bout that! Probably a nova or maybe even a supernova. What are the chances of that?"

"Must be astronomical." Abby chuckled. "But it's marvelous."

"Well, technically, since you are the discoverer, you get to name it."

Abby focused on it, taken in by the spectacle. It appeared so small, but yet it was a big event somewhere. "It's sort of like us, Denny."

"Meaning?" he drew out slowly.

"I know what supernovae and novae are."

"Yeah, a star in its death throes. Much or most of it gets thrown back out into interstellar space back into the galactic medium from where it originally came."

"But it's also life." She paused for just a moment to collect and connect the direction of her thoughts. "Just like the salmon back home when they spawn and die. They return to nature and the whole cycle starts over again. By itself, in the bigger scheme of things, like us, it's small and insignificant. In a year few will remember our purported passing. To us though, personally, it's our fate…the biggest event ever to befall us. It's what we are, how it defines us, and how we cope. It's how our life is playing out now for the two of us."

"Our life died back there on Earth," Dennis contemplated, following along, "and from the debris new life arises."

"And here we are, starting all over again. Even the rest of this journey will be filled with its challenges and dangers we can't even begin to imagine."

"And then there's Lindsey," he reminded her on a sober note.

"I was not going to bring that up. But yes, you are correct, Denny."

The conversation died off as they again took in the exquisite panorama. The non-twinkling stars and the numerous smears of light that were nebulae, star clusters, and galaxies near and far painted a serene tapestry no artist could hope to capture. They of a certainty had been through much, much more than anyone back home on Earth. And they had survived. What lay ahead was guaranteed to be uncertain at best. Dangers? That *was* guaranteed.

But she had Dennis and the warmth of his affection. That overwhelmed any fear that tried to make its presence known, even her weird dreams that were now on the periphery of her mind or Mil's ominous complaints about *Mistress's* propulsion. That was all she needed to bolster herself up. Mil and the others were icing on the cake.

There's no ordeal so grim when faced together with those you care about, she told herself. *To be right here and secure now with Denny...*

The thought never finished.

Without warning and caught off guard, Dennis swept her up in his strong embrace. As he found her lips, she melted in the strength and warmth of his body. Time and the universe evaporated as he smothered her soul in his long, passionate kiss.

THE END

ABOUT THE AUTHOR

Though he has written several science fiction stories, Shadow Guardians is Brett's first published novel. He is involved in such diverse interests as his church, donating platelets at the local donation center, astronomy and space exploration, and rockhounding and lapidary. He and his wife, Sherry, are both Air Force brats and have made the Lakewood, Washington area their home for over forty years, thirty-six of it married. They have two sons, four grandchildren, and two cats to keep them busy. Both are employed by the State of Washington in Lakewood.